THE
DUEL

Center Point
Large Print

Also by Giles Tippette and available from
Center Point Large Print:

Slick Money
The Button Horse
Mexican Standoff

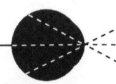

THE DUEL

A WARNER GRAYSON NOVEL

Giles Tippette

CENTER POINT LARGE PRINT
THORNDIKE, MAINE

This Center Point Large Print edition
is published in the year 2019 by arrangement with
Betsyanne Tippette.

Printed in the United States of America
on permanent paper.
Set in 16-point Times New Roman type.

ISBN: 978-1-64358-166-8

Library of Congress Cataloging-in-Publication Data

Library of Congress Cataloging in Publication
Control Number: 2019003085

1

I looked at it as a damn dangerous move from any viewpoint. It involved leaving the country I was raised in and where I came to manhood and where I was the best known, to move up to northeast Texas damn near to the Arkansas and Louisiana borders. It meant selling the five-thousand-acre horse ranch I'd been paying on for a good many years and then taking on more debt than I'd ever expected to bear to buy the east Texas land. It also meant taking on a full-time partner, something I'd sworn never to do, no matter how much I cared about her.

But the biggest change was in the very risky direction I was taking in my career as a horse-man. For most of my thirty-two years, I had been making my living with horse, either breaking them or trading them or training them. And for a big chunk of that time, since my grandfather had died, I'd been on my own. My parents had been carried off by the yellow fever when I was a small child and, if I'd got a raising, it had been at the hands of my grandfather, a gentle-man of the old school who believed in right and wrong and knew the difference and who believed in honor and the value of a man's word and who knew pretty nearly every word in the Bible and went a good ways toward practicing it.

He had also known considerable about horses and had been at some pains to pass on that knowledge to me.

Consequently, by the time of his death, I could pretty well hold my own with any horseman in southeast Texas and could get the best of most of them in any sort of trade or race.

But new horizons had beckoned. For years, I had raised the best cattle horses and pleasure horses and traveling horses and short-distance running horses in that part of the country and had grown famous doing it. The word was that if you wanted a finished horse of the best quality, you went to see Warner Grayson and I would treat you fair.

And I was proud of that reputation and proud of the stock I'd turned out through the years and the prominence of the names on my list of customers. But I wanted a piece of the premier end of horse handling and that meant Thoroughbred, blue-grass racing stock horses that ran at a mile or better.

Of course we'd had horse racing in south Texas for years; all over Texas for that matter. But they were mostly small, brush-track county-fair events that featured quarter horses and were usually run at distances of three hundred yards to less than half a mile. This was not to say that a quarter horse wasn't as fine a piece of horseflesh as there was; he just couldn't run fast for any great distance. However, there wasn't any reason that he should. The quarter horse had been bred off the Morgan and he'd been originally intended as a cow horse. And for that purpose—quick bursts of speed over short distances—he had no peer. For a distance of three or four hundred yards there wasn't anything that could stay with a quarter horse, not even a Thoroughbred. But once past that distance, the quarter horse's chunky muscles became a handicap instead of a help. A Thoroughbred, with his big chest and long, supple muscles, would run away from him.

I could see the future and I knew it was Thoroughbred racing, even in Texas, and I wanted to be in there right from the first. In that year, 1886, they were already starting to talk about building mile tracks with grandstands in Houston, San Antonio, and even in Dallas. There was already one in Del Rio and a man could get on a train and go to Louisiana or Tennessee or Kentucky or Virginia and see big racing tracks that were putting up big prize money.

So I'd felt that if I was going to keep on

climbing the ladder I had to get in the big show.

But it was a dangerous move to contemplate. You didn't go into that business with a prayer and a promise. It took money and quite a little bit of it. First, I had to sell my ranch in south Texas. The five thousand acres I'd worked so hard to earn wasn't worth ten cents for raising Thoroughbreds. The grass was too poor. The land had been salt-leached for centuries and all it would grow was a kind of buffalo stubble that wasn't much better than straw. You could run blooded Morgans and quarter horses and saddle-bred stock on it because you mostly fed them grain and hay. But a Thoroughbred needed lots of room when he was a colt to run and play and let those long, lean muscles develop. And the grass you turned him out on had to be top quality or he'd never amount to anything or come to promise.

I hadn't wanted to leave Texas so I scoured the areas up near Arkansas and Louisiana until I'd found eight thousand acres covered with lush grass and pine thicket and pecan groves. It was beautiful ground and the grass was as good as any bluestem I'd ever seen, but, my, was it dear. I simply couldn't swing the deal on my own, not even after I'd gotten a pretty good price for my little spread. The eight thousand acres had cost plenty and then there had been the cost of locating a headquarters on the new ranch—building a house and barns and bunkhouses, not to mention the money I'd have to pay for Thoroughbred broodmares and the big cost of the Thoroughbred studs.

But, if it was to be done, it had to be done right.

And that meant money and money had meant taking in Laura (or the widow Pico as I sometimes called her in embattled moments) as a full partner.

Oh, there had been other sources. I could have gone to the Williams brothers who owned the Half-Moon ranch and were probably as wealthy as anyone in south Texas. I'd felt sure they would have been willing to back me. Or I could have approached the man I considered my best friend, Wilson Young. Wilson was a bank robber who had been pardoned by the governor some few years back—some said at the behest of the lawmen who were tired of chasing him. He had a very profitable casino and saloon and cathouse in Del Rio. I'd first met Wilson when I'd sold him a horse with a chase party hot on his trail. I'd been fifteen years old and him not much more, but he'd taken the time to dicker over the horse and had paid me and gotten a bill of sale. Throughout the years, I reckoned I'd sold him every horse he'd straddled.

But I didn't go to any of them, because maybe I figured it would end up being in one name anyway. Besides, Laura was already a partial partner in my operation. She had brought six Andalusian stallions in with her, a horse that was as rare and wonderful as she sometimes was. It had been through the Andalusians I had met Laura. She had married a rich man named John Pico and insisted he buy and import the six Spanish stallions. She'd had some hare-brained idea that she could produce a better cow horse by breeding the Andalusian's prodigious endurance and smooth gait in with common range mares. Of course, that idea was plain silly because the Andalusian had no cow sense at all and all you'd get out of such a breed would be a worthless cow horse that could make mistakes all day long.

She and her husband had had a ranch down along the border near Del Rio. It had been attacked by Mexican bandits, who'd stolen the Andalusians along with a number of other horses. Since they had also stolen from me and killed one of my hired hands, I was already on their track.

Laura's husband had been killed when he had foolishly run out into the open trying to drive off half-a dozen armed bandits.

My background up to that point had strictly been the experience of a man who dealt with horses. I had never so much as shot at another man, much less set out to kill a half a dozen or more. But after my treatment at the hands of the bandits I had determined that only death was going to stop me from recovering and revenging in the endeavor and I had also recovered Laura's horses as well as mine. It had been no mean accomplishment, since Laura said, and I believed her, that the Andalusian stallions had cost two thousand dollars apiece to import from the Andalusian district of Spain. They were an old breed, the grandfathers of the Arabians and a wonderful mixture of gait and manners and endurance. Laura had proposed that I throw in with her on her silly scheme, but I had just laughed. To persuade me she had tried her feminine wiles, but I let her know right quick that I had been to two county fairs and a prairie fire and wasn't as green as I looked. The upshot had been that she'd moved to Corpus Christi, which was about fifteen miles from my ranch, and I had used the Andalusians to develop as fine a road and traveling horse as a man could want.

We loved each other, though the word got damn little exercise on either one of our tongues. Sometimes I didn't know if we were in love or just in bed, which we were a considerable amount of time. Laura was the most strikingly handsome woman I'd ever seen. I figured her for a couple of years older than me, but that was something I was never going to find out from her. She had butter-colored hair that looked

11

like it had been stained at the ends with the juice of wild strawberries. She wasn't what you could call beautiful, because her facial features were too regular and perfect. They even had a kind of sharp look about them, especially when she had her stern face on, and that was more often than I cared for. And she hid her figure under severe gowns and riding pants and blouses. Only when she undressed in the dim glow of a lantern could a man see the fullness and swell of her breasts with their cherry-sized nipples, and see the flare of her hips and the little mound at the place where her legs met that was forested with blond hair like strands of fine silk.

She was a fine, fine looking woman and if the bargain had quit there a man couldn't have been more happy. But the widow Pico was of an arrogant disposition that matched up well with her sharp tongue. About the only time we didn't fight was when we were talking horses or making love. We didn't fight about horses because she knew I knew a hell of a lot more than she did. And we didn't fight in bed because we were too busy otherwise.

I think we fought more for recreation than for any sensible reasons of disagreement. I was not a combative man by nature, but it seemed as if it didn't take no effort at all for Laura and me to suddenly be in a pitched battle.

Surprisingly, she went along with my plan without a murmur, even though it was going to take a considerable amount of her money. I will give Laura her due: she was as honest as the day is long. John Pico had left her well fixed because he'd been a rich man. And Laura had never made any bones about the fact that she was marrying him for his money and his willingness to let her have a business in horses. She was Virginia born and bred and I think all Virginians are of the fixed opinion that they invented the horse, the women being just as bad as the men.

The only stipulation that Laura put on the move was that she be allowed to have the ranch house built the way she wanted. She had hated my four-room adobe cabin on my ranch in south Texas and had refused to stay there for longer than three- or four-day visits that she sometimes cut to one night depending on her temper.

She had built herself a ten-room house in Corpus on a bluff overlooking the bay. In the three years we had been together in south Texas, I had never passed a night under the roof of that elegant house. It was not my way of showing my displeasure at Laura's refusal to accept my way of living, it was just that the place was too damn *nice* and I just couldn't get comfortable for fear I was going to break something.

So it was with some trepidation that I agreed to her condition about the ranch house. I had told her my feelings about her house in Corpus and had added that if she did up the east Texas house the same way she'd find me sleeping in the bunkhouse on more than a random occasion.

I would have been almost willing to believe it shocked her into considering my feelings if I hadn't known her better. But the result was some kind of compromise that I found livable even if it wasn't as fancy as I think she wanted.

It was, however, the first all-frame house I'd ever lived in. Lumber in the country down toward Mexico that had been my home grounds came mighty dear, too dear to waste on such things as a house. Trees were a scarce article and any tree that was tall enough and straight enough to make lumber out of would have been such an oddity that a stone fence would have been built around it and admission charged just to view it. As a consequence, houses in south Texas were built out of rock or adobe brick or, later, concrete brick plastered over with limestone.

But, of course, east Texas was rife with pine trees and lumber yards and sawmills. Lumber was cheap. It was the rock and brick that were scarce. So, as a consequence, Laura had a big, eight-room house built on a hill overlooking a twenty- or twenty-five-acre lake that was full

14

of bass and perch. It was a beautiful, white-washed affair with big porches on three sides. It even had running water to the kitchen and the two bathrooms by virtue of the raised cistern that collected rainwater. And one of my hands, Les Russel, who was good at such things, was even at work on a boiler scheme to pipe hot water right into the house.

The whole business, which included finding and buying the land, building the house and the outbuildings and the feedlots and corrals, and moving the stock from my ranch, had taken the better part of a year. Within another two months, we had moved into the new place, got it running, and I had succeeded in buying eight Thoroughbred broodmares, two of which were in foal. But the most important part was yet to come—the purchase of my basic line of stallions, through which I would create my own bloodline. It was an endeavor that would not allow for a mistake or a foot put wrong. The Thoroughbred mares were important, make no mistake, but it was through the studs that you established yourself.

And they were not cheap. Try and buy too cheap and you were throwing your money away. Go at it with a completely open purse and you were fair game for every swindler and sharp trader, who were as ready to expose your ignorance as they were to rob you. No, it was a proposition that you had to approach as carefully as you would a highbred woman.

I'd had some little education in high-blooded Thoroughbreds through my friend Wilson Young who had dabbled with them as a consequence of gambling debts owed by gentlemen from Mexico who had paid off with running horses rather than cash. But the horses were not of the genuine bluegrass variety that I was determined to base my stable on. Of course I had studied every bit of written material I could lay my hands on and had talked with every dealer and trader I knew that I thought had the least knowledge of the subject.

But even with all that, even with all my years of nibbling around the edges, it was still going to come down to me going to where the horses were and pitting my knowledge and skill and money against men who'd been in the business for generations.

And I was about to undertake such an endeavor in the form of a buying trip up into bluegrass country.

But all my studying was by no means preparation enough to put me on an equal footing with horsemen who'd been in the Thoroughbred game as long as I'd been in the western horse business. And I couldn't afford to make a mistake. I had limited funds and I had to deal myself a winning hand first rattle out of the box or everything I'd worked all my life to build up would be lost within a few years.

Not to mention the money that Laura was putting in. I could safely say that I could have accepted being broke and ruined a hundred times easier than I could face losing a dollar of her money or dropping an inch in her estimation. So maybe in the life-or-death sense of bullets flying, what I was setting out to do couldn't be considered dangerous. I'd been shot at and missed and shot at and hit and surrounded and overwhelmed and routed and run, but I don't reckon I had ever been as scared as I was about the venture of going to buy those stallions that my stable's bloodline would rest on.

Maybe it was that fear that made me nervous and maybe it was that little jitteriness that got me and Laura into a fight the morning before I was to leave on my stud-buying trip.

Actually, it was a double-barreled fight, because we got started good on one subject and then, slick as clabbered milk churning into butter, we slipped right into the main one. It commenced in the kitchen, at the breakfast table, where me and Laura was having a last cup of coffee after our meal. It was a beautiful May morning and the kitchen was lit up by the sunlight streaming in through the big windows. Outside I could hear the satisfying sounds of my four ranch hands getting on about the day's business. Rosa, our cook and the wife of my best vaquero, Juanito, was going on about her duties of cleaning up the dishes. I had just made a remark that I reckoned had passed my lips no less than fifty or a hundred times without it drawing the response it did.

I'd said, "Do you plan to go on being Mrs. Pico the rest of your life? I mean, it ain't like we're not certain the man ain't coming back."

She'd been about to take a sip of coffee, stopped with the cup halfway to her mouth, and said, "What's that?"

"You heard me. How many times have I asked you why don't you use your maiden name? Longstreet is a perfectly good name. John's dead. Hell, he don't care."

She put the cup down carefully in the saucer and turned slightly in her chair to face me. Laura can make her voice colder than the north end of a west Texas cow in a blizzard when she's a mind to and the one she turned on me was so cold you could nearly see the blue in it. She said, "The floor under your boots and the ceiling over that hat you insist on wearing to the table were paid for with John Pico's money."

It was a back-alley attack and she knew it, which only made it worse. She knew I was damn sensitive about using her money, and

18

even more touchy knowing it had been earned by another man. It made me hot right off. But I held my trigger for a few seconds. Truth be told, I was always a little worried about Laura. We had been together for four years and, fight as we did, I had a hard time imagining what my life would be like without her. I guess the fact was I could never figure out what she saw in me. I was tall and lean and had good shoulders and hands, but nobody had ever gone out of their way, except Laura on a few occasions and some silly girls I'd sparked in the past, to call me handsome. And certainly I wasn't no scholar, even though I'd gone through the tenth grade of school and followed my grandfather's example of reading everything I could lay my hands on. But I wasn't the gentleman to match her as a lady and I reckoned I was a little rough and certainly wouldn't rank very high in the manners department. Best I could figure, it was the horses that drew her to me. Though, God himself knew, there had been no less than ten thousand times when one or the other of us had sworn we were through and enough was enough.

Except we never quite parted. To other people, we presented ourselves as being strictly partners in a venture, but, hell, you'd've had to be deaf and dumb and simple not to know we were much more than that to each other. We had never married. We had gotten close on at least half a dozen occasions but something had always come up or one of us had had second thoughts. It was as if marriage was something we'd both agreed to but there was other business to take care of first. We knew that there were people who thought we were living in sin but neither Laura nor I had ever cared overmuch about what people thought of us personally.

There was a whiskey bottle sitting in the middle of the table and I took a moment to reach out, uncork it, and pour a good dollop in my coffee before I looked up at Laura.

The only physical trait that Laura and I shared, since I was dark where she was blond and light and I was muscular where she was slight, was the color of our eyes. Both of us had hazel eyes except when we got angry. Then they turned green. Hers were snapping green. And I reckoned that mine were also. I'd just as soon she'd have kicked me in the balls as passed the remark she just had. I was so mad, I nearly bit the coffee mug when I took a sip of the whiskey.

I said, slowly, "Well, if you are going to put it like that there ain't but one way I can reply. I never took a cent of money in my life I didn't earn and this floor and this roof you spoke of ain't no different. But the way I calculate it, having earned them by living with you for four years, they ought to be paved with gold."

It set her back on her heels. She don't mind fighting dirty herself, but she doesn't like to get it back. By her lights a lady is allowed to poleaxe you from the back, but she ain't supposed to get the same treatment in return. She drew herself up and used what I called her January voice, still and cold and frozen.

She said, "That is the most insulting remark that has ever been made to me."

I said, "No, it's not. You're forgetting a few years back when we were in bed and supposed to be making love, only you were in a snit and I told you let's not waste that thing of yours, but for you to go into the kitchen and make me a pitcher of lemonade and sit on it until it got real cold."

It made her face blaze. She glanced over at Rosa, but Rosa was placidly going on about her duties in that slow, careful way that fat people have. Rosa didn't speak a word of English so far as I knew and, even if she had, she'd heard enough of our fights to know them by heart.

Laura leaned across the table and hissed at me. She then said, "You said you had not meant that and would never make reference to it again."

"Fine. I'm a sonofabitch. But so are you, if you get right down to it. What kind of remark was that that you passed at me? I reckon I'm supposed to just take them little rusty knives and say, Why, thank you kindly, ma'am? Before we went into this, it was agreed that I could find another partner but that you wanted to be the one. I said all right, but I agreed on the condition that where you got your money wasn't to ever come up."

"This is different."

"Bullshit. Did you or did you not agree to that?"

"God damn it, am I supposed to remember everything we agreed to? Do I have to go around watching my tongue every second for fear you'll accuse me of being an iceberg in bed? That one time. You forget how you'd been treating me before. You very conveniently forget that. In fact, you very conveniently forget a lot of things, *Mister* Grayson!"

"Like what, *Widow* Pico?"

"Like the time my name would have been Grayson in very short order except the famous Williams brothers of the famous Half-Moon ranch needed you urgently to wet-nurse the youngest on a trip to Mexico to buy some counterfeit Arabians and that was more impor- tant than our wedding."

I gave her a disgusted look. She'd used that situation on me in more arguments than I cared to remember. I had given up trying to defend my position that we could have put our wedding off a week, but I'd been waiting a good ten years to do business with the Half-Moon ranch. That explanation hadn't held water the first ten times I'd advanced it and I knew better than to try and defend it at that moment. Instead, I stood up and held out my hand. She looked up at me.

She said, "What?"

"What? Hell, get up and go get your bonnet while I tell Charlie or somebody to hitch up the surrey. There are enough preachers in Tyler to marry half of Texas and if we can't find one or be hitched by noon I'll put this ranch in your name."

She jerked her head back and then from side to side, making her hair swirl. "Oh, go to hell, Warner Grayson. You know I'm not going to just get up like this and go to Tyler and get married. Don't act anymore the fool than you already are."

I still kept my hand out. "Come on. Get up, woman. I'm ready to do something about that last name of yours. It has bothered me for four years and I'm convinced you keep it just to irritate me. You didn't love John Pico, you've said so yourself. You've said you married him for his money and he agreed to it. Why, I ain't got the slightest idea."

She gave me a look and said, "I ought to get up and call your bluff. But Tyler is five miles away and you'd probably contrive to have an accident of some kind before we made it. The horse would probably drop dead under your direction."

"We'll see who is bluffing, missy. Get up. Hell, being married to you can't be no worse than living with you, and I've managed to tolerate that."

She suddenly came to her feet with her face blazing. I caught the wild right-handed slap she'd intended just before it reached my face. I held her by the wrist and smiled into her eyes. I said, "If you ever do succeed in hitting me and I find out about it you are going to be in trouble."

With that she brought her knee swiftly up between my legs. It wasn't the first nor the second nor even the third time she'd caught me so off guard. She was the first woman who'd ever treated me so and I just couldn't prepare myself for such an attack because I couldn't imagine a lady doing such a thing.

The blow doubled me over and left me holding my private parts and groaning. I heard Laura say something to Rosa and then laugh. Then she yelled at me, "Still want to get married?"

I heard the heels of shoes tapping fiercely as she marched out of the kitchen. When I could, I sat back down in the chair and tried to straighten up. Without a word, Rosa came over and poured me a drink of whiskey in my coffee cup. I took it down in a gulp, glad for its fiery warmth to distract my mind.

I sat still for a good ten minutes, waiting for all the pain to go away. I had another drink of whiskey and then got out a cigarette and lit it and thought of how I could get back at Laura. I was damn good and mad. I'd been nervous before about the upcoming trip not being successful, but now I was angry as hell at Laura and determined to get back at her. If she'd've been a man, I'd have beat the hell out of her, but she always pulled such stunts on me and then hid behind her femininity, knowing I couldn't do a thing except boil over.

I figured she was having herself a hell of a good laugh at my expense right at that moment. And there wasn't the slightest doubt in my mind that the damn woman kept using Pico as her last name just because I'd once been so foolish as to make something out of it. If I'd never let on it bothered me, she'd have gone back to her maiden name three years before.

Hell, she hadn't been married to Pico even a year and she claimed, and I believed her, that he hadn't wanted her for bed so much as for show. He was one of them sons of immigrants who'd come up poor and then made a ton of money in some business up north and went looking for a proper lady to buy. Naturally, the first kind you went for were Virginia bred and there had been Laura, a perfect fit for what he was seeking. I wondered if he'd gotten a good enough taste of that wonderful temper of hers. She once told me she'd run off half the beaus in Virginia because she was tougher than they were and I believed her.

I thought she'd come back down and continue the fight. That was her usual tactic. She'd fire off some hard-hitting remark—or in this case a knee—and then walk out before I could reply. But it appeared that this time she wasn't going to employ her hit and run and return strategy.

Ours was a two-story house and I could hear her walking around overhead, our big bedroom being at the end of the house that was situated partly over the kitchen. I sat there stewing, trying to think of some way to get back at her. Here we were, leaving the next day on what was as important a horse trip as I'd ever taken and she'd left me with a kick in the balls. That right there was enough to put a shadow over the trip.

So I sat there, thinking it over. I'd had plenty of experience with women in my life. Circumstances had forced me to grow up before my time so I'd come early to the matters of a man. But she was the first and only woman I'd ever been in love with—that is, if I understood what love was. As near as I could figure it, it involved needing to be around the one person in the world that exasperated you the most. Laura could make me madder, make me happier, make me sadder and gladder than any woman I had ever known. If love was needing the woman who drove you the craziest then I was as much in love with Laura as any man was with any woman. I sometimes hated to be around her, but then I missed her like sin when we were apart.

Of course, I had never communicated any of these thoughts to her. I wouldn't have done so any more than I'd have told my deadliest enemy where my hideout was or how fast was the horse I was riding. The funny thing, though, was that, even with the temper and the unpredictability, I wouldn't have changed Laura. Not one whit. I guess that one fact was what made me pretty sure that I loved her. Not that I threw the word around much. I'd heard other folks do so all my life and I always felt like they either knew more than I did or were just more careless.

Laura liked to give names to horses and would have made pets out of them if I'd let her. I'd never named a horse in my life. A horse was for using, for work, and if I wanted a friend I'd buy a bum a drink in a saloon, not make one out of an animal with four legs and a brain about the size of a pecan.

But, if I said a horse was good at what he

was wanted for, you could bet that he would perform. I wasn't a man much given to sentimentality or overstatement. If a thing was a fact it was a fact and didn't need discussion. If it wasn't, all the exaggeration and words of praise weren't going to change it.

Which was a hell of a way to try and explain my feelings, even to myself, about Laura. How she felt about me was something I never pursued. The fact that she was still with me after four stormy years, was, I figured, statement enough.

I got up from the kitchen table and walked through the formal dining room that Laura had insisted on us having—though everybody I'd ever known had found the kitchen a good enough place to eat—passed through the parlor and went out the front door onto the big, wide porch that looked out over the lake. I went up and leaned against the whitewashed railing that fenced in the porch and stared out at the still water. Occasionally, I could see a little dimple and then ripples as a fish rose to have a taste of the mayflies that were lighting on the smooth surface of the water.

I looked around. We'd been established in the house with furniture and all the other household gewgaws folks needed for less than a month. My stock, the Morgans and quarter horses and the Andalusians had been moved much earlier, coming under the care of Charlie Stanton, my young foreman, and Juanito, who had lived out of a tent while they'd seen to getting certain areas fenced and the stock used to the country. They'd hired carpenters and laborers out of the town of Tyler to do the work, but Charlie had overseen it.

It was new, fencing pastures. That wasn't done in south Texas because cattle and horses had to be allowed to run free because of the lack of grass. But it was an accomplished way of life in the area we were in and, besides, I'd have had to have done it anyway. You don't turn five-thousand-dollar stallions loose on the open range, especially when you are planning on charging a five-hundred-dollar breeding fee.

I stood there, leaning against the railing, smoking a cigarette and looking out over the country. As short a time as we'd been there, I'd already come to like the place. We were located about five miles west of the town of Tyler, which claimed to hold twenty-five thousand inhabitants, though I privately figured they were counting strangers and the folks in the grave-yard as well. I reckoned you'd call it a sawmill town, because that was the main industry. It was a pretty little town, with neat houses and, being the county seat of Smith County, the courthouse, and enough saloons to start a man on the road to perdition and enough churches to have a fair chance of dragging him back. I hadn't really gotten to know many folks, just the tradespeople we'd done business with and the workmen that had built our house and other buildings, but they seemed like a friendly enough lot.

Certainly, the country was something to see after a lifetime on the flat, gray plains of south Texas. Of course, when a man grows up near the coast he sort of feels closed in when he moves as far inland as we had. We had located up in the extreme northeast part of Texas. The Louisiana border wasn't but about sixty miles due east and a tip of Arkansas not much more than that to the north and east. Oklahoma Territory was no more than a hundred miles to the north, just across the Red River.

I had never seen such green country before. Our little ranch headquarters were protected on three sides by groves of pine trees and my land and pastures were here and there cut by strips of pine or pecan or oak, or all three, making natural wind breaks and protection for any stock that was turned out.

Out across the lake I could see the five-hundred-acre pasture of rolling hills where I'd turned out the eight broodmares. The two that were in foal were not very far along and it would be late winter before they'd be dropping their colts. They had been sort of a gamble on my part. The owner had claimed they were bred to a stallion that carried quite a reputation, but he couldn't seem to find proof of the breeding. For that reason, he was willing to sell them cheap.

I'd bought them for a thousand dollars apiece, buying the mares for their own bloodlines, and not ever figuring that the colts they dropped would be worth anything more than good saddle horses. But they would be their first colts and if they threw those successfully, I'd feel a lot safer about breeding them to the high-quality stallions I was hoping to buy. A first colt is an iffy thing for a mare—and for the colt as well. It's best to get it out of the way with as little risk as possible.

The trip was as planned out as I could make it. After much study and consideration, I had settled on six breeding stables and written them my wishes and intentions and had heard back from all six. Our trip, by train, would take us first to a farm in Louisiana, thence to Tennessee, and from there up to Kentucky to two breeding farms, and finally to Virginia.

Part of the stay in Virginia would be social, as we expected to see Laura's kin. I wondered idly and with no little malice what they were going to think when she turned up there with a man she wasn't married to, still calling herself the widow Pico. A few times, the thought flitted across my mind that she might have the gall to suggest we present ourselves to her kin as a married couple. The thought made me smile grimly to myself. My luck would never be that good for her to present me with such an opportunity.

I stood there, looking out over the pastures, watching how the stock was faring. That was the horseman in me. I could be as mad as a wet settin' hen and yet it would not affect my eye nor my judgment as I looked over the stock. I could tell at a glance that Charlie was leaving a small herd of Morgans too long on a stand of timothy hay stubble. They'd end up with galled intestines if he let them keep on eating that much straw. He ought to have known better and I made a note to myself to speak to him about it. Charlie was only twenty-two years old, but he had been working for me full time since he was seventeen and I judged him to be nearly as good a horseman as there was around. The four men that worked under him never seemed to mind his age, which was just as well, because it would have been them getting paid off and sent packing.

I shook my head thinking of how Laura was going to go swelling around among her Virginia kin telling them we were going into Thoroughbred racing. Hell, she loved horses, but she didn't know a damn thing about them.

She could tell an Andalusian from a Morgan, but you had better not get into crosses or she was lost. If she called a horse by some pet name I would say, "You talking about that roan short coupled Andalusian quarter horse cross or that Morgan with the off-legged stocking?"

Of course, I might as well have been talking to her in Dutch for all she understood. Usually it made her stamp her foot and swear at me, but it didn't break her of naming horses, nor make her understand that they were a commodity like beef or corn or house paint.

Standing there, thinking about her putting on the dog around her relatives in Virginia, gave me a sudden idea. She had been looking forward to the trip as soon as I had first planned it and had gotten more and more excited as we neared the day of departure. Now it appeared I'd be making the trip walking a little sore.

Well, I decided right then and there that I would have me an apology off that woman. As best I could remember, she had never really apologized to me for anything, but I figured I had enough ammunition to get her to see the error of her ways.

I pushed away from the porch railing and went back inside. Before I went upstairs to beard the lioness in her den, I made a pass through the kitchen and had another pull at the coffee cup that still had whiskey in it. I wasn't afraid of Laura, but just to be sure my nerves were steady, I poured myself out another good shot and downed that. Then I got a cigarette and lit it and gave the whiskey a moment to work.

Laura didn't drink in the morning. So far as that went she didn't do all that much drinking period. She'd take a little wine at the table and maybe a brandy here and there, but that was about it. The first time she'd seen me take a morning whiskey, she'd been shocked enough to wonder if I was some kind of drunkard, except she called me a dipsomaniac.

Hell, damn near everybody I knew took a morning whiskey to get the day started. Even my grandfather had done so and if there was ever a man was moderate in habits, it was Carver Grayson.

But I was putting off doing something I might end up being sorry for. Right then I didn't much care. She hadn't ought to have given me the knee in the balls.

I was fixing to teach her that she wasn't the only one could play dirty. I put out my cigarette and wiped my mouth and started up the back stairs behind the pantry.

2

She was sitting in our bedroom by a window that looked out over the back part of the ranch. She was sitting in a big, wing chair that I generally sat in. I had taken note that she had changed out of the frock she'd been wearing at breakfast and into riding pants and boots and a crisp, white blouse.

I came into the room and stood just inside the door, waiting for her to acknowledge my presence. Finally she turned her head my way ever so slightly and said, "Did you want something?"

I pointed a finger at her. I said, "Laura, there is a price for everything. You can't knee me in the balls and then walk off with a laugh and think it will go away."

"Oh, for heaven's sake," she said, "don't go to carrying on like you're hurt. It can't be that bad."

"I wish you had a set," I said, "so I could give you a good swift kick and let you see how it felt."

She waved her hand at me. "Oh, pshaw. You upset me. It was your own fault."

I stared at her. "My fault? That's a hell of a way to look at it." I pointed my finger at her again. "How would you like it if I gave you a little pain every time you pulled that stunt? I don't reckon it would be long before you learned better. I could take a razor strop to your bare bottom and I bet you'd remember that a good while."

She gave a laugh. "You wouldn't dare. I know you too well for that, Warner Grayson."

"That's it," I said, nodding rapidly. "That's goddamn well it right there." I was getting up a full head of steam again. "You know I won't do nothing back to you so you figure you can do anything you please to me. Well, missy, them days is coming to a quick end. I ain't gonna take a razor strop to your ass, but you're going to wish I had instead of what I'm going to do."

She waved her hand nonchalantly. "Oh? And what would that be? Sleep in the other bedroom for a few nights until you can't stand it any more?"

"No."

I turned on my heel and started out the door and toward the stairs. "I'm going to leave you here on this buying trip. No trip, no Thoroughbred horses, no reunion in Virginia."

I heard her gasp as I started down the stairs, clumping my boots loudly. I knew she'd be right after me so I went straight out the kitchen door and back to the horse barn where I kept my regular saddle horses up. I figured to ride off and give her plenty of time to stew. Miguel, our man of all work, was busy forking hay down from the loft, getting ready to put it out into the corrals for the horses that were being kept up close. Besides Charlie and Les Russel, who was an odd case in himself, I had two vaqueros, Juanito and Raoul, who did most of the work aboard green horses. They had seats and hands with nervous horses as good as anybody I'd ever come across. Les Russel was a fair enough hand with horses, but he had other uses.

I was about to tell Miguel to saddle me a horse, when I glanced back toward the house and saw Laura coming at a pretty good clip. She had never been one to let any grass grow under her feet. I could tell by the tilt in her chin and the way she was walking that a good fight was in the offing and wouldn't be long in coming. She'd be on me before I could mount a horse and ride off and I didn't want a fight out in the middle of the ranch headquarters with most of the hired hands for an audience. When she was about half way, I came out of the barn, walking as fast I could to intercept her. As I got close enough to speak, I said, "All right, Laura, let's don't put this on parade. Let's take it back in the house. Be more things handy there you can throw at me."

She was about five yards off. She said, "Hell no. You just see to getting that surrey hitched up. We're going into Tyler and get married. You don't like my last name? You can damn well change it. And right now!"

I put my hands out, palms down. "That offer got withdrawn in the same spirit it was rejected. A woman don't come up to a man whose testicles are still aching from his last encounter with her and propose they jump right up and get married. It ain't a help on the honeymoon."

She put her hands on her hips and faced me. "Damn it, Warner Grayson, you are not going to keep me from going on that trip. Half this ranch is mine."

It appeared she intended to have it out right there in the middle of the back yard. Well, that didn't mean I had to be a party to it. I just walked right by her. "You want to talk to me I will be in the parlor at the medicine cabinet pouring myself a shot of snake venom."

It left her no choice but to follow me. I could hear her coming behind me, but I stretched out my long legs, making sure she couldn't get near enough to start a brawl. She was mouthing words, but I couldn't catch any of them, a situation I counted myself lucky in. I mounted the back porch, went in through the kitchen door, and passed through the kitchen into the hall and into the parlor, and went straight to the liquor cabinet and had it open and was pouring myself a large whiskey when she came storming into the room.

"God damn it, you cannot keep me from going! I am half owner of this place!"

The parlor was cool and dim after the late-morning sunshine of outside. Laura had her head back and her legs slightly spread. The posture served to thrust her breasts out against the thin linen of her blouse.

I took a sip of my whiskey. It was commencing to look like one of those days we had about once a month. It did appear to be coming at a damn inconvenient time. Laura had been packing for the trip for the past week. Naturally, I could do all of mine in about half an hour, though she had been making some noises about me buying a suit of clothes with a foulard tie and a waistcoat and some other foolishness, like a swallowtail coat. I hadn't paid her much mind but she had vowed that I would be dressed properly by the time we saw her family in Virginia. I'd said I'd be dressed like what I was: a horseman who was living in sin with one of the coldest-jawed women ever came down the pike. And that was true. If Laura had been a horse, a bit would have done a man no good. She'd have paid it not the slightest mind.

I said, "As you well understand, and as you signed papers to that effect, you are a partner in the profit and loss of this ranch. You are not a partner in the management or the decisions of this ranch other than those that have to do with domestic arrangements. You ain't got a single vote when it comes to the business of horses and this trip is a horse-buying trip. That answer your question about who has a say as to whether you can go or not? You ain't no different from Charlie or Les Russel or Raoul around here. You are just another one of the hired help."

She was so mad she nearly had tears in her eyes. She stamped her foot. She said, "You are the meanest thing on earth! You know how much I have been looking forward to this trip. You can't do this to me."

I took another sip of whiskey. "You ought to have thought of that before you ended the other argument the way you did, Missus *Pico*."

She stamped her foot again. "Oh, damn you! Damn you!"

"That's the right way to go about it. Everybody knows you catch more flies with cuss words than honey."

She glared at me. "If I thought honey would work I'd try it. But you'd just listen and then laugh. I'd even apologize, but you wouldn't take it."

"No, because you wouldn't mean it and I know that and so do you."

"Listen, damn it, you are talking about spending large sums of money on those stallions. That's my money. Or the better part of it is."

I said, dryly, "A little while ago it was John Pico's money."

She steadied herself and crossed her arms over her breasts. She said, "You are determined to make an issue out of that, aren't you?"

I had to laugh. "Me make an issue out of it? Somehow I don't reckon it's been me going around here for the last four years calling myself by a name that wasn't mine no more. Aw, yeah, I'm the one making the issue."

She took a moment. "I can go on my own, you know."

I nodded. "That you can. You can go see your kin in Virginia. I wouldn't never interfere with you on that. But was I you I wouldn't tell them you were getting into the Thoroughbred horse racing business. Somebody might have some questions you couldn't answer."

Her lip trembled in spite of herself. She said, "I've got a right to go to those other ranches, too."

"Farms," I said. "For some reason they call them Thoroughbred farms up in that part of

41

the country. Don't know why. Guess it makes them seem more high toned than an ordinary ranch like we have down here. See, right there you would have given yourself away."

"Well, I've got the right to go to those *farms* then. After all, it is my money, no matter what you say."

I shook my head. "No, it ain't all your money. Or John Pico's either. I got a pretty good chunk of change in this operation myself. Not to count a lifetime of experience. But you can't say it was Pico's money as bought the floor my boots were on or the ceiling over my head and then turn around and claim it's his money going to buy them stud horses. There is a place where his stops and mine starts."

She got a stubborn look on her face. "Say what you will . . . I still have the right to go to those farms and see what the money is buying."

"Of course you do." I downed my whiskey. "That is if you knew which stud farms they were. I'm the only one who knows where I'm going and when."

Her lip began to tremble. I didn't know if it was real or put on for my benefit. Laura had once told me in a moment of uncommon weakness (or a couple of brandies too many) that the reason she had to keep her guard up with me and be so hard-shelled most of the time was that she was afraid I would overpower her, that she cared more for me than was good for her own interests. Well, she couldn't have said it any better for the way I felt about her. I felt like the second I showed weakness she'd eat me alive and then walk off, leaving the skin and bones for the coyotes.

She said, "I can't believe you want to deprive me of the chance to see my family."

I laughed. "Visit your family. Hell, Laura, in four years you've never showed the slightest interest in going back home to Virginia. The only reason you want to go now is so you can go swell around and show off that you're a highbred race horse owner."

She took a step toward me and uncrossed her arms, letting them hang at her sides. She had some kind of trick where she could go from hard and sharp around the edges to taking on a kind of vulnerable softness that made you want to take her in your arms. She said, "What makes you think it's not you I want to show off?"

I shook my head and poured myself out another drink and leaned against the liquor cabinet. "That one is way below your style, Laura. I'm kind of ashamed for you. You can do better than that. Why now?"

She took another step forward and her voice kind of got whispery. "Before, they wouldn't have understood what kind of genius you are with horses. They wouldn't know about Morgans and quarter horses and cattle horses. But Thoroughbred, Thoroughbred racers they understand."

I sipped my whiskey. "That ain't much better, Laura. Pretty thin, mighty thin."

She bit at her lower lip. "I don't understand you, Warner Grayson. We have had fights before. God only knows we've had fights before, but you never stooped this low before. I didn't do that much. For heaven's sake!"

I stared at her in disbelief. "You didn't do that much? Woman, were you and I at the same rodeo? First, you tear into my manhood with that remark about using John Pico's money and then you try to kick what's left of it up into my belly. Didn't do that much! Hell, I'd rather you'd shot me. At least that would not have damaged what little dignity I've got left after four years with you."

She stared at me a long time. "What if I were to say I was sorry?"

"I'd say that you were sorry that I wasn't taking you. I wouldn't believe you were out and out sorry on your own for cutting me down with words and then lifting me up with your knee. You laughed before you walked out of the kitchen, remember, Laura?"

She gave at me another long, slow look. Finally she stepped back. She said. "I guess you are not as tough a man as I have always thought you were. Maybe this new endeavor is too much for you. I should have realized."

It was another one of her leave-the-room remarks. As soon as she'd delivered the blow she turned on her heel and went straight out of the room. In a second I could hear her climbing the front stairs. She was climbing briskly, as if she had something to do or someplace to go.

Well, it scared me. I might have gone too far and that is a dangerous and indistinct line with Laura. You approach it at your peril and you cross it to your destruction. I stood there with a feeling of uneasiness running all through me. I had never meant to not take her with me. Hell, besides the fact that she did, indeed, have the right to see what her money was being spent on, the trip was going to last a few weeks, and I didn't want to be without her that long. I had wanted to bring to her attention that she'd crossed one of my lines, and I'd wanted her to be damn sorry she'd done so, but I hadn't wanted it to go so far. There had been a certain finality in the way she'd left the room, a kind of sad seriousness to it that I'd never seen before.

My first urge was to hurry right after her and say she could go, that everything was all right. But that would have put the saddle squarely on my back and handed her a file to sharpen her spurs with. I was going to have to give this matter a little thought and figure out a way for her to ask me again to please let her go and for me to grudgingly give in. But right then and there I didn't have the slightest idea how to go about it.

I got out a cigarette and lit it and stood there, leaning against the liquor cabinet, thinking. One thing my grandfather had taught me was how to think. You start off with where you are, where you want to get to, and figure out what you need to do or say to arrive at the situation or circumstance or place you want to be. It was clear I was in the hole with Laura. What I wanted was for the whole mess to get patched up and forgotten. But I wanted to do it in such a way that I wouldn't be giving in to her, or at least be perceived that way. It would have been easy to have followed her up to the bedroom and said, "Oh, hell, forget it. We both got carried away. Let's start the day all over again."

The only problem with that was that Laura would look as pleased as a cat with cream on its whiskers and figure I was weak as the next man.

And Laura didn't like weak men, she only thought she did.

I thought the whole matter over for a good long while, testing out approaches and different varieties of strategy. None of them seemed to be worth a damn, because they didn't pack any punch. If you want somebody to do something you've either got to make it worth their while or make it too costly not to do. There ain't no other approach when you are in a showdown. If you ain't got the cards that give you the best hand then you'd better have enough money to make your opponent scared to call your bet. A lot of folks would call that a bluff, but Carver Grayson, who was as good a poker player as I reckon I'd ever seen—and I was watching him at an early age—always said it wasn't a bluff if you won the hand. If nobody calls you, you don't have to show your cards and it doesn't really matter what you had. Another thing that Carver used to say was that if there wasn't a gate in a fence where you wanted one then make one. Or else content yourself with staying on the wrong side of the fence.

Well, I didn't like the side of the fence I was on, because Laura was on the other and I had to figure out either how to make a gate or how to get her to come over on my side. I had examined my cards and I did not have a very strong hand. All that left me was the option of making the bet so high she'd have to give it serious thought before she called.

I took a last drink of whiskey, put out my cigarette, and went upstairs.

Laura was sitting in front of her dressing table

brushing her hair. She brushed her hair as a regular thing, but always had at it when she was agitated. You could tell how agitated she was by how fast she was brushing it. Her hand was moving so fast the brush was just a blur.

I stopped in the open door and leaned up against the jamb. She glanced in the mirror at me but in no other way recognized my presence. After a minute I said, "I want to tell you about a horse I had a little trouble with a few years back. Maybe ten years ago." I waited, but she made no sign she'd heard, didn't even glance in the mirror at me. "Reason I want to tell you this story is that the horse kind of reminded me of you."

I saw her face tighten but she didn't even glance at me in the mirror, just seemed to brush a little faster.

I said, "This was a cow horse that had been turned out for a year and had gotten spoiled. Which is the worst condition a horse can get in. A green horse is not so bad because he ain't learned all the tricks, but a spoiled horse knows what to do, he just don't want to cooperate. Anyway, I was working this horse, trying to get him back to where he was some kind of useful. One morning I went out and threw a saddle on him, figuring to let him get the hump out of his back. Soon as I got next to him he started cow-kicking. Cow-kicking is when a horse kicks forward with his hind leg. It's natural in a cow, but ain't in a horse. That's why they—"

She said in a flat voice, "I know what cow-kicking is."

I nodded. I was grateful for any kind of response. I was fixing to run a hell of a bluff and I was plenty nervous. Of course, as my grandfather would say, it hadn't been determined if I was bluffing or not. If I got called it was a bluff, if I made the heavy bet stand up nobody would ever see my cards and I could always claim I had a royal flush.

I said, "Well, with his kicking out like that I stepped into the stirrup and swung aboard as fast as I could. But his last kick knocked my boot out of the stirrup and damned if the horse didn't get his hoof caught right in the iron. And there we were. He was hopping around on three legs with his fourth hoof in the stirrup and I was only half mounted. I had his head pulled around with the reins so I was looking him straight in the face. I said, 'Well, if you are going to get on, I'm gettin off.' So I jumped off his side and stood there and watched him trying to complete the business of riding himself. I could have told him it wouldn't work but he had to find out for himself." I stopped and folded my arms and looked at her reflection in the mirror, waiting.

For a moment she kept on brushing, but then her hand finally slowed. She stopped and looked at me in the mirror. "Is there supposed to be some sort of deep meaning to that story or are you just trying to impress me with another of your horse adventures?"

I said slowly, "No, I was trying to make a point." I took a quick little breath. I was about to shove a whole lot of chips into the pot. "Can't but one of us ride, Laura, can't but one of us handle the reins. You seem to want to ride double and handle the reins at the same time. Won't work."

My heart was beating like a galloping horse. I was not at all sure how far I wanted to push on with what I had started. But she slowly turned in her chair and looked at me. The hell of it was she always looked so damn desirable at the worst times in our fights. Now her features were softened and her breasts looked round and soft in her blouse. One of the buttons had come undone so that I could see a good deal of her milky skin. She was resting the hand with the brush on one of her legs, her thigh looked perfect in her riding pants. She said, "What are you trying to say, Warner, other than to make an unflattering comparison of me to an unruly horse."

I cleared my throat, wishing I had another drink. "I reckon it's pretty obvious. There can't be but one boss here and that's the one that knows the business, not who has got the most money. All your money bought you, excuse me, *John Pico's* money, was the chance to make more. It didn't buy you the right to make the decisions."

"You are still not saying what you mean."

I took a deep breath. I said, "I reckon I had better go and find the money to pay you back what you've put in. With a profit if I can raise it."

She almost brought it off cold, but not quite. I saw her flinch. I saw her take a quick little breath and her eyes widened for an instant. Just an instant, but it was enough to tell me I'd hit a nerve.

But that was all she let show. When she spoke, she was icy cool. She said, "I see. And what if I don't want to see? What if I want to buy you out?"

I laughed. I wasn't exactly relieved, but I had seen that slight crack in her armor. I said, "Don't be silly. You know I ain't boasting or stretching it when I say I'm the biggest asset this enterprise has got. All the money in the world won't buy my horse sense."

She looked at me, considering. I tried to avoid locking eyes with her, but she kept after mine until she had them. Then she said, "And you'd let me go? Just like that?"

Now she was starting to try and hem me up in a corner. I knew her tactics. I said dryly, "I don't reckon it's been, just like that. I reckon four years of a running fight is hardly just like that. But you are pushing me further and further every time, Laura. And I reckon I've come to my stopping place."

She still had my eyes. "You'd let me go. Out of your life?"

"You don't have to put it like that."

"No, there's no other way to put it. That's what you're saying."

And then, in a sudden gesture, she put both her hands to the front of her blouse and ripped it and the sheer camisole underneath wide apart so that her round, erect breasts stood seductively out from her chest. She said, "You'd let this go." She sat there, her shirt front pulled gaping wide, her breasts presented to me. "This, all of this. You'd let it go."

I turned my head and looked away. I said, "Aw, hell, Laura, now you are really fighting dirty." But even though I knew her purpose I couldn't help what the sight of her was doing to me. I said, "That ain't fair."

"Fair?" She laughed. "How many times have I heard you say that the only way to fight was to win. Whether it was poker or pistols, you played to win by any means. Isn't that so?"

I still wouldn't look at her. I said, "It ain't

52

the same thing. You and I ought not to be fighting in the first place."

"Why don't you look at me, Warner? You're the one continuing this fight. The last thing I said to you was 'Let's go to town and get married.' That would change my name."

"You said it when you knew there wasn't time."

She got up. I could see her out of the corner of my eye. She was walking with her shoulders back to make her breasts even more obvious. Her nipples looked like big, over-ripe strawberries. They were erect and hard and they only got that way when she was cold or aroused and it damn sure wasn't cold in the room, not even cool for that matter. She said, "We've got time if you want to make time. I'm willing right now. You put your name on me and there'd be no question of who was in the saddle." She took two steps toward me.

I said, "Stay right there, Laura. We are talking business here, not romance, and certainly not marriage."

She stopped. She said, "We were talking my last name. That hasn't got a damn thing to do with the ranch."

"No, we were talking about you coming on this trip. That's when you declared you'd do as you damn well pleased and give me the knee to make your point." I still wouldn't look at her.

She got a little tremble in her voice. I judged it to be calculated. She said, "Would you believe me if I told you I was sorry that I did that, that I wish I could take it back? And it has nothing to do with whether you let me come on the trip or not. I've been thinking about it and I know I was wrong. I was wrong to have done it in the first place, but I was unforgivably wrong to have done it in front of Rosa. I'm spoiled, Warner. That's the only explanation I can give. I'm spoiled rotten. Men have always spoiled me. You're the first man I've never been able to push around. You confuse me and sometimes I . . . I do things I don't—"

I looked at her quickly. There was a tone in her voice that damn near sounded sincere. "Don't what?"

She dropped her voice to almost a whisper. "Don't mean. Don't mean to do. Maybe I have been keeping John's name to anger you, using it on you because you didn't like it. Doing something I didn't really want to do."

"Then why do it? Why create all this damn trouble for nothing?"

I saw her swallow. She said, stammering just the slightest, "Because I . . . I . . . I'm afraid of you Warner."

She was only a few feet away. She looked so beautiful my heart ached. But I said, "Afraid of me? Hell, Laura, I never so much as raised a finger to you."

A hint of impatience flitted across her face. "Damn it, Warner, you know that is not what I mean. I'm afraid of losing you. There, I've said it. You satisfied?"

I gave her a long look. This was going a shade too easy. I said, "Is that why you keep walking away from me? You sure you ain't more afraid of me not taking you on this trip?"

She sighed and let her shoulders droop a little, which only served to call further attention to her breasts. I could feel my jeans getting a little tight in spite of the damage my balls had suffered. They were probably wondering what in hell my leader was getting them up to.

She said, "Are we back to that?"

"Back to that? Hell, Laura, I come up here to discuss dissolving this partnership with you. We ain't *back* to nothing." It kind of scared me to say it, but I figured in for a penny, in for a pound.

She searched my face. "I don't think you mean that." She narrowed her eyes. "I don't think that's what you came up here for."

I waved my hand at her. I said, "Hell, cover up will you? That pair of yours is beating my one of a kind."

For answer she ripped her shirt and camisole off and threw them on the floor. Then she started to unbutton her riding pants, which buttoned at the waist on the side like women's britches did.

I said, "Now, damn it, hold up there."

She gave me a defiant look. "Why? If I'm going to leave I've got to change clothes. I'm not going into town dressed like this."

Now that scared the hell out of me. I said, "You don't have to leave. Not right now. Hell, nothing is settled. I thought we'd talk about it."

She went back and sat down on her dressing-table chair and took off her short, jodhpur riding boots. "Why? You think I'm trying to take the reins out of your hands. You think I'm trying to push you out of the saddle. I never in my life heard such a ridiculous thing. We had a fight, I got a little too angry. I could see I had gone too far. I felt bad about it. I wanted to apologize but you wouldn't let me. So I finally told you something I never thought I would. There's nothing left to talk about. You're leaving tomorrow on the trip, I'm leaving for town today."

She stood up and took off her riding pants and then her silk step-ins. She was standing there before me as smooth and as rounded and as delectable as it was possible for a woman to look.

My chest was so tight and my breathing was coming so hard I was having trouble getting any words out. Finally I said, "It's damn silly the way you are acting."

She said, "I think you came up here to see if you could make me knuckle under. All right. I did." She took two steps toward me. I was looking at the little mound where the silken forest of blond hair grew. She said, "I told you why I had done what I did. I asked you to forgive me. I said I was sorry. What else? Did I forget to say you were the boss and that I knew it? All right. You're the boss. I recognize that fact. You make all the decisions where the ranch is concerned."

Then she stepped right up to me, very close. She tapped herself between the breasts. "But I make all the decisions where *I'm* concerned. You understand?"

I put my hands out to cup her breasts, but she pushed them away.

She said, "Do you understand?"

"About what?"

"That I make the decisions about me. I'm not part of the ranch that you're the boss over. You're the boss over that part that involves my money, yes, but not me. Not yet. Not as long as we're not married."

Well, she'd done it again. She'd backed me around until she had the upper hand again. Five minutes before, her lip and her voice had been trembling and she'd been begging to get back in my good graces. Then I'd pushed it one inch too far and she'd taken off her clothes and I'd lost the hand. It had happened often enough that I ought to have seen it coming, but I hadn't. Now I was suddenly flung in the position of having to talk her out of leaving and taking up residence at the hotel in town while I supposedly dissolved the partnership or at least set the lawyers to the task.

I was of half a mind to turn around and walk out and leave her to her own devices. Just once, I told myself, I ought to call her bluff.

I slowly shook my head. I had my breathing under control. I said, "Naw, I ain't gonna wear that, Laura."

"Wear what?"

"That coat that's got about one too many colors in it. You want to make me out the bully that pushes you around and won't marry you and takes your poor dead husband's money and then is mean to you in the bargain." I shook my head again. "Naw, I ain't all them things. What I am is a man who cares a great deal about you and who is also a little scared of you. I'm also a man a little scared he might be in over his head on a new business enterprise and who sure as hell don't need no devilment from you. But I'm also a man who knows you as well as anybody does and I know you didn't take your clothes off so you could get dressed to go stay in town. You took your clothes off because you know it turns my brains to mush when you do. Ain't that about the size of it?"

I stared at her and she stood there, staring back. For a long half minute nothing happened and then a little smile tugged at the corner of her mouth. "You think that's why I took my clothes off, do you?"

I stepped up until we were almost touching. "I don't think it, I know it."

She started unbuttoning my shirt. "You going to take me with you?"

I let her finish taking my shirt off while I kicked off my boots and unbuckled my jeans and then stepped out of them. I hadn't worn underwear since I figured out it was just something else to get in the way. I reached out and took her by the arms and leaned down and kissed her upturned mouth. The bed was a few yards away to the right. I said, "Yeah, I'm going to take you." I started her toward the bed. "Right over here."

"You know what I mean."

"Yeah, I know what you mean. But right now, I'm taking you here."

As we eased down on top of the spread, she said, "We ought to get married. I think it would save ever so much trouble. At least then we could have decent fights without scaring one another to death."

I said, "Shut up. You are talking too much again. You always get in trouble with that mouth of yours."

"Are you going to take me?"

Just before I kissed her I said, "We'll see."

Which was a damn fool thing to say because we both knew that I was. But I was also conscious, as I think she was, that we'd almost gone too far. She was right. It was becoming necessary that we get married before something really bad happened.

Laura was a very easy woman for a man to lose himself in. In bed with her a man didn't ordinarily have much else on his mind except what he was holding. But I couldn't help wondering the whole time if I'd won or lost. It didn't seem like anything had changed. We'd got up that morning with a trip planned for the next day. That was still going to be. A lot had happened in the meantime, but it really hadn't changed anything except to make my balls sore.

Luckily, they still worked just as well. So, toward the end, I went ahead and accepted the fact that me and Laura had fought to another Mexican standoff like we had so many times before.

3

We left about ten the next morning for the drive into Tyler to catch the eastbound noon train. Due to the amount of Laura's luggage, we were forced to take the buggy in order to provide room for us and the number of valises, hat boxes, trunks, and other paraphernalia that she deemed necessary to take. Judging from the amount of gear that she was lugging along, I calculated that she figured to change clothes at least three or four times a day during the extent of our trip. Laura and I sat on the rear seat of the surrey facing forward, staring at the mass of baggage piled in front of us. For myself, I was taking a fair-sized valise that held plenty of clothes, maybe more than I needed, for the trip. And even though I wasn't taking a horse, I took along my old saddlebags. For some reason I always felt more comfortable carrying them around with me. My valise would be in the baggage car of the train, but the saddlebags would stay with me.

It was another beautiful May morning and Laura was bright eyed and smiling, happy at the prospect of some excitement in her life. I sometimes had to wonder if she didn't create enough in her daily getting about to last most folks a lifetime. But she looked enormously pretty in a light yellow frock with a little white ruffled collar fastened at her throat by some kind of brooch or pin that women will wear.

Charlie Stanton and Les Russel were up on the driver's seat, with Les doing the driving. Ordinarily, I would have had Les drive us in, leaving Charlie at the ranch. But with us being gone as long as I figured, I thought some last-minute details might come into my mind that I might want to pass on to Charlie.

Charlie was my height, only a good deal slimmer. He was sandy haired and friendly looking. Right off the bat, you would take him for a country hick, but he was one country hick that you didn't want to get into a horse trading match with. The way our outfit worked was that Juanito and Raoul brought the green horses along until they were nearly ready for finishing—that job belonged to me and Charlie. Of late, as plans for the new ranch had taken most of my mind, I had left a good deal of that work to Charlie. As I've said, he was as good a hand with a horse as anybody I knew of, outside myself. Les Russel was a good all-around man. I had even considered taking him along on the trip with me just in case we ran into trouble or needed another hand with all of Laura's luggage.

We were going down a country road that led into town, going up over the gentle little rises and drops. All around us were green and brightly colored flowers just coming into bloom. I had to admit that it was beautiful country. Laura saw it only that way, as beautiful country. I saw it as beautiful and good for horses. That made it all the more beautiful to me.

Charlie turned and looked back at me. He said, "Boss, do you want to move those Thoroughbred broodmares off that grass we got them on? I'd really like to have those two that are in foal up nearer to the barn. You know, neither one of us have much experience with those delicate Thoroughbreds and I don't want to take any chances, least not while I'm minding the store."

I said, "That might be a good idea, Charlie."

Les Russel said, "Boss, how in hell are me and Juanito and Raoul and us that don't know things by instinct like you and Charlie gonna learn about them high-toned Thoroughbreds?"

I said, "Les, you have made it this far in life without knowing about anything. Why would you doubt your instincts now?"

Les laughed. He was a man who laughed easily. "Boss, somewhere in there might be a compliment, but I'm damned if I can find it."

Laura said, "Would ya'll stop talking about

business for the moment? Let's enjoy this drive into town. I am ever so excited."

Charlie said, "Miss Laura, you sound like you've never been nowhere before. I've always kinda got the impression that you were a well traveled lady."

The remark made me cut my eyes sideways at her and give her a slight grin.

She gave me a sharp slap on the thigh for what she imagined I was thinking. She said in demure tones to Charlie, "Thank you Charlie. Yes, I have seen my fair share of the civilized world. I do not, however, count this part of Texas as being in its confines. I would not call this the most sophisticated area that I have ever been to but if this is where Mr. Warner Grayson says that we can raise the finest Thoroughbred racing horses, then of course, who am I to argue?"

Laura and I had gotten up that morning as if the day before had never happened. It hadn't been long, however, until she had expressed her thrill at leaving what she chose to refer to as a godforsaken wilderness where there was no society, no gentility, and damned little civilization. I had replied that, of course, nothing could possibly compare to the life that she had led in Corpus Christi, especially considering the meager amount of Spanish she spoke. That had led to a few sharp words, but in the end, peace had reigned, at least the kind of peace that you would normally find between Laura and me. She had, however, assured me that once I had seen the real gentility of the South in Louisiana, Tennessee, Kentucky, and most assuredly in Virginia, that I would never again be content with such a lifeless void as where we were presently settled, and, if I was any man at all, my sights would be aimed much higher, viewing our present circumstances only as the first stepping stone in a long climb to some higher form of society where the men for some reason wore boiled shirts. I didn't choose to comment on that one.

She had, however, objected to my taking my handguns along. I wasn't wearing a gun, but I had both of my Colt .42/.40s in my saddlebags, along with an amount of ammunition. The revolvers were specially made for me. They were .40-caliber guns set on a .42-caliber frame. The .42-caliber frame gave a heavier feeling in the hand and cut down on the barrel deviation. If you couldn't stop what you wanted to stop with a .40-caliber slug, then you weren't hitting it in the stopping place. One of my revolvers, the one that I normally carried as a side gun, had a six-inch barrel. The other, kept in reserve and used for work at longer range, had a nine-inch barrel.

Laura had assured me that if these weapons

were found in my possession in the cultured homes that we would be visiting in the cultured states that we would be going through, that I would be viewed as a barbarian. She had said, "We are leaving the frontier, Warner. There will be no necessity for drawing your gun and shooting someone at the slightest provocation. The men you will be dealing with are gentlemen. They are not given to common and ordinary scuffles in the main street in full view of the entire town's populace."

If I hadn't known better, I would have thought that Laura was a snob, but I was taking my guns just the same, no matter how genteel the gentlemen were.

I looked at my watch. It was a quarter to eleven. Up ahead, the trees began to break and I could see the town of Tyler lying before us some half mile distant. It nestled down in a small, broad valley, though there weren't really enough hills to create a valley. It was a pretty enough place and I suspected that someday we'd get to know a good number of folks there. But for the time being, we were newcomers who appeared to have more money than we ought to be keeping.

We'd had visitors out to the ranch looking over the stock. By and large, most of them had never seen such animals, especially the Andalusians. Quarter horses and Morgans were faintly familiar to them, but all most of the old nestors in that part of the country had ever really looked at was the hind end of a mule while they were plowing. Even though the country was good ranch land for cattle, most of the spreads were small and there were more farms than there were ranches. It did make a good selection of viands for the kitchen. I didn't reckon that we had ever had such good pork and hams and beef and vegetables as we had since we had moved to Tyler. I was well taken with the place and thought we were moving along at a good pace to get established.

That was, if I was able to find the kind of studs that would breed a line of horses that could outrun other folks' horses. Sometimes I found it frightening to find that our livelihood depended upon my ability to breed a horse that could run faster than the other fellow's. That was a little strange when you thought about it, but then, I suppose when the first two men riding horses got together, the first thing they did was to see which one of them could run the fastest. I reckon it was just part of human nature, at least for the horseman. But knowing that and understanding that didn't make it any less scary, realizing that I was going to have to come home with horses that could make us winners or else the whole shebang would be down the drain.

We came into Tyler in good style, driving down the main street toward the depot that lay near the north end. There were a good many people out and about on the boardwalks in front of the stores. They stopped and stared, mainly, I think, at Laura's luggage, though the surrey itself and the matched pair of blacks that were pulling it made a handsome sight. A few of the women waved, and Laura waved back. Me and Charlie and Les tipped our hats and nodded at a few of the men. They all knew who we were. Newcomers in these lonesome parts were a bit of a rarity. I reckon that the word had already gotten back to the womenfolk that the widow Pico and I didn't share the same last name. We'd never volunteered any information, so for all they knew, she might have been my widowed sister. That is if they were willing to give her the benefit of the doubt. But knowing women as I did, I didn't imagine that they could look at that brilliant head of hair of hers and her stylish and smart clothes and not do a little hard and fast gossiping behind their hands and behind their doors. I reckon they figured that we were rich. That thought brought a smile to my face. If they only knew how close to being mighty unrich we were, they sure as hell wouldn't have envied us.

We pulled up in front of the train station with a good forty-five minutes to go before the train was due to depart. But that was all right. Buying tickets would take some time and it would take an even greater time to get the luggage assembled so that we could load it on the baggage car before the train pulled out. Les pulled the surrey into a hitching rack next to the depot and Laura and I got out and went on into the station house. She sat down while I went up and bought the tickets. The first leg of our route would take us east through Longview to Shreveport, Louisiana, and then on east and a little north to Lafayette, Louisiana.

While I was busy with the tickets, Les and Charlie were making several trips with the luggage, leaving it on the passenger platform where the train would pull up. I only bought our tickets as far as Lafayette. From there we'd go on to a farm in Tennessee near Nashville.

Laura sat on a waiting-room bench, looking as excited as a little girl. I had my saddlebags over my shoulder. Besides my guns, there was a bottle of whiskey in each one. I was a man who liked to be prepared when I traveled. The trip to Lafayette would get us in about five or six o'clock that afternoon. They had a dining car on the train where it was said that we would get lunch. I'd been told about such things, but never had eaten a regular meal on a train. I was about halfway looking forward to it, but so much had changed of late, so many new things, modern life moving so much further along, that I couldn't keep up with it.

Once the tickets were settled, Charlie and I wandered off to talk about the business of the ranch while I was gone. Laura sent Les over to a nearby store to get her some newspapers and other odds and ends.

Charlie said, "Well, Boss, I guess we'll just wait for you to get back. I can't think of anything that needs doing."

I said, "Charlie, make damned certain that we don't have any trouble with the new neighbors about any of that fencing that we put up on that south eight hundred acres. That's pretty near some water that's common water around here. Make sure that we haven't fenced anybody's cows off from that water."

He said, "Don't worry about that, Boss. I'm not gonna get you crosswise with any of these folks around here."

And then the train was coming in, huffing and puffing, blowing out clouds of steam, its bell clanging as it skidded to a stop, steel screeching on steel. The conductor got down from the first of the passenger cars, setting his metal step down so that the ladies would have an easier time climbing up. I hustled down with Charlie and Les and helped them get the luggage into the baggage car. Then I shook hands quickly and went back up and escorted Laura into the chair car.

Laura and I got settled in a seat toward the back of the train facing forward. There was a seat facing us, but it was empty. The car was about half full, which I was glad of because one of the reasons I hated to ride in the chair cars was that they were generally crowded and you always had somebody jammed up against you or somebody's kid wailing and making all kinds of commotion. But it looked like it was going to be a pretty easy trip.

Before long, I could feel the train tremble as the engineer got up steam and then the cars went to jerking as the locomotive's forward motion began to take up slack between the couplings. Within a few moments, we were moving along at a pretty good clip and the houses and farms of Tyler had fallen behind us. I settled back in my seat and put my boots up on the seat opposite me. I said, "Well, Laura, we're off."

"Yes," she said, "we're off. How do you feel?"

"I feel like taking a drink."

She said, "Oh, not yet." I stood and reached up into the overhead where I had stowed my saddlebags and got out a bottle of whiskey. I sat down, pulled the plug and had a pretty good drink. I smiled and offered it to Laura, certain that she would turn it down. Instead she surprised me by taking the bottle by the neck, putting it to her lips, and taking a small sip. She made a little face.

She said with a wry smile, "For luck."

"For luck," I said.

By now, the train was picking up speed to about thirty or forty miles an hour. Laura said, "Are you worried?"

I said, "Hell yes, I'm worried. Aren't you?"

Laura said, "No. I don't have to be worried. Remember, I'm the silent partner."

"Well, you could worry silently."

She said, "It has been made clear to me that I am not to even think about the horse part of the business."

I patted her on the thigh. "Just keep it that way, honey."

She motioned with her head at the rack over her head and said, "I suppose that you've got those two huge revolvers of yours up there."

I said, "Yes, they're in my saddlebags."

She said, "I suppose they're loaded?"

"They are loaded for the same reason that I don't carry a dull knife."

She said, "What's to keep them from going off and shooting someone?"

I said, "Guns don't go off by themselves."

She said, "Well, then why have I heard that men keep an empty cartridge under the hammer?"

I said, "That's an empty chamber under

the hammer and they don't do that anymore. Something called the floating firing pin has been invented and now you can load all six chambers without fear of an accidental discharge. I assure you that the least of our worries is that one of my revolvers is going to go off all by itself. In fact, so far as I know in the history of mankind and guns, there has never been a revolver that fired itself."

Laura said, "But it's up there on the overhead rack, being jostled around by the motion of the train. Surely that might be enough to set one off and send a bullet crashing through some innocent person sitting in front of us."

"Laura, this is one of those things that you are going to have to trust me on."

She gave me a look, unconvinced, and then returned her attention to the scenery outside. Laura had always, so long as I had known her, had a healthy timidity about guns. She didn't like them. She did not understand them, she thought they made too much noise, and ever since she had been shot accidentally by Jack Fisher during the race I was having against him in Del Rio, she didn't even like to think about guns. Nothing that I could say or do was ever going to convince her to the contrary. But I had lived in the day and age when if a man didn't know how to use a gun, he could very well die of his own ignorance. I understood

Laura's feeling about guns after the gunshot wound that had penetrated her side. I had tried, in the intervening two years since that time, to reintroduce her to guns and how they could be used for good purposes in the name of law and order and for a man's protection.

On several occasions I had taken Laura out to try some target shooting. With trembling hands she had grasped the butt of a revolver. Once she had even gone so far as to pull the trigger, but the explosion had been so loud, she'd immediately dropped the gun. After a couple of those incidents I had given up. But I still told her that I thought that she was making a mistake. A gun was nothing but another tool, and a tool was to be used. She'd never know when the time might come that she would have a use for such a tool.

Our first stop was to be at a breeding farm outside of Lafayette called The Gables. When I had first written them, I thought that the name was the same as the man who owned the place, but Laura had told me that a gable had something to do with architecture. She had assured me that I was going to see a fine, Southern mansion, something that I had never seen before.

But I cared less about the man's house than I did about his horses. The breeder's name was Clive Clatterbuck. He had been breeding for some twelve to fifteen years and with pretty good success the last ten years. Several of those years he had horses in the big derby in Kentucky. He hadn't won, but some of his stock had run on up in the money. His biggest achievement on his record sheet was winning the derby in New Orleans where the prize was ten thousand dollars. That was quite a nice piece of change to win in a single horse race. The back end of his stable had been built on a stallion named Slewfoot Bob, who went way back in Thoroughbred racing lineage. The horse himself was now about twenty years old, but he had produced some colts who had created impressive records and had gone on to produce colts with even better records. It was that strain that went back to Slewfoot Bob that I was looking to get a stallion or two from.

About the man Clive Clatterbuck, I knew very little. I understood that he had two sons and that his wife was deceased and that by all accounts he was successful. The Williams's family banking connections had done me the favor of doing a kind of check on him through the bank they owned, and he had come up all aces. I was very hopeful that out of that Slewfoot Bob line I might be able to make a good buy that I could intermingle with some other studs from good farms and begin the Warner Grayson bloodline. Maybe we'd get a chance in a few years to win us some of those ten-thousand-dollar purses.

The day wore on. The train clattered along and we crossed the Louisiana border. We pulled into Shreveport about three in the afternoon. We had a meal in the dining car that was surprisingly good. I had beef stew and Laura had some kind of chicken with a sauce on it. They had waiters in there—Negroes wearing starched white coats—and it was just as fine a restaurant as I had ever been in.

Us sitting there, having our meal with the countryside tearing by outside—I didn't know what they were going to think of next. The meal had cost us about two dollars apiece, which I reckon was a little high, but then you had to add in the forty miles an hour that you were racing along at while you were eating it. I guess if you did that, it would come out to a pretty good price per mile. First time I had ever judged a meal by its distance.

About four o'clock, Laura was starting to get restless and I asked her a question that we never had gotten around to discussing. I said, "Laura, we are going to be met at the station by the Clatterbucks and then they are going to drive us out to their plantation. How are we going to introduce ourselves?"

She said, "Well, whatever in the world do you mean?"

I said, "Are we going to play the dumb bunny, Laura? That really will suit you."

She made a little fluttering motion with her hand. She said, "Do you mean, shall we present ourselves as husband and wife?"

"That would be passing strange since we don't bear the same last name," I said.

She said, "Well, should we present ourselves just as we are? As business partners?"

I said, "That will mean two separate bedrooms." I gave her a look.

She looked back at me squarely. She said, "Well, would that be so bad?"

I folded my arms. "Won't bother me."

She said, "Then it is settled. We shall present ourselves as business partners."

I said, "Are you sure that you will be able to keep your hands off me?"

She gave me a sharp slap on the thigh. That woman was the hittingest woman I had ever seen. She said, "I don't see that we should make an issue out of it, Warner. Why don't you behave properly? After all, you're going to buy studs, not act like one."

I gave her a look and shook my head slowly. Sometimes she was more than I wanted to handle.

4

It was still daylight when we got into Lafayette. Laura and I descended from the train and were met almost immediately by a tall man in his early thirties. I reckon the wrong kind of woman might have thought of him as handsome. He had long sideburns, and a thin mustache above a pouty mouth. He was wearing a waistcoat and a string tie with a white frilly shirt and a wide hat that I was to learn was called a plantation hat. But all I noticed right off was that here was a man wearing a coat and a tie in the middle of the afternoon. He marched himself straight up to us, swept off his hat and said, "You would be our visitors from Tyler, I presume?"

I gave him my name and then presented Laura. Damned if the fellow didn't give her a bow. He said, "I am mighty pleased to make your acquaintance, ma'am. I am Royce Clatterbuck of The Gables plantation. My father, Mr. Clive Clatterbuck, has sent me to fetch you folks out to the plantation."

He made me feel kind of foolish standing there in my jeans and hat and blue work shirt with my saddlebags over my shoulder, but I gave him a handshake and thanked him for meeting us and then we got on with the business of getting Laura's luggage off the train. He had a man there to help him and we managed to load it all in a fine, big carriage. After that, we got on board and set off for what he said was a three-mile ride out to their place. As we rode, I studied young Mr. Royce Clatterbuck, who was studying Laura at the same time. He seemed to be rather pleased with himself. Judging from the quality of his clothes, I figured he probably had reason, so far as what he was worth in his wallet, though that didn't count as much to me as what he was worth inside. I can't say that I took a dislike to him, but I didn't exactly warm to him either. There was something a little slippery about him. I hoped his horses would turn out to be more genuine than at first glance he appeared to be.

Lafayette was a pretty little town that Mr. Royce Clatterbuck informed me consisted of some five thousand souls. He said that during race meetings, the population swelled to over twenty thousand. They had race meetings twice a year, lasting upwards of a month. I noted that the houses looked different from what I had been used to seeing. It was the widow Pico who informed me that it was French architecture. I thanked her for that insight.

She asked Mr. Royce Clatterbuck how long he and his family had lived in Lafayette. He seemed to almost make another bow, and said that while they were newly arrived in the country in relation to some of the older, established families, they felt no less a part of the southern sporting life.

I had to confess that I had never heard anybody talk like Mr. Royce Clatterbuck talked. I also had to confess to myself that I was getting a little tired of how big his eyes were getting, especially when they rested on Laura.

I thought it a little presumptuous of a man who, without knowing the relationship between another man and woman, starts making forward gestures, unobtrusive as they were, in the presence of the other man. True, the way I was dressed, I perhaps could have been mistaken for Missus Pico's handyman, but I resented it nonetheless.

We got out of town and into the pretty countryside. The grass was lush and green. There were big oaks with moss hanging off the sides of them. It was a different looking country than anything I had ever seen. The air was a trifle sultry for my taste, but all in all I could tell that it was a rich country by looking at the fat cattle grazing in the pastures. Even the range horses looked sleek and well fed.

I pointed this out to Mr. Royce Clatterbuck

and he acknowledged that yes, they did have the benefit of particularly nutritious grass. Then he set in to instruct me—I could find no other word for it—on the fact that Thoroughbreds, in order to develop those long, sleek, flowing muscles, needed large pastures during young years to run and play and those pastures had to be filled with nutritional grass. Laura, to her discredit, looked at me and then fluttered her eyes at Mr. Royce Clatterbuck and said, "Why, Warner, whyever didn't you think of such a thing?"

I did not reply.

Mr. Clatterbuck gave me to understand that there was a swath through such parts of the south where the Thoroughbred racing horse absolutely bloomed, not only because of the wonderful grass, but mainly because of the natural expertise of the horsemen, the like of which was to be found nowhere else in the country. Laura gave me a sly look on that one, but had the good grace to keep her mouth shut.

My estimation of Mr. Royce Clatterbuck was not growing.

We rolled along in the splendid carriage pulled by a couple of fine-looking bays, with the driver up on his perch. Mr. Clatterbuck was sitting opposite us, directly across from Laura. I assumed that it gave him a better view of her ankles and anything else that he cared to look at.

I said, "Well, Mr. Clatterbuck, I assume that your father is in receipt of my letter. I am hopeful that you will have some horses up for me to look at."

Mr. Clatterbuck took a thin panatela cigar out of his pocket. He started to light it and then made as if to offer it to me. I waved it away and took out a cigarette. When he had his cigar lit and drawing, he said, "Yes, we have some horses up that we felt would suit your needs. According to your letter, you are seeking studs to create a bloodline. We are proud, of course, of the Slewfoot bloodline and are a little particular to whom we sell our studs."

I lit my cigarette. I said, "Would that particularity have more to do with the character of a man or the character of his money?"

Mr. Clatterbuck drew on his cigar and didn't say anything. Laura, however, gave me a look as if I was a barbarian and a ruffian and some sort of white trash that had come in through the back door and didn't know how to behave in front of proper company.

After a few minutes, Mr. Clatterbuck inquired of Laura if she played whist. When she said that she did, he said, "Delightful, then we shall have a game tonight."

As it happened, I knew what whist was. It was a card game that involved four people. He hadn't said anything to me about it. I said,

"I was rather looking forward to playing poker."

Mr. Royce Clatterbuck raised his eyebrows at me and said, "Why . . . yes, but of course that would exclude the lady, here."

I laughed slightly. I said, "It might exclude your money if you play poker with this lady."

Clatterbuck looked surprised. He glanced at Laura and said, "Am I to understand that you play poker, ma'am?"

Damned if she didn't flutter her eyelashes at him. She said, "Well now sir, I understand the rules of the game, but as far as being an actual player, I wouldn't want to go so far as to say that."

My Lord, I thought, the damned woman is going to have a southern accent before we go another mile.

Mr. Clatterbuck said, "Well, by all means, then it would be a pleasure to try your hand at a game of poker. We can certainly arrange that. There is my brother, Cloyce, and then of course, there is our father."

I thought I should get things back to where they ought to be. I said, "Excuse me, Mr. Clatterbuck, our main business here is to look at horses. Perhaps when that is out of the way, then we could tend to the recreation."

He gave me an annoyed look.

In another five minutes we had come around

a curve in the dirt road, past some great oaks. Suddenly, we were going up a gravel drive in front of a huge white mansion. Good Lord, it was the biggest house that I had ever seen. It had columns out front and all kinds of windows sticking out from the roof—I was to find out later that these were gables.

As we came driving up, a Negro came out dressed in some kind of uniform and caught the horses as we came to a stop. Mr. Clatterbuck jumped out of the carriage so as to be sure to help Laura down. I said, "What do we do about the luggage?"

Mr. Clatterbuck informed me that that would be attended to by other people. He then motioned to the widest set of steps I had ever seen, giving Laura his hand, which I'll be damned if she didn't take. I followed along in the wake, looking back over my shoulder to watch the carriage being driven off. We got up on this big cement porch and then went through a set of double doors and then into a room that I reckoned was big enough to hold a good-size dance in. It was cool and light and furnished with expensive looking furniture. We walked a few steps further, and then a large, heavyset man came out of a side door and marched forward to greet us. He was dressed much as his son was except he was wearing a brocade vest. For the life of me, I had never seen people dress up like they were going into town just to stay at home.

The man came forward with his hand outstretched. I put his age somewhere in the middle fifties. He had a goatee beard and a mustache and the same muttonchop sideburns that his son wore. He said, "Mr. Grayson, I would imagine. I'm Clive Clatterbuck. Welcome to The Gables. I trust that you had an enjoyable trip down?"

He almost had a southern accent, but not quite. Every now and then he bit a word off hard like I've heard Yankees do, but he looked like a southerner and he tried to act like one. That peculiarity of his speech threw me. I gave him my name and then Royce presented Laura as if it was his job. "And this is Mrs. Laura Pico. She is Mr. Grayson's business partner, Father."

Well, Mr. Clive Clatterbuck done the same as his son had done. He bowed over her hand like he was going to kiss it. I was good and disgusted. What made it even worse was that she acted as if she liked it. But then, that's Laura for you. She always likes to be the center of attention.

While Laura was talking to the elder Mr. Clatterbuck, I had a look around. I was having misgivings about my decision. When Mr. Clatterbuck had written me inviting me to please come look at his horses, he had offered me the hospitality of his house. Well, like any man with common sense, I know a free room beats paying for one at a hotel, so I had accepted. Now I wasn't so sure. It was a mighty grand place. It didn't look like the sort of operation where you would feel comfortable haggling over the price of a horse. But that was my style. I'd haggle you down to the last penny if I could. Now I felt somewhat at a disadvantage, being Mr. Clatterbuck's guest and being in such elegant surroundings. I resolved, however, that if Mr. Clatterbuck thought I'd be so impressed with his hospitality that I would pay his asking price, then he was in for a rude shock. It might embarrass Laura, but it sure as hell wasn't gonna embarrass me to get down to the bedrock of what I thought a horse was worth. Those Thoroughbreds were going to be expensive enough as it was. I didn't plan to leave any money lying on the table.

Then Mr. Clatterbuck was saying, "I know you two are fatigued from your journey and I'm sure you'd like to refresh yourselves. I'll have someone show you to your rooms." He suddenly stopped and gave both of us a look and said, "You would be wanting a room each, would you not?"

Laura spoke a little too quickly. She said, "Well, certainly, of course. Whatever would you think?"

Mr. Clatterbuck said, bowing a little as he did, "Why, of course, ma'am. I meant no offense whatsoever." He turned to me. He said, "We will be dining at seven-thirty if that meets with your pleasure, sir."

I said, "That'll be fine with me."

He said, "I will see you." He gave Laura another courtly bow, nodded at me, and then went back into whatever room he'd come out of. Next thing I knew, Laura and I were following an old man in a starched white jacket like the man in the dining car on the train had worn, to the upstairs part of the house. If anything, it was more grand than the first floor. He led us down a long hall about the size of a hall you'd see in a big hotel. First he deposited Laura in a room on the right and then he took me several doors down and put me in another room. He kept wanting to take my saddlebags from me, but I insisted on hanging on to them. I took careful note of the door that Laura had disappeared behind.

Once we got in the room, this Negro fellow in the white jacket—there seemed to be a considerable amount of them around the place—pointed out to me the water jug and the basin and also made note of the fact that there was a bottle of brandy in the room in case I cared to refresh myself, as he put it.

I sat down on the bed and looked at my

boots, which were dusty, and looked at my Levi's, which were dusty, and thought about my throat, which was dusty. I had the whiskey in my saddlebags, but there was that decanter of brandy over on the dresser and I figured that so long as I was going to be doing business with Mr. Clatterbuck, I might as well try his brandy, though as a general rule I did prefer whiskey. I poured myself about half of a water glass full and knocked it down, then lit a cigarette and wandered around the room. It was bigger than the biggest hotel room that I had ever been in. It had a tremendous bed, a chiffonier, a bureau, and two or three chairs. My heavens, I could have done business in the place. I was wondering what I was supposed to do next when in came another fellow in a white jacket carrying my valise. He informed me that the bathroom was at the far end of the hall, that there were towels and soap aplenty, and that the house was furnished with running hot water, and could he draw me a bath. I had never heard anybody offer to draw anybody a bath in my entire life.

I did not know what he meant by it and I did not know what to say, so I said, "No, I reckon I can handle it myself."

After he went out, I took another shot of brandy and then slipped down the hall and knocked at Laura's door. She called out, "Who is it?"

I said, "Who the hell do you think it is?" Then I opened the door and went in. She was half undressed and was sitting at a dressing table looking at her face in the mirror.

She looked happy, excited, and she turned around to face me. She said, "Didn't I tell you what a grand place it would be? Didn't I tell you?"

I said, "Laura, we need to go into town and get us a hotel room."

She said, "Why? Whatever for?"

"Because this man is gonna try to make me feel cheap with all this grandeur and froufrou so that he can stick me good for the price of a horse."

Laura said, "Warner, you've never met a southern gentleman before. You don't know how to act around them. You don't know how they act. Why don't you mind your own manners? They'll mind theirs."

I said, "Is old Royce minding his manners by the way he is looking you over, like something he'd like to have on his plate?"

She said, "Oh, are we getting jealous?"

"If I thought that you'd have anything to do with that snake, I wouldn't be jealous, I'd be ashamed."

She said, "We can talk about this later. I've got to go take a bath."

I said, "Well, I guess you'll have to wait until

after me, because the man is drawing my bath right now."

She shook her head at me. She said, "Warner, must you always act like a Texas ruffian? Don't you know that they have more than one bathroom in this mansion?"

"No, but I'm pretty sure that you will occupy them all at the same time if they do."

Supper that night was good, if a little strange. The main dish was something done out of shrimp and fish. I always thought that shrimp and fish were pretty good by themselves without being dressed up with all kinds of fancy sauces and whatnot. Mr. Clatterbuck give me to understand that it was creole cooking and everything was supposed to be a delicacy. Well, I could see Laura giving me the kind of look she gave me when she almost said out loud "You're embarrassing me again," so I just smiled and nodded and acted like I liked it. Mr. Clatterbuck's other son joined us for supper. His name was Cloyce. Mr. Clatterbuck explained that his deceased wife's name was Joyce, and it was from a combination of their names, Clive and Joyce, that you got Cloyce. I could have gone all night without him telling me that but it didn't seem to embarrass the boy any. Well, he wasn't really a boy. I figured him to be in his mid-twenties.

The dining room was big enough, and the table we were eating at was long enough, that there could have been most of the hired help come in and eat with us, but as it was, we all sat around one end. We had some wine that Mr. Clatterbuck said was Madeira, which was a Spanish wine. It tasted like wine to me.

Laura was in her element. She had dressed in an elegant gown, sort of white with a little yellow in it, that was off the shoulders and revealed a little more of her bosom than I cared to have other men looking at. Naturally, she was the center of attention and fairly aglow. I mentally made a note to myself to mention to her that if she kept on occupying center ring, that we were going to have a hell of a time getting around to the business of trading horses.

Mr. Royce Clatterbuck continued to pay court to Laura. They were seated together on the same side of the table, while I was across from them with Cloyce. Mr. Clatterbuck sat at the head of the table. I took note that Royce was very attentive to Laura, explaining to her all the creole dishes and how they were made. He did it with such enthusiasm, you'd have thought that he had made them himself. The younger brother wasn't too talkative, but I could see his eyes eating up Laura's bosom and that creamy white skin of hers. Even the old man didn't seem averse to having a stare every once in a while. But what I couldn't get over was that they had changed clothes again, as if they weren't dressed up enough before.

I thought the meal was never going to end. I was anxious to get off with Mr. Clatterbuck and have a look at the pedigrees of some of his horses. They must have served us seven or eight dishes. I couldn't keep up with them— all I knew was that it was way more than a body needed to eat. But finally they brought in dessert, and damned if it wasn't ice cream.

But then finally the meal was over and I made mention to Mr. Clatterbuck that I would like to have a conversation with him about the purpose of my visit. He said, "Well, yes sir, by all means. Let's you and I retire to my office. I've got some fine old brandy there and some mighty good cigars. I'm certain that my sons can entertain the lady to her satisfaction."

I darted a look at Laura. She gave me a little smirk and sort of patted Royce on the arm. She said, and I swear her voice was turning southern, "Why yes sir, Mr. Clatterbuck. I am sure that these fine, strapping young sons of yours can more than keep me entertained."

Mr. Clatterbuck went out into that big dance hall of a parlor and then off into a room about the size of my old ranch house that he referred to as his office. We got sat down and he poured us up a glass of brandy and we got cigars lit.

He was sitting on a swivel chair at his desk and I was sitting in an armchair catty-cornered to him. He lifted his glass and said, "To your mighty fine health, sir."

I said, "Luck," and then knocked mine back as befits the toast.

He said, "I judge from your letter that you are a man setting about developing a fine string of running horses."

I nodded and said, "Yes sir. It's my belief that Thoroughbred racing is going to become very popular in Texas and I intend to be in the forefront."

"I congratulate you, sir, on your foresight. I hope that we here at The Gables will have the kind of breeding stock that you are looking for. Your letter mentioned that you were interested in three to four stallions with bloodlines to support their ability to run with the best horses in the country."

I nodded. "That's about the size of it."

He said, "I'm certain that you have some idea just how dear that sort of breeding stock is."

I smiled. I said, "Mr. Clatterbuck, I don't reckon it's time to start talking price yet. I haven't seen your horses, but I would like to see your breeding book that goes back to this Slewfoot Bob that I've heard about. That's what I'm doing here, Mr. Clatterbuck. That's what myself and Miz Pico have come for."

His eyes lit up a little. "This Mrs. Pico, or is it Miss?"

I said, "No, it's Mrs. She is a widow. Her husband was a dear friend of mine who was formerly my partner." I told the lie without shame or fear of contradiction. It was the only way I could think to stake some sort of claim on Laura to maybe hold Mr. Royce Clatterbuck at bay. For all I knew all three of them were going to have a run at her.

Mr. Clatterbuck said, "I understand that Mrs. Pico is a Virginian. A wonderful state, a true flower of the old South."

I wondered if he was talking about the state or about Laura. I said, "Yes, she is from Virginia. It is our plan to visit her family there as well as some Thoroughbred farms near her home."

"It may surprise her to know that I am not originally from Louisiana. My home was in New Jersey, which is not far removed from Virginia."

Well, that explained that clipped, Yankee accent to me, even though it was overlaid with a slab of southern molasses talk. I said, "Well, I am taken by surprise. I thought that you were a native of Louisiana."

"Oh, no," he said. "I've only been here some twenty years. I was fortunate enough to come in right after the Civil War."

Well, naturally. That explained a lot to me.

Hell, he was no southern gentleman, he was a damned Yankee carpetbagger who had come south with greed in his heart and an empty carpetbag to gather up what he could. I would gamble that The Gables belonged to some poor southern veteran who had it taken away from him during the Reconstruction. I said, "By any chance, did you come in as an official of the federal government?"

"Why, yes. As a matter of fact, I did. I came in here in charge of an attachment of Union troops who were here to regulate the freeing of the slaves and to make sure they were given their rights."

I wanted to laugh. From the looks of his place, he had kept on a good many of those slaves that he was sent to free. But I didn't say anything. I was here to examine the man's horses, not his politics or his character, but I did have to smile inwardly to myself. I couldn't wait to tell Laura that her fine southern gentleman was nothing but another Yankee carpetbagger who had gotten rich at the expense of the southern states, of which one was Virginia. I reckoned that most of that had been forgotten by his neighbors. I always noticed that once a man had money, most people tended to forget how he got it.

I was surprised that Mr. Clatterbuck's two sideburned heirs weren't with us learning the horse business at their daddy's knee. I asked him as much. His fat face creased into what I took to be a grin. He said, "Well, sir, we couldn't leave the fair and enchanting Mrs. Pico to her own devices, especially on her first night in Louisiana. That wouldn't be the gentlemanly thing to do, sir."

I said, "No, I reckon not."

After that, we got down to his bloodline books and he showed me the direct lineage from Slewfoot Bob through any number of first-rate mares producing generation after generation of top-flight colts—colts that had run in the money and colts that were still running in the money at various tracks in Louisiana, Tennessee, Kentucky, and the other states where Thoroughbred horse racing was much in favor. I had to admit that on paper his horses were impressive. I asked him how many colts he had to show me that went directly back to Slewfoot Bob.

He began ticking off a list of names, then finally turned back to face me and said, "Sir, these seventeen right here."

I said, "I would like to take these charts up to bed with me tonight and study them. Do I understand that you have these studs up now?"

He said, "They will be ready for your inspection in the morning. We'll have breakfast at whatever time you may choose. After that, you and I will inspect the animals. Will we have the pleasure of Mrs. Pico's company during this part of the business?"

I smothered a smile and said, "Mrs. Pico leaves the choosing of the horseflesh to me. She's my business partner in the financial sense only."

He appeared to get a smirk on his face. He said, "And that would be your only relationship, in the business sense?"

I thought he paused a long bit between saying relationship and business. I didn't much care for it, but I didn't say anything. I didn't like his son Royce, and I didn't know his son Cloyce well enough to have formed much of an opinion, but I was rapidly growing to dislike the old man. They all seemed to be walking around with some kind of damned smirk on their faces.

We concluded our preliminary business around ten o'clock. No prices were mentioned. There's not a whole hell of a lot of reason to talk about a horse until you've looked at it, so far as price is concerned. You can see his bloodline from here back to the horizon, but what you really want to look at is what's standing on four hooves and what kind of look he's got in his eye.

We came out of Mr. Clatterbuck's office to find, to our surprise, Mr. Royce Clatterbuck and Mr. Cloyce Clatterbuck playing poker with Mrs. Laura Pico at a table in a recessed part of the big parlor, if you could call it that. I still felt like calling it a hotel lobby.

Now three-handed poker wasn't my game and it ain't the game of anybody who is a serious poker player, but the Clatterbuck brothers seemed to be having a good time, in spite of the fact that most of the greenbacks and silver were in front of Laura. They were playing five-card stud and Laura was the dealer. I said to Royce, "Didn't I warn you about playing poker with her?"

He turned around and smiled thinly at me and said, "Oh, there are compensations for the loss of a little money."

Mr. Clatterbuck laughed. I said to Laura, "I reckon you need to wind this up pretty soon. You need to be getting to bed. We'll be looking at horses pretty early in the morning."

I said it with just a little edge in my voice that she would hear, but that would not be obvious to the others. For an answer, she gave me an irritated look that seemed to say "I can take care of myself. I don't need your advice and I damned sure am not going to listen to your orders."

Mr. Royce Clatterbuck said, "There's plenty of time. The night is young. It's the shank of the evening. I'm sure Mrs. Pico is enjoying herself."

I said, looking Laura directly in the eyes, "Mrs. Pico is here on business, which she full well knows."

You could almost touch the tension in the air with your finger—like wetting it and sticking it up in the north wind. Royce Clatterbuck turned around and gave me a hard look. He started to say something, thought better of it, and then returned to his cards.

I said, "Laura, I am going up. I need to discuss a few things with you before bedtime. We have some horse business to talk over, *financial* horse business."

I hit the word hard, assuming that she would get it.

I had one more drink with Mr. Clatterbuck. He himself sat down to watch the game. I took my drink standing up to emphasize to Laura that I wanted her immediate presence upstairs. Finally, when it seemed fitting, I made my good-nights and started up the stairs. I went up to my room and closed the door but I didn't make myself ready for bed. I got my own whiskey out of my saddlebags and poured myself a shot. I noticed that during the time we had been having dinner, somebody had come and turned down my bed. Made me almost laugh. It was the first time in my life, far as I knew, that anyone had come and turned down my bed for me.

But then it was the first time I had ever stayed in a southern gentleman's mansion with three gentlemen, none of whom were southern, who seemed more intent on paying court to my business partner than they did on selling me a horse. I looked at my watch. It was only a little after ten. If Laura wasn't tapping on my door within the half hour, she was going to hear about it.

5

I said, "Laura, I think we're being worked."
We were in her room, she was sitting at the
dressing table brushing her hair. She turned
around to me.

She said, "Why? Whatever do you mean?"

I said, "We're getting the ten-dollar treatment
for a five-dollar bag of tricks. I don't trust any
of this bunch any further than I can sling them."

"Oh, you're just mad because a couple of
harmless young men have been trying to flirt
with me." She was sitting there in nothing but
her camisole, which was made of the shearest
silk. It was enough to unsettle any man, but
right then my mind was more on business.

I said, "Oh, by the way, you'll be interested
to know that your fine southern gentleman is a
Yankee carpetbagger. He came from New Jersey."

She turned around and looked at me with pure
shock. She said, "You're just making that up."

"No, I'm not. He told me so himself. He came
down here right after the Civil War. I would
imagine that some real southern gentleman at
one time owned this place and this scalawag
managed to take it away from him."

Absolute horror came over her face. I had never seen such a change in Laura. It was as if I had slapped her in the face with the most unacceptable truth that she could imagine. She was coming home to the South, only our first stop in the South had turned out to be owned by a Yankee. I would have laughed if she hadn't looked so upset. When I finished telling her the whole story, she was grim faced.

She said, "Why, that son of a bitch. No . . . all three of them sons of a bitch. That hominy-grit accent of theirs, they've got no more right to that accent than . . . than . . ."

"Than a pig has to a ballroom gown?"

"Yes!"

I said, "Now, don't go getting yourself so hot and bothered. We're here to do business. You keep your feelings under wraps. Personalities and personal feelings haven't got any place in business. We're here to buy horses, do you understand me?"

She was brushing her hair furiously. She said, "I've got a good mind to tell those watermelon-mouthed sons of bitches off."

I said calmly, "Laura, now you're not going to do any such thing. We got it settled back in Tyler who was the boss of this operation. Don't you forget that."

She said, "Why, yes sir, Boss. Yes sir."

"Is that your best southern accent?"

"It's the best that I'm gonna give a son of a bitch like you."

I turned to head to the door. I paused. "By the way, how much did you win in the poker game?"

She pulled a face. "Not much over fifty dollars. The cheapskates wouldn't play but a dollar limit. They were afraid anything else would have been too steep for a lady." She said it with a sarcastic accent to the la-dy, like it was two or three words.

"You're really something, you know that? You just keep that temper in check and mind what you are told."

She said, "Why, yes sir, Boss."

I shut the door hard behind me. As I stepped into the hall, I caught the motion out of the corner of my eye of another door being closed down the hall. It wouldn't have surprised me if Mr. Royce Clatterbuck hadn't been doing his best to spy on Laura and me. I shook my head, went on to my room, and went to bed, hoping that the morrow would bring the kind of horses that I was looking for.

The elder Clatterbuck and I had breakfast alone the next morning at about seven. It appeared that it was not Royce or Cloyce's habit to rise early. I damned sure knew it wasn't Laura's.

We didn't eat in that long dining room that I figured you could have run a horse race in.

103

Instead, there was a small breakfast room off the kitchen connected by a swinging door, something that I had never seen before.

We had a good view through some big windows out toward the stables, the corrals, and the other pastures. I could see several men working about the place and was gratified to see that they were dressed like normal cowhands. At least not everybody around the place dressed in brocade vests and pinched-back long-tailed suits. This morning, Mr. Clatterbuck had dropped the vest, but he was wearing a white linen shirt with a string tie and a wide plantation hat. He called it a panama. I didn't know what that meant, but it was his hat and I reckon that he could call it anything he wanted. It looked like straw except that it really didn't look like straw. I had never seen one like it before. We were served by the same black man in the white starched coat that had served us supper the night before. He seemed to be the general hand around the house, although he wasn't the one that had shown me to my room. I guess there was one for serving meals, one for showing rooms, and one for turning down beds.

I made a good meal out of ham and eggs and grits, something I didn't get as often as I liked. The coffee was good, too, though a might strong. Mr. Clatterbuck informed me that they put chicory in their coffee, another creole specialty. I put whiskey in mine.

After we finished breakfast, Mr. Clatterbuck lit up a big cigar, offering me one in the process. I declined, and lit up a cigarette. He said, sounding like he had the night before, "Now, Mr. Grayson, before we go look at the horses, I assume you do have some idea of the value of this type of animal?"

"I will as soon as I see them, Mr. Clatterbuck. You can depend on that. I've been looking at horses for a mighty long time."

He nodded and got up and put on his hat. We headed for the back door and then on toward the stables.

I had expected to walk into the stables and go from horse to horse, looking them over, but Mr. Clatterbuck had a setup that turned my head. He had a show-ring with a set of bleachers set up in it. It was the damndest thing I'd ever seen. The fence was built out of dressed lumber and the bleachers would have seated at least fifty people. He said that sometimes he had bunches of people out when he had yearly sales and they held auctions. I had never heard of a one-man auction before, but then I was starting to realize just how expansive Mr. Clatterbuck's operations was. He said that he owned more than ten thousand acres of pasture land. For Louisiana, with its rich soil and good grass, that was a hell of a lot of good grazing.

We sat down in the bleachers. The ring wasn't particularly big, maybe twenty or thirty feet across and maybe, oh, a little longer. It wasn't so much a ring as it was an oblong. It backed up to the stables so that the horses could be led straight out.

After we sat for a moment, Mr. Clatterbuck gave a signal and a succession of hired hands, he called them grooms, started bringing out one horse at a time. It took me a minute or two to get used to the procedure, but Mr. Clatterbuck was giving me the description, the record, and the lineage of each stud as he was walked out into the ring for our inspection. The groom—he had to be called that—would walk the horse all around the ring, bring him to a stop, back him up, wheel him in a circle, and then walk him up close to where we were sitting so that we could get a firsthand look. They did the same with each horse and as soon as one was shown, he was taken back into the stable and another one was brought out in the same way. Once I got the hang of it, I saw it was a pretty fair way for a fellow to look over horses, especially with the owner sitting right there with his blood book, reading off the history of the horse and who his mamma and daddy and his grandmother and granddaddy were.

It wasn't long before I became aware that Mr. Clatterbuck was trying to point me in the direction of about four horses. I could hear the tone in his voice, the same kind of tone that you get from a drummer or a dry-goods salesman when he's got some product he particularly wants you to have—at your expense, of course.

Those four horses, however, were not the ones taking my eye, but I didn't say anything.

There were two horses that I especially liked the look of. One was a dun and the other was a roan with a star-shaped blaze on his forehead. The roan's off eye had a milky cast to it but that didn't matter none. I didn't notice anything particular about the dun, but then I hadn't had my hands on either of them. All I saw was the will to run. And that's breeding. They were both big horses, standing, I figured, seventeen to seventeen and a half hands high. Of course they both had the long, classic, lean lines of a Thoroughbred, but there was something about the way they carried themselves that I liked. They had a certain cockiness about them, a command, a presence. I can't explain it, but I've always been able to look in the eye of a horse and tell what that horse has inside. It's not an ability that I have an explanation for, but it had stood me in good stead down through the years.

Of course, the last thing that I wanted Mr. Clatterbuck to know was which horse I was interested in, so I proposed to him that we go down and mingle among the horses and let me get a good close look at them and run my hands over a few of them.

He waved at what I took to be the head groom and called for him to bring the whole bunch into the ring and then he and I made our way from the bleachers through the gate and into the ring. I had to say, they were all magnificent looking animals. I guessed the dun to be about nine years old and the roan about ten. Mr. Clatterbuck's records indicated that they were eight and nine. Of course, both were well past their racing prime and neither one of them had had particularly impressive records. The best the roan had done was second in an important race in New Orleans and a few third place finishes at some tracks in Tennessee and Kentucky. The dun had started out like a house on fire at some smaller tracks but then had run into some stiff competition when he ran at larger tracks. He had been retired early to stud. I got that kind of information, not solely about the two horses, but about all of them. This horse and that horse, not showing any particular interest in any of them.

I had twenty thousand dollars to spend on studs. For that amount, I was hoping to get at least four horses. I didn't know what Clatterbuck was going to ask, but I knew that I had to start stretching my money from the very beginning.

We went down the line of horses, me making

a show of mouthing a few of them and running my hands over their shiny coats. I felt the bones in their legs, patted them on the flanks to see how jumpy they were, taking note of their hocks and their hams—those big, driving muscles that a horse has got to have to be a quarter horse or a Thoroughbred. I looked them straight on, to see how they carried their ears, and noted the size of their chests, which is a good indication of how much lung they've got.

Noting all that, I stepped back and surveyed the whole bunch. Mr. Clatterbuck kept pointing me at a couple of blacks and a chestnut. Just to get the bidding started, I casually asked him how much he was asking for the chestnut.

He made a great show, standing there in the middle of the ring with his hired hands all around, of looking in his book at the chestnut's background, his record while he was on the track, and what the colts that he had sired had done. Then he stood there chewing on his cigar, looking off into the sky like the figure that he was looking for was written among the clouds. Finally, he took a deep drag on his cigar, let out a good puff of smoke, and said, "Well sir. I reckon I'd have to have ten thousand dollars for that horse. And a mighty fine horse he is. As you can see from his record right here, he has sired colts that have already run at the big tracks in New Orleans and some that are expected to run in Kentucky. I have had good success in selling his progeny."

I didn't know what progeny meant, but I reckoned it meant colts. I said, "Well, he appears a little weak on his mamma's side. According to your book, Queen of Sheba never really did much racing."

He said, "Sir, I'd like to acquaint you with the fact that it is the stud that produces most of the racing quality in the offspring. The dam, or mamma, is not as important from the racing standpoint as she is for providing good solid stock."

I said, "Well, be that as it may, I don't think that you can discount the dam, as you call her, but just for the sake of argument, I kinda like these blacks here, especially the one with the white stocking foot and thirty-four brand on his hip. What would you be asking for those two horses?"

He had to go through the motions of checking his records again. Then he squinted his eyes and said, "Well, you're getting into . . . well, the first one will bring twelve thousand five hundred dollars. And the other, hmmm, I might let you have that horse for around twelve thousand dollars. They are both eight-year-olds and you should be able to get another eight years of breeding out of them."

I nodded like I was listening to him. Both of the horses, as far as I could tell, were too short coupled to be able to last in races much over a mile. I didn't like the looks of either one of them and I doubted the record that he claimed they had, but I still didn't want to show my hand on the dun and the roan. I just said, "Mr. Clatterbuck, I guess we have taken advantage of your hospitality on false pretenses. I had written with the objective of buying a couple of stud horses and now I discover that you are trying to sell me your plantation."

"Why, what do you mean, dear sir?"

I said, "Well, from the price of these two horses, I figure at least five thousand acres of your land must go with each one of them."

He made a weak attempt to laugh, but I could see that he didn't think it was very funny. He said, "I had assumed, sir, that you were acquainted with the price of this kind of horse-flesh. Perhaps at your Texas ranches, cow horses go for fifty dollars or a hundred, but we're not talking about cow horses here."

I said, "Personally, I've never owned a fifty- or a hundred-dollar cow horse. That's a mighty cheap horse."

He said, "Then you shouldn't be surprised at the price of these horses."

"Well, let me mull this over," I said. "I'd like to take a little ride around your operation here. You wouldn't have a riding horse I could borrow, would you?"

He said, "Well, certainly." He turned to what I took to be the honcho of the four or five grooms and said, "Lem, saddle Mr. Grayson a horse and put a western saddle on it."

I nodded my thanks and said, "I'm gonna go into the house and confer with my business partner and I'll be back out in an hour, Lem."

He nodded and said, "I'll have the horse tied out here."

Mr. Clatterbuck and I walked back to the big house. His manner to me seemed distinctly cool.

I went to Laura's room and opened the door. As I entered I could see she was up—well, sort of—having breakfast. Somebody had brought her a tray with coffee and bread rolls and jam. She looked mighty pretty with a pillow fluffed up behind her. She was wearing a silky-looking white nightgown that almost, but not quite, was cut down to the nipples of her breast.

I said, "You mustn't be so hard on yourself, Laura. You've really got to take things a little easier."

She said, "Well, they may all be Yankees, but at least they have adopted some of the more appealing local customs."

"I don't know what they are, but I know what they think I am. They think I am a hick from Suckersville. You ought to hear the prices Clatterbuck is quoting on those nags of his."

Laura said, "Are they much too high?"

I sat down and shrugged. "I really don't know. I haven't gotten around to pricing the two horses that I am interested in. He has been trying to steer me on to three that he is looking to get rid of. He's asking an average of around twelve thousand dollars."

She looked startled. "For each horse?"

I said, "Laura, it's really not that much money. Not if you can get some progeny," I had to laugh when I said that one, "out of them and then charge a stud fee of anywhere from five hundred to a thousand dollars. A horse like that can be well worth the money. It so happens that these three horses that he is trying to unload on me ain't worth anywhere near that much money. The man does have some good stock though."

She said, "How long do you expect us to be here?"

I shrugged and got a cigarette out and lit it. "Long as it takes, I guess. You in any particular hurry to leave? I'd have thought from all the attention paid to you, you'd be as satisfied as a cat with cream on his whiskers."

"If you are referring to Mr. Lothario Clatterbuck, I am not welcoming his attentions."

"Oh, well, you could have fooled me."

She said, "I am simply trying to be sociable for the purpose of business, but I am certain that you wouldn't understand such sophisticated behavior."

"Sociability hasn't got anything to do with it, Laura. It's all price—what a man wants and what you'll pay and what you'll finally settle on. And you can do that cussing or caressing, it don't make a damn bit of difference."

She took a sip of coffee. "What's the plan, now?"

"I'm going to take a ride around to make sure I know enough about what a Thoroughbred horse farm looks like. Then I'm gonna go back and see if Mr. Clatterbuck will let me get alone with his bloodlines book and sort of cross match a couple of horses that I very definitely am interested in."

"Are they pretty?"

I gave her a sour look and said, "Yes, and they've got the cutest names."

"Oh? What are they?"

I didn't bother to answer. I got up, shaking my head, and went downstairs.

I found Mr. Clatterbuck in the breakfast room with his two sons. He was having a cup of coffee with them while they ate. I wanted to ask his permission to have a leisurely study of his registry book after I had ridden around the plantation.

As I came into the room, Royce looked up and bid me a good morning. Cloyce did the

114

same but without much enthusiasm. Mr. Clatterbuck said that by all means his books were open and that I should pursue them at my leisure. I thanked him and then began to wonder about the younger of the Clatterbuck brothers as I left. Even though he favored his older brother, there was a sort of somberness about him that was unusual for a lad in his mid-twenties. He was thinner, but there was a sort of meanness around his mouth and eyes. It seemed unusual, for one so quiet, but I suppose it was my imagination. I somehow got the feeling that he didn't like me.

The horse was waiting for me as promised and I mounted and set off for a ride around the far pastures of The Gables plantation. It was a beautiful place, with big oaks and lush pastures and enough streams and lakes to have outfitted a dozen west Texas ranches. Mr. Clatterbuck ran whiteface cattle in addition to his horses. They were prime looking, heavy and sleek. I imagined that there wasn't much part of that fertile land that didn't turn a profit.

I rode for about an hour, and while I was impressed with the place, it confirmed what I had been hoping—that I had an equally good facility in east Texas. That told me that I ought to be able to raise better horses than him because I figured to be a better horseman than he was.

The Gables was perhaps the biggest ranch that we were going to visit. In addition to the seventeen horses that Clatterbuck had standing at stud, he had anywhere from fifty to seventy-five somewhere in their racing careers, coming along anywhere from colt stage to that six- or seven-year period where a horse is no longer fit to run. Finally, having seen everything that interested me, I rode back to the ranch. One of the hands was waiting to meet me as I rode up. I dismounted and he took charge of the horse.

I went inside. Mr. Clatterbuck was in his office. I could hear laughter coming out of the breakfast room as I passed it, walking by the big dining room to my right with the hotel lobby, as I called it, beyond that. The door to Mr. Clatterbuck's office was half open and I stuck my head in and said hello.

He got up from his desk and said, "Ah, Mr. Grayson. Please come in, set yourself down here at my desk. I've got all of my registration books laid out and you can look them over to your heart's content, sir. Is there anything I can have you brought? A pot of coffee? A cigar? Anything that might take your fancy?"

I took off my hat and sat down and said, "No sir. A few hours of peace and quiet would suit me fine."

"Make yourself at home, sir."

He went out, closing the door behind him.

I settled in to look deep into the background of every horse that I had seen that morning. There was a decanter of brandy with some shot glasses near the desk. I poured myself a couple of fingers of the smooth-drinking stuff, knocked it back, and after I had lit a cigarette, settled to my work.

It took me the better part of two hours, but I found what I was looking for. I found the link that had drawn me to the dun and the roan. They both shared a common grandmother, Cajun Rose, and she was the direct granddaughter of old Slewfoot Bob. Her own record had started off very impressively some fifteen years past when she won her maiden race as a filly at the age of three and then went on to finish her next nine races in the top money, mostly on the Louisiana tracks. Then she had obviously suffered an injury to one of her hooves—she had come down with a split hoof that wouldn't heal—and had been turned into a broodmare.

It was very clear that her get had not been used to the extent that it might have, possibly because whoever was managing the horse, and as near as I could figure the horse was registered in the name of Cloyce Clatterbuck, hadn't realized what they had in the filly. So I had my Slewfoot Bob breeding, except that I had it on the distaff side. I found that very interesting. She had apparently inherited his racing qualities as well as what horsemen call the good stock qualities that you get from a mare. That's the build, the conformation, the bones, the good blood. As near as I could figure, I had exactly what I had wanted. I had a couple of stallions that had gotten the best of both the Slewfoot Bob line and the line from Cajun Rose. You could have founded a pretty successful stable just on her. Studying the records, it was clear to me from the way that they had bred Cajun Rose so offhandedly that they didn't realize what they had. The roan and the chestnut had been bred to two fairly outstanding Tennessee stallions. One was Foley's Boy and the other, Little Big Man, was a stallion that had run in the money in the big derby in Kentucky.

My prejudice about naming horses did not apply to racing horses, horses that you raced in front of the public. The public had to have some name to call them. They had to have a name to put in the racing program so the public would know who they were betting on. It was all damned foolishness.

About a half an hour before noon, I closed the book and went out of the office feeling well satisfied with myself. I was searching for Mr. Clatterbuck, but instead I found Mr. Royce Clatterbuck and Laura. They were in the kitchen. They seemed to be in close conversation standing by the counter that ran along beside the sink. Laura looked around as I came into the room. She did not look pleased. Mr. Clatterbuck had been saying something in an earnest voice. I heard the tone, if not the words, as I stepped into the kitchen. Now he looked at me with annoyance.

I said, "I'm looking for your daddy."

He tossed his head toward the door. He said, "He would be at the stables at this hour." He said it like it was something that I ought to have known right off the bat.

I thanked him and, giving Laura a glance, went on out. I didn't know what was going on, but I figured that I would find out from her later.

I found Mr. Clatterbuck out beyond the corral, sitting in a lawn chair located so as to give himself a view of his plantation. There was another chair handy, so I dropped into it.

I said, "Well, I can see why you are proud of those horses."

He nodded. He was smoking another of his long cigars. "Good bloodlines, sir. Good bloodlines. You can't beat quality."

I said, "Well, sometime after lunch, I'd like to have a talk with you about maybe some horses that I can afford."

He said, "I thought you would be well pleased with those two blacks."

"I'm well pleased, all right, but they don't please my pocketbook."

"Sir, I will not presume to give you advice, but as I understand it, you intend on starting a bloodline in Texas. I would not recommend that you try it with anything but the best."

I said, "Oh, I agree with you, Mr. Clatterbuck. However, you are the first farm on our trip. I appreciate your hospitality, but I am not certain that you have the horses that I am looking for."

His face got a pinched look at my words. "I'm sorry to hear that, sir. Perhaps you would like a closer look. The horses that we have assembled for your inspection are still up in the stables."

I said, "I'd like to do that sometime this afternoon."

With an effort, for he really was a heavyset man, he heaved himself out of his chair. "Speaking of afternoon, I believe that noon is almost upon us. I can almost smell another fine dish awaiting us. Shall we go in for luncheon?"

Laura and the brothers Clatterbuck were already at the table when we arrived. Royce had once again placed himself conspicuously near Laura. Cloyce sat across the table from them, his head down, his attention on his food. Mr. Clatterbuck and I faced each other. The meal was some sort of chicken, which would have been just fine, but instead, they had to pile on those creole sauces and flatter it up until it had long since ceased being chicken. I never could understand that kind of cooking. If a man liked chicken, why not give him chicken? Or beef? Or pork? Or whatever it was? Most things, I'd discovered, were best in their natural state, like a good-looking woman for instance.

I'd taken great note that Royce was paying more attention to Laura than to his food. Every once in a while, I'd noticed her giving me a little glance. I smiled benignly at her. It appeared to me that she had attracted an admirer, an admirer that she was not so anxious to have.

For my part, I talked horses with Mr. Clatterbuck, telling him about what we had in Texas. How cow horses worked, how you bred them, how you crossed the Morgans and the Standardbred to get the quarter horse. I told him a little about my early life as a horse trader. He seemed interested, or interested in the way a man who wants to sell you something is interested. Not so much interested in what you have to say, but interested in making you think he is interested.

We finished lunch with a pudding. It had rum in it, I could taste that, and it had pieces of cake all mixed in. Well, that convinced me that they didn't know what they were doing. How somebody could set out to make a cake and wind up with pudding was something beyond me. But it was far more than I cared to know.

My mind was busy on how I was going to approach Clatterbuck about the dun and the roan.

After lunch, I let Laura go on upstairs ahead of me and engaged the two brothers in what conversation I could. Royce was fairly easy to talk to. He didn't have anything to say that anyone would want to hear, but he was easy to talk to. He could tell you about the different dances that were all the vogue and what clothes a man ought to be wearing to go where. He could also tell you who the right people were in society in southern Louisiana, but since I wasn't very interested in these matters, I didn't pay any more attention to him than his daddy had to me.

Cloyce was another kettle of fish. He didn't say much. I asked him straight out if he was interested in the horse business and he gave me a direct look and answered, of course, that since his family was involved, certainly he was interested.

Didn't much sound like it to me.

After about an hour, I went on upstairs. I gave Laura's door a slight knock and then went in. She was lying on her bed. She had changed from the little frock that she had been wearing all morning into her riding clothes. She said that Royce had insisted that they go riding that afternoon.

I sat down on her dressing-room chair and

said "Ya'll seem to be getting on about like a house on fire."

She sat up and swung her legs around. "Warner, honestly, I don't know what I am going to do with that boy—and I call him a boy even though I reckon he is as old as I am—because he is pressing his attentions in a most distasteful manner."

I laughed. "Well, we've been here for less than a day, less than twenty-four hours, and already you are using such expressions as 'pressing his attentions in a distasteful manner.' That's pretty funny, Laura."

"I'm serious, Warner. I am getting very tired of it and I don't know how to stop him without interfering with your horse business."

"Just stop him, Laura. Tell him to cut it out."

"He's not doing anything that I can directly say, 'Don't do that.' It's the way he keeps sidling up to me. He sort of oozes up to me."

"Oozes at you? What, like molasses in the winter or molasses in July?"

She frowned. "It's not funny, Warner. The next step is that he is going to try to kiss me or he is going to try to put his hand on me and then we're going to have trouble."

I stood up. Even straddling it, the little chair was uncomfortable. "Laura, you've been handling men all your life. I imagine that you came out of the cradle knowing how to handle men. I can't imagine you can't handle some hick from Louisiana, no matter how fine his clothes are."

Laura said, "Well, I cannot assure you of what's going to happen on the ride. I am going to try to stay within sight of the house but if he thinks that he is going to haul me off into some bushes somewhere . . ."

"Laura, Laura, Laura. Didn't you tell me that you could handle anything, me included? Are you now telling me that that little boy with those muttonchop whiskers is frightening you?"

She stood up. "Damn it. Don't you understand? If you have any interest in these horses here, we might well lose our welcome the first time I slap his snide little face."

I started to the door and said, "Well, try not to slap his face until this afternoon when I get a chance to maybe make an offer on a couple of stud horses that have taken my eye."

She said as I went out the door, "You better hurry up."

I went down to my room and poured myself a good honest shot of whiskey. I felt like it was about time to get down to business.

I had to wait until Mr. Clatterbuck woke from his nap, and then about four o'clock, he and I went out to his stables behind the house, out beyond the show-ring. We went into the cool, dark, hay-smelling, horse-smelling interior. I always like the smell of stables, of barns, or any place that horses are kept. The horses were now in their box stalls. Most of them had their heads through the top half-door that had been left open. I walked casually down the line, stopping now and again to glance at first one then another. I gave the dun a cursory look and then moved on. I passed the roan with no more than a glance, stopped and pretended to admire the two blacks and then came on back up the line again.

Mr. Clatterbuck and a couple of his hired hands stood by awaiting my orders. I wondered to myself how many hands he had taking care of the stables, not to mention the cattle and the horses out on the range. The man was wealthy, there was no mistake about that, but I didn't think he had made it from horses or cattle. I think he had made it from robbing a ravaged country after the Civil War. But those days were over and who and what Mr. Clive Clatterbuck was wasn't any of my business.

The next time up, I paused at the roan. I said to the head groom, "Let's have a look at this one. Would you bring him out?"

The groom hustled to open the door and said, "Yes sir, yes sir, yes sir," when once would have been sufficient. He led the horse out for my inspection. The roan was a little flighty, but I liked his eyes immediately. You could see deep into them. You could see that the horse studied and thought about things and that there was a kind of fire in him. Don't ever let anybody tell you that a racing horse don't want to win. There are some horses that don't know that they are in a race; there are others that do. The ones that do are the ones that win. This one knew that he was in a race and wanted to win.

I went through all the normal motions. I felt his legs, looked at his hooves, mouthed him, and ran my hands over his neck. Then I felt his ears and the bump on top of his head before running my hand down his back. I did all the normal things that I was supposed to do when looking for a horse.

I inspected his private parts—those are kind of necessary when buying a stud. It is understood, however, and it is part of any contract, that when you by a horse for breeding purposes, the seller guarantees that the horse will perform, and, if he doesn't the buyer is entitled to his money back plus any damages.

Finally I motioned for the groom to put the horse back up.

I could feel Clatterbuck watching me but I didn't let on. Instead, I inspected two or three more horses that I wasn't the slightest bit interested in before getting around to the dun. I thought the same about him as I did about the roan. He had that feel, he put off that vibration that told me that this was a competitor. This was a horse that was going to sire me some fast running Thoroughbred horses, but I still didn't let on.

I had them bring out a chestnut and went through the same motions. This time I asked Clatterbuck what he would take for the horse. Clatterbuck didn't have his registry book with him—the small one, not the big one that he kept in his office—so he had to go on memory.

He said, "Well, I could be corrected on this, Mr. Grayson, but I believe that this horse is priced at nine thousand dollars."

I crossed my arms like I was studying on the proposition. I was studying but it was not on the price of nine thousand dollars for the chestnut. What I was studying was when would be the proper time and what would be the proper way to begin feeling Clatterbuck out about the roan and the dun. The dun had the milky-white right eye, which might or might not have been blind. I wasn't interested in whether he could see or not, it didn't make any difference. Stallions, as a general thing, don't care what the mare that they are about to mount looks like.

The roan had a bowed tendon in his left leg. Again, that didn't make me any difference. I didn't know if Clatterbuck was aware of the defects in the two horses or not, or if he was aware that they had absolutely no effect on the value of the horses as studs.

For the moment, I decided that it was better to bide my time and not approach him so directly about the dun and the roan. After shuffling my boots in the sand of the stables, I started walking toward the door. Mr. Clatterbuck fell in beside me and said, "Well, what do you think?"

I said, "Mr. Clatterbuck, maybe you spend this kind of money before supper as a regular thing every day, but I don't. I got to give it some thought. I reckon you and I could have a talk later on this evening in your office."

"Mr. Grayson, I don't want you to feel no rush on yourself, sir. You and your lady friend are free to make yourselves at home here as long as it interests you. If my horses don't suit you or your pocketbook, then say no more."

"Well, that is mighty kind of you, Mr. Clatterbuck. I can see you're a handy man to do business with. I am much obliged."

I had expected Laura to be back by the time I had finished my dealings in the stables, but as it turned out, I had a longer wait. I was in my bedroom sipping a glass of whiskey and looking out the window at the beautifully manicured back yard of the plantation house when my door suddenly burst open and a very angry looking lady that I mostly called the widow Pico came bursting in. She had a riding crop in her right hand and she was beating a tattoo against her thigh with it as she stopped and stood fuming at me. I took a drink and said, "Well, it looks like you enjoyed your ride with young Mr. Royce Clatterbuck."

"You go to hell, Warner Grayson. You just go straight to hell and stay there."

Without another word, she came over to the table by my bed and poured herself a glass of whiskey and tossed half of it off. That was a strong statement for Laura to make.

I said, "Now what's the matter?"

She whirled on me and said, "You know damned well what is the matter with me. That little love-sick puppy is pursuing me a little bit closer than I care for."

I gave her a disgusted look. I said, "Laura, I cannot believe that you are not capable of handling a kid like Royce Clatterbuck."

"You don't understand, Warner. He's all hands. When he helps me out of the saddle, he manages to get them all over me. I swear, the man has more than his normal share of hands. I'm tired of it. I came very close to slapping his face."

I said, "Now wait a damn minute, Laura. I brought you along on this trip to hold the horses. And if you can't even hold the horses while I rob the damn bank, I don't know what good you are."

"Now what is that supposed to mean?"

"It means that you are to keep the distractions to a minimum while I tend to the real business. The real business, as you no doubt have figured out by now, is that I am here to buy stud horses. And I don't want any business between you and young Mr. Clatterbuck to interfere with the business between me and his father. Now is that clear?"

She put her hands on her hips and glared at me. "Where did you get that wonderful expression I'm supposed to hold the horses while you rob the bank? Is that from your friend, Wilson Young?"

"As a matter of fact, it is. But even if it wasn't, it suits the situation just fine because sometimes Wilson took along a man that wasn't suited for the business of robbing a bank but he could at least hold the horses for the men that were."

Flames shot through her face. She stamped her foot and said, "Well, damn you, I've got a good mind to slap your face."

"You start that hitting business again and I'm gonna put you on the first train back to Texas and that's not a promise, that's a guarantee."

She gave me a grim look. "You don't want much do you? Are you asking me to play the whore?"

I shook my head in a disgusted fashion. "Of course I'm not asking you to play the whore. I'm asking you to tend to the two younger men while I tend to the father. I'm about to zero in on the two horses that I want. I'm planning to discuss them tonight. Don't you think you can keep Mr. Clatterbuck happy or satisfied or at least content until I get that tended to?"

She gave me a long hard look, then she finally sighed. Our business was as important to her as it was to me and she knew it. She also knew that she was being a little silly.

"Well, I suppose so. I have to tell you, Warner, that I consider this above and beyond the call of duty."

"Is he all that bad?" I asked.

She gave a short laugh. "You go sit with him under a tree for half an hour and listen to his silly prattle, then tell me if it's all that bad."

"What about the other one, Cloyce? The one with his momma and daddy's names?"

"He tags along sometimes but he never says anything. I promise you though, that between the two of them, I haven't had a moment's peace."

"Well, it won't be long now." I nodded my head at the glass she still held in her hand. "Why don't you finish the rest of that? Maybe it will give you a little courage."

131

She put the glass down. "I don't see how you can drink that vile stuff. It tastes horrible."

"You don't drink it for the taste, Mrs. Pico. You know, I hate to tell you I told you so, but if we had gotten married before we left like I wanted to, none of this would have happened."

She stared at me, her eyes going wide. "Gotten married like you wanted to? I'll be damned if you are not the biggest liar, Warner Grayson, in nine counties. At no time did you make any serious effort to see us married before we came on this trip." She stamped her foot. "How dare you say that? You are the outlyingest man I think I have ever met in my life."

I said, "Laura, the next time I say that we are going to get married I am going to say it right in front of a preacher or a judge so that there can be no way that you can back out. Do you understand me?"

She stuck her tongue out at me. She said, "Why on earth would any woman want to marry a man who simply uses her as some sort of bait while he concludes a horse deal? You're not a man at all, you're just a horse trader."

I smiled. "Not every day that you pay me such a fine compliment."

She turned. "I'm going to have a bath and then get ready for supper. I hope to have a bath in privacy. I don't suppose there is any chance of you guarding the door?"

"Oh, I can guard the door all right, but I don't know what I can do about the hole they have drilled in the ceiling."

For a second her eyes widened, and then she gave me a smirk and said, "Well, I am sure that if anyone knew about the hole in the ceiling, you would."

With that she turned and flounced out of the room. I have never seen a woman wearing riding pants flounce before, but she managed to bring it off. I picked up my glass and finished off my whiskey before pouring out some more. I glanced at my watch. It was going on six. We'd be having supper in about an hour and a half so I thought I'd have me a bath and put on some clean clothes, too. I didn't ordinarily take a bath every day but that seemed to be the standard around the place so I didn't want to be caught lacking. I even thought I'd put on that suit of clothes that Laura had me buy, but I'd be damned if I was going to wear the tie. A pinch-back suit was bad enough and them sack-cloth trousers, but I was damned if I was going to put on that foulard tie.

Sometimes Laura could be a mite overbossy.

6

At about ten o'clock, me and Mr. Clatterbuck went into his office for what I reckoned to be a brass-tacks talk. I had expected Mr. Royce Clatterbuck to join us for the experience, if nothing else. His father had asked him but he had pled off with the excuse that he felt that it was his duty to entertain the lady, Mrs. Pico. Mrs. Pico had looked none too happy about the move and had even talked faintly about a headache. One thing that I had noticed with some glee was that she was wearing as severe a gown as I had ever seen her wear. It didn't exactly close at the throat but it left everything to the imagination because there was damn little skin showing. If the dress had been black, she'd have been all set to go to a funeral.

She gave me a fleeting, accusing look as I left that mile-long dining room to go with Mr. Clatterbuck to his office.

We got settled with brandy and him a cigar and me a cigarette and then started talking over the whole string of horses. He kept pushing the blacks and I kept sounding uncertain about what I was looking for. He asked what I thought of the chestnut at nine thousand dollars and then offered, after another check of his books, to come down to eight thousand dollars on the horse. I still hung fire acting like a man who was in a little bit over his head.

Finally I decided that it was time to move things along. I got myself another glass of brandy and sipped at it like I was thinking. Finally, I said, "Well, Mr. Clatterbuck, I figure that you ain't got but two horses there that I can afford and I'm just gonna have to hope that you can see yourself clear to sell them to me. One is the big, raw-boned dun and the other one is the roan with the star blaze on its forehead, the one with the milky eye. I reckon he's blind in that eye, ain't he?"

Clatterbuck looked surprised, to say the least. He drew on his cigar for a second and he said, "You interested in those two horses? Is that my understanding, sir?"

"Well, I'm interested in them according to the price."

He sat there for a moment with a puzzled frown on his face, puffing on his cigar. Then he turned to his desk and his registry books and began turning pages. I sat there patiently smoking my cigarette, sipping my brandy, hoping like hell that he wouldn't find the connection of their grandmother, Cajun Rose, as I did. If he did, I hoped like hell he wouldn't put together that that's where the blood came from, straight back to old Slewfoot Bob. A lot of folks don't know to look on the distaff side. They think it's all stud. A lot of folks are wrong. If it's true in quarter horses and Morgans and American Standardbreds, it's true in Kentucky bluegrass Thoroughbreds.

I waited at least five minutes while Mr. Clatterbuck looked at his registry book, scratched his head, turned pages, and then scratched his head some more. He finally sat back in his chair and went to studying the ceiling.

I said, "Is there something written up there that I ought to know about?" It kind of brought him back to where I was.

He said, "What?"

"Well sir, you were staring so hard up to the ceiling, I thought maybe that there was some information up there that I ought to be the beneficiary of also."

He laughed, but without much humor. He said, "Oh. You've caught me off guard. I never expected you to show any interest in those two particular studs. Certainly, you have never evidenced any interest in them before."

I said, "Well, I wouldn't normally have, except that the rest of your horses are so damn high. Here you have a horse that is blind in one eye, the roan, and the dun has a bowed tendon on

136

his near front leg. So I figured that you wouldn't be setting such great store by them."

He frowned. "What makes you think that dun has a bowed tendon?"

"Because I felt it. I've felt a considerable amount of bowed tendons in my days and one bowed tendon feels pretty much like another one. I reckon that's why that horse didn't race very much."

He narrowed his eyes at me. "So you did look the books over pretty thoroughly this afternoon."

"That's what I sat in here two hours doing. But that's not what we are sitting here to talk about. We're supposed to be talking about buying and selling some horses. Now, I've named the two I'm interested in, are you going to name your price?"

That brought the frown back on his face and a little more attention to the ceiling.

I said, "Come on, Mr. Clatterbuck, it can't be all that hard. You whipped out a price on those blacks like it was nothing and that chestnut like it was nothing. And I'm just asking you for a price on these two damaged animals."

He said, "Well, sir, I don't quite share your opinion of those fine stud horses as being damaged goods. 'Course, I do understand that that is one form of bargaining, to run down the other man's property to the benefit of your purse. But I have had that tried on me before."

I said, "Yes sir. And I've been to a rodeo before myself, even to a county fair. So I guess you might say that we are starting even. Now you wanna look at that book there for a while and then name me a price?"

He said, leaning back farther in his chair, "Oh, I already have a figure pretty well in mind. I'd say that I'd have to get fifteen thousand dollars for that pair of horses."

I kinda smiled. I said, "Would you like me to run upstairs to my room and fetch my revolver for you?"

"Whatever for, sir?"

"Well, if you've a mind to rob me, then you ought to at least do it by gunpoint."

He got a pinched look on his face that I think he thought passed for a smile. It missed by a good bit. He said, "Do you find that price out of your range, sir?"

"I find it way *off* the range. My range or anybody else's range."

"Would you like to make a counter offer?" he asked.

"I'm thinking four thousand dollars each."

"Eight thousand dollars for that pair of stud horses that have bloodlines going back yonder to the best stock in this part of the country?"

"There. You put your finger on it. This part of the country, sir. That's not Kentucky bloodstock, sir, that's Louisiana bloodstock you're talking about. You're not talking about Slewfoot Bob, now."

It set a frown on his face. He said, "There is no possibility, sir, that I would sell you that pair of studs for eight thousand dollars. Why, I get five hundred dollars stud fee for each one of them."

I gave him a questioning look. "Oh yeah? Done any business with them lately?"

He hesitated, contemplated lying to me, but then he knew that I had gone over his registry books, which included the stud service that had been performed by his different stallions and the dates and the prices. He said, "I don't reckon that information has anything to do with the conversation that we are now conducting. I will come down a thousand to fourteen thousand dollars for the pair of them."

"I will raise my offer a thousand to nine thousand dollars for the pair of them." What he didn't know, and I sure as hell wasn't gonna tell him, was that I was willing to go to ten thousand dollars for the dun and the roan. That would halve my available money and would leave me a pretty short supply of cash when I went to dealing in three other states. But they were two horses that I knew would provide me with a solid basis for a bloodline and I wanted the horses badly.

Mr. Clatterbuck reached out with one of his

fat hands and closed both of his registry books. He drew on his cigar and then knocked his ash off into a dish. He said, "Well, sir, we seem to be quite far apart on this matter. I don't see any way that we can reconcile these differences."

I said, "Sir, why don't you sleep on it. Think about it. I don't see those two studs earning keep around here and I'd at least be giving them work."

He said, "Would you be willing to go thirteen thousand dollars and the first get from each one of them?"

That made me laugh. If I was to give him the first colt that they sired, I would be taking a giant step backwards. I wouldn't be starting a breeding farm, I'd be starting a giveaway store.

"Well, Mr. Clatterbuck, as appealing as that offer is, I don't see the benefit in it for me. Now if the first bred turned out to be both mares, I'd consider giving you one of the first mares."

"Oh no, no, no," he said. "They'd have to be colts. I wouldn't be interested in mares from either one of these two horses."

He was wrong there, only he didn't know it. I got up. There was a clock on the wall beginning to chime eleven-thirty. I said, "Why don't we discuss this in the morning?"

"I'm willing to do that, Mr. Grayson. I just don't see us getting any closer unless you come to realize the quality of the stock you are trying to buy."

I said, "Oh, I admit to their quality or else I wouldn't be trying to buy them. I just disagree with the price. Remember, I still have a good many stops to make, all the way up to Virginia. I can't leave all my money here, Mr. Clatterbuck."

He gave me kind of a disdainful look. "If eight thousand dollars was all you started out with, I'd say that you have little chance of getting into the serious Thoroughbred horse racing business, Mr. Grayson."

I had expected to find Laura all tucked up in bed and half asleep when I looked in on her. She was in her nightgown, all right, but she was sitting on the side of her bed sipping wine out of a bottle, not even bothering with a glass. I came in and sat down crosswise on the little dressing-table chair.

I said, "I don't want to get too close because you look about as mad as a wet setting hen."

She gave me a dirty look.

I said, "Do you want to tell Uncle Warner about it?"

"That son of a bitch, honest to God, expected me to go walking in the moonlight with him. Can you imagine something so juvenile, that we should go walking out in the moonlight?"

I thought about it, as if I was going to give it

serious consideration. I said, "You're getting a little long in the tooth, Laura. I'd say that the moonlight might favor you better than them bright lamps they got in this house."

She gave me a sour look. She said, "I do not find you funny, Warner. Either we leave tomorrow or you tell that young man to stay the hell away from me or I'm going to slap the hell out of him the next time he touches me. He makes me feel slimy." She ran her hand down her arm and shuddered. "He's obsequious."

I blinked. I said, "I don't know what that means, but it sounds kind of bad."

"Oily, slimy. He oozes at me."

"I'm starting to get the idea that you don't like him."

She said, "Do you have to be a damn smart aleck? I mean what I say, Warner. Either warn him off, let's leave, or I'm gonna claw his eyes out. I don't know what that'll do to your horse trading but whatever it does, it'll have to be."

I laughed and said as I got up, "Put your mind at ease, madam. I will deal with the situation. I am sure that all the man needs is a gentle word of guidance and I will tell him that it is not the proper time of the month for such advances. That otherwise, you would entertain him and enjoy him."

I think that if she had had something to

throw at me, she would have thrown it, but instead she said, "Oh, go to hell."

I said, "Does that rule out a goodnight kiss or maybe even something beyond that?"

"I would say that it rules out everything. I don't want to even shake your hand. Do I make myself clear?"

I said, "It really must be that time of the month."

Then she did throw the wine glass at me. I caught it neatly and then set it on the dressing table. I went over and bent down and forced her to raise her head and kissed her on the lips. I said, "Now you get in bed and get some sleep and I'll speak to the young man in the morning. I've just about got my business concluded with Clatterbuck."

"Are you going to be able to buy the horses that you want?"

"I don't know. It depends on his whim. If he thinks that I've got more money than I've got, he might make it hard on me. I'll go half our stake, but that is as far as I will go. Now, you get in bed and turn out your lamp and get some sleep."

As she got into bed and laid her head on the pillow I leaned down and kissed her again. This time, she put her arms around my neck. When I lifted my lips, she said, "How did you manage to catch that glass?"

I smiled. I said, "Because I knew that you were going to throw it."

"Get out of here."

As I left her room, I again had the impression that a door had been swiftly closed somewhere along the hall. I guess either Royce or Cloyce was spying on us. I didn't much give a damn. Tomorrow would see our business pretty close to complete and then we could continue our journey. I was going to feel a lot better if I had a couple of solid studs in my hand before we left. I went on into my room and had a good drink of whiskey before turning in. I hoped that I would finally get used to the over-soft mattress before we left the next day.

Mr. Clatterbuck and I had breakfast together the next morning, though we did not talk about the price of the roan and the dun horses. He told me something about the other horse farms in the area and offered to take Laura and me to the oval one-mile track that they had just outside Lafayette. He said that the grandstands would seat fifteen hundred people and that I would be surprised at the amount of money that would be changing hands there, even at such a small track. He said that the season would be beginning in about a week but the owners were already bringing their horses there to get them stabled. He said that it would provide me with a fine opportunity to see a Thoroughbred being worked early in the morning by his jockey. Now I knew what that was, so I didn't expose my ignorance by asking where they got those little men. First of all, I figured I already had a couple in Raoul and Juanito that could ride with anybody.

The thing that I found curious was that each jockey wore the colors of his stable. I thought that meant some kind of ribbon or something, but no, it turned out to be the colored shirt that he wore during the race. That, to me, was an interesting fact. My main business, however, was having a quiet word with Mr. Royce Clatterbuck. It was eight o'clock before the elder Clatterbuck finished breakfast and the young Mr. Royce Clatterbuck hadn't as yet made an appearance. I thought to myself that it was odd the way I kept referring to him as the young Mr. Clatterbuck when indeed, he was possibly my age or even a little older. I suppose it was just the way he acted. The fact was, his younger brother seemed more mature than he did.

I wanted to get that business settled before Laura went and did something that would queer my prospective deal with Mr. Clatterbuck. As a consequence, I excused myself when Mr. Clatterbuck declared that he was going to the stables for his morning rounds and would I accompany him. I told him that, no, I felt like hanging around the house and giving it a good looking over, as I hadn't had a chance to do so before.

He took my answer with good grace and went on out leaving me to await Royce's coming and to see what kind of time I was going to have. I settled back with a cup of coffee and some brandy and a copy of a day-old local newspaper. I didn't expect much trouble over the business. I'd catch Mr. Royce Clatterbuck at a quiet moment and put a flea in his ear and that ought to about handle the business. Most likely he was going to get his feelings hurt but that couldn't be helped. Any man who dealt with a woman like Laura could expect to get his feelings hurt sooner or later in one way or another. The fact that I didn't like Mr. Royce Clatterbuck made the job that much more savory. I had to admit to myself that I was kinda looking forward to it, but I really didn't expect to rub his nose in it. I was going to tell him that the lady would prefer that he backed off and fell into a swamp somewhere. Maybe I'd tell him that he ought to take a bath once in a while. Maybe I'd tell him that he had bad breath. Maybe I'd tell him that Laura didn't like men that wore more perfume than she did. That made me chuckle to myself. That ought to really dig him good.

My wait was soon rewarded. There was a

146

small garden outside the breakfast room windows. It was a pleasant little place covered over with lattice work. There was a pool in the middle and benches placed around it. I knew that Royce had more than once managed to trap Laura there and pour some of his earnest entreaties over her. I thought it would be an excellent place for me to pour some cold water over him. I was elated when I saw him come strolling into the garden smoking a cigar, one hand in the pocket of his waistcoat. He sat down on a bench. Off a little farther, I could see Cloyce on the lawn, strolling along, his hands clasped down behind his back, his head downturned, studying the ground under his feet. He was the strange one, all right, make no mistake, but right then my business was with Royce.

I took the last drink of coffee in my cup and finished a last shot of Cognac and hurried out through the kitchen into the back. Royce was still sitting on the concrete bench where he had taken up residence, to watch for Laura, no doubt.

I came up to him and said, "Well, good morning, Mr. Clatterbuck. I hope that this day finds you in fine fettle."

He glanced up at me. I didn't think he was very fond of me either. I'd arrived with Laura and for all he knew there might be some connection between us. At any rate, he certainly didn't want me there in case Laura was to come along, but he gave me a good morning of sorts. He asked how the horse trading was coming along.

I said, "Well, I'm rather surprised that you haven't wanted to be a part of it. Your daddy and I have gone at it pretty hot and heavy. I'd have liked to have you in there. You might have been on my side."

He flicked the ash from his cigar. "I doubt it." He had an annoyed look on his face. "I find the horse breeding business tiresome. All this haggling over money. It's a tiresome pursuit for a gentleman."

I said, "Oh, gentlemen don't haggle over money?"

He gave me a look that nearly took the skin off my face. The look clearly implied that I didn't know anything about gentlemen or their ways. He said, "Gentlemen are more concerned with the finer elements of life. Money, however, is not one of those."

That made me kind of laugh. I said, "I guess then that you can only be a gentleman if you're rich enough not to have to worry about it, is that about the size of it?"

He said, "I don't expect you to understand, Mr. Grayson. Now if you would excuse me, I'm waiting on someone."

I got a cigarette out and lit it. I said, "I know

that, Mr. Clatterbuck, and that is what I am here to talk to you about."

That got his attention. He said, "What do you mean?"

I said, "I assume that you are awaiting Mrs. Pico."

"Would that be any of your business?"

"Yes, that would be my business, Mr. Clatterbuck, especially since she is not particularly interested in your advances."

I swear his face went dead white. He stood up slowly, his eyes wide and staring. He said, "Would you care to repeat that, sir?"

I laughed a little. I said, "Royce, the thing is, the lady is not interested in you right now. She is on a business trip and she finds your advances less than welcome. Is that clear enough for you?"

He stood rigidly straight, his face still pale. He said, "Sir, had I in my possession a pair of gloves, I would slap you across the face. But as it is, you may consider yourself challenged."

I stared at him. I didn't have the foggiest idea what he was talking about and I said so.

"Perhaps you are not acquainted with a gentleman's code, sir. I don't know why I would have thought that you would be. Let me enlighten you. However, I will need a witness." He turned his head in the direction of his brother and yelled, "Cloyce! Cloyce!"

I stood there in some amazement, wondering what these proceedings were all about, while I watched his brother slowly walk toward us. As he neared, Royce motioned impatiently to hurry. When he arrived in our midst, Royce turned to me. He said, "Now, would you care to repeat what you said before, in the presence of a witness, my brother Cloyce Clatterbuck?"

I looked at Cloyce, who stared back with nothing on his face. I looked at Royce and asked, "Are you sure you would not rather keep this private?"

Royce said, "I have challenged you, sir. It is necessary I do so in the presence of a witness. That is in accordance with the code duello."

"The what?"

"The code duello. However, I will make you acquainted with that gentlemen's code in enough time. Now, will you repeat that statement, sir, or will you withdraw it?"

Hell, he was about to annoy me. I was about halfway tempted to slap the living shit out of him, but because I had a horse deal cooking with his daddy, my hands were kind of tied.

I said, "All right, if you want your brother to know, then I'll tell you. Mrs. Pico does not welcome your romantic advances, if that's what they be, and would prefer you to cease and desist right now. In other words, cut it out. Now, is that clear enough for you?"

Cloyce, to my surprise, sighed and shook his head slowly. Royce turned to him triumphantly. He said, "You heard it."

Cloyce nodded his head and said, in an almost inaudible voice, "Yes, I heard."

Royce swiveled his head back to me. He said, "You may now consider yourself challenged, sir. I request that you go immediately to your room so that my second may call upon you to give you the particulars."

I said, "What in the hell are you talking about?"

He said, "I am challenging you to a duel, sir. Are you not familiar with a duel?"

I said, "You mean like you read about in a book? Swords and pistols and all that other stuff? Slapping people in the face with a glove? Standing back to back and walking ten paces? That kind of stuff?"

"Unless you prefer the sword, sir."

"Hell, I ain't never even picked up a sword." I just shook my head at him. "Listen, son, we take these kind of challenges in Texas pretty seriously. Now if you are setting out to get yourself killed, you're making a damn good start at it. Was I you, I'd let this matter drop. I'm willing to forget it."

Then Cloyce said, with a kind of misery in his voice, "He can't forget about it. He is a gentleman. You've insulted him by interfering in his personal life."

I gave both of them a puzzled look. I said, "In the first place, the lady is here with me. That makes it more of my personal business than it is yours. And secondly, I am not going to fight you in no damn duel, no matter what you say."

Royce acted like he hadn't heard me. He said, "My second will call upon you in your room at your earliest possible convenience. I assume that you do not have a second, so we will provide you with one."

I gave a disgusted sound. I said, "Oh, go to hell, Royce."

I flipped my cigarette away, turned around, walked across the garden, and entered the house through some doors that led into what I figured was a library. Then I went upstairs looking for Laura. I wanted her to know just what her foolishness had gotten me into.

She wasn't in her room, so I closed her door and went on down to mine. I poured myself a drink and sat down on the bed to contemplate the situation. Of course, the whole matter was complicated by the fact that I wanted to buy those two horses from Clatterbuck. Why his son should take such a wild hair as to want to fight me in a duel because I told him that Laura wanted to be left alone was beyond my comprehension. The way it was in Texas, you didn't tell a man you wanted to fight a duel. You made your gripe pretty obvious and you settled it right then on the spot. I didn't know about the business of seconds or what part they played, but I didn't need a second. Neither did he, because there wasn't going to be any duel. The whole thing got sillier and sillier the more I thought about it.

I was about to pour myself another drink when there came a light knock on the door. Thinking it was Laura, I called out, "Come in."

The door opened and Cloyce Clatterbuck came in. He had a thin book in his hand and a dour look on his face.

He said, "Mr. Grayson, I am here acting as my brother's second."

I said, "You can be his second, his third, his fourth, or his tenth, I don't give a damn. I'm not having anything to do with this foolishness."

He gave me a sorrowful look. "I'm afraid he will not be dissuaded. He will force you to fight him."

"He can't force me if I'm agin it, and I am agin it. If he shoots me, then that's murder. Now if he thinks he's going to shoot me, then I'm going to slap on a revolver. He might want to have second thoughts about having a duel, because what he is doing now is playing a dangerous little game."

Cloyce sighed. "I'm going to try to explain my brother to you if I can, Mr. Grayson, though I doubt that you will understand, for you seem to be a pretty sensible man. The way he thinks and the way he acts are not sensible to any one with the slightest bit of intelligence. He is acting out a dream he has invented. It is absurd, it's ridiculous, but unfortunately, it's also dangerous."

I was amazed. I didn't realize that Cloyce could talk that much. I said, "Well, why don't you try and explain this dream or whatever it is that your brother has."

Cloyce looked over across the room. "I'm almost embarrassed to tell you this because it is also shared by my father. Neither one of them are southern born and to them that is the greatest tragedy of their lives. They envision themselves as part of the south, even though my father came to the south as an official of the federal government. You may well know by now that he is originally from Fort Lee, New Jersey. I am the only one who can even claim a southern upbringing and I was about five years old when we came here. Royce has taken to this life just as my father has. Royce has taken to some of its more dangerous forms, however. This dueling business, for instance, is very much the vogue among the young gentlemen of the smarter set, if you can call them that—the more sophisticated set."

I said, "Am I to understand that they actually do fight duels here? That they actually do clang swords and shoot at each other?"

He nodded. He said, "Yes, they do. They draw blood."

"Do they ever kill anybody?"

"On occasion."

"But isn't that illegal?"

"You must understand, Mr. Grayson, these are all sons of very wealthy families. The law can be bought off here. The law can be asked to turn and look the other way. You must realize that they are playacting, but it is a very dangerous form of playacting."

I said, "Listen, I came here to trade horses with your daddy, not to play games with your brother."

Cloyce sighed. "I wish it was that simple. However, I have explained the situation to you the best that I can. There is nothing further that I can add except that this is real to Royce. He considers himself to be insulted and he considers that the only way the wrong can be righted is for blood to be drawn. Therefore, you have been challenged. The choice of weapons is yours, since you are the challenged party— the choice of weapons and the choice of grounds. I would warn you against the épée or the foil, since Royce studied fencing under a master in New Orleans."

For a second I was confused and then I realized that he was talking about swords. I laughed.

He said, "You find something funny, sir?"

I said, "Oh, I don't know. When you mentioned fencing, I thought that maybe we were going to go at each other with coils of barbed wire."

A thin smile appeared on his face. It was as close as I had come to seeing him display any emotion.

I said, "Well, it's not going to be swords or fences or coils of barbed wire. And it's not going to be pistols or cannons or anything else, because I simply am not going to duel."

He gave me a sad look. He said, "Then I am afraid that your mission to buy horses from my father will fail."

"You're not trying to tell me that your daddy is going to refuse to sell me horses because I refuse to kill his son?"

"I must warn you, Mr. Grayson, my brother is very proficient. He has fought five duels. He has killed three men and has wounded two others."

I said, "Were his opponents of a high caliber?"

Cloyce shrugged. He said, "I don't know. I don't care for this sort of affair. Right now I must discharge my duty by handing you this volume called the *Code Duello*, which you may study at your leisure. I will await your answer. If you have a second, have him seek me out, naming the weapon, the time, and the grounds. If not, we will provide you with someone who can act for you. I suggest you read the book. I bid you good day."

With that, he turned on his heel and left the room, leaving me stunned and startled. For a minute, I just sat there shaking my head, wondering how I managed to get myself into such messes. I was going to have to talk to Laura. She had gotten me into this mess, and it was up to her to get me out.

The book was still in my hand and for the lack of anything better to do, I opened it and idly began scanning its few pages. It had been written by some Frenchman with some title back in seventeen something. It claimed to be the rules of conduct for personal engagements. That was a hell of a way to describe two men setting out to kill each other. One item that caught my attention as I leafed through the book was that, both parties being agreeable, a doctor should be on hand at the time of engagement. Now if there was ever a silly arrangement, that was one. Here, two men planned to do the most harm they could do to each other, and they planned to have a doctor there to repair the damage. That was the silliest damn thing I had ever heard of.

Another point that struck me was that the challenged party got to pick his weapon and the ground that he wanted to fight on. It said that while the sword and the pistol were the accepted weapons of choice, any weapon capable of deadly force could be used. Well, that ought to give you thought right there if you were planning to go around challenging folks. If you challenged an Indian, that gave him the right to pick the weapon and he was liable to pick bow and arrow and fill your ass full of arrows like a pin cushion. So here this young man had given me the choice of weapons and grounds. That didn't seem to be too sensible of him. I was a stranger to him and he didn't know how capable I was or wasn't.

That ain't real good poker playing, but according to his barometer, he had five engagements, as they were called, and was still alive, so he had to be a fair hand. But that didn't really answer the question at hand. I was going to have to talk to his father. I doubted if Clive Clatterbuck would sell me those horses if I killed Royce and I damned sure wasn't going to let his son kill me.

All of a sudden, it made me as angry as hell to think of what Laura had gotten me into. If the damned fool woman had had the good sense to marry me before we left, or to introduce herself as Mrs. Grayson, anything but that damn Pico that she insisted on going by, none of this would have happened! Royce, being the southern gentleman he claimed to be, would certainly have had the sense to leave her alone.

Just as I was coming to a slow boil, there was a slight tap at my door and Laura slipped in. She was wearing another severe frock and had her hair pinned up in a most unbecoming fashion. From the look on her face, I could tell that she already knew. I glared at her.

She said, "Warner, I can't believe what I just heard."

I said, "Well, believe it. Since you are the cause of it, I reckon that you ought to believe it."

"Do you know that Royce just marched up to me downstairs and said that my honor and his honor were at stake. What kind of lunatic is he?"

"He's a southern-fried lunatic. Haven't I heard you prattle about that southern chivalry? Well, even though he is from New Jersey and a damned Yankee, he has bought the whole farm."

"He has actually challenged you to a duel?"

"Must be. I got the book right here."

She said, "You can't fight him in a duel. You can't kill him."

"Nothing gets by you, does it, Laura? You're as sharp as a bear trap."

She said, "Don't take that tone with me, Warner Grayson."

I had been a little heated when she came into the room and I was even more heated now. In the first place, I blamed her for what I thought was good cause. I said, "I'll take any damned tone with you that I want to. All I asked you to do was hold the horses. That was the only purpose for you to come along on this trip. And yet you have managed to flaunt yourself around until . . . this mess."

Her eyes blazed. "Don't you dare blame me for this. Don't you dare."

"Well, if you had handled things a little bit better, I don't reckon that we would be in this situation. Or if I had left you at home, then none of this would have ever come up."

She glared at me with her fists at her sides. "That's unfair."

"Oh it is? Well, what's the situation as it is? On top of everything else, I am challenged to a duel and I don't even have a second. Now how does that make me look down here in this wonderful South? You can't be my second. It says right here in this damn book that if a third party is the subject of the alienation between the two principals, that that third party cannot act as the second for either one of the principals. Now, I don't know exactly what that means, but I gather that the pair of tits that caused us to have the falling out can't act as my second."

Her mouth tightened. She said, "All right. You're angry. I'm angry. We're both angry and I'm going to let you blow off steam. Go ahead. But when I think that I've gotten as much as I've got coming, I'm going to tell you to stop and you damned well better stop."

I said, "Laura, you're not going to tell me

one damned thing." I glared at her. "What you need is a damn good whipping with a smart stick. You weren't near this ignorant when I took you up."

She put her hands on her hips. "I've got some news for you, Warner. Any woman that takes up with you has got to be ignorant to start with."

My face fell. "Now, Laura, that's downright cruel. You ain't got no call to say such a thing. That ain't very ladylike."

"But according to you, it's all my fault. *I* made the mistake."

"Aren't you the cause of the dispute?"

"All right, then it's up to me to go and settle this whole mess."

I said, "Oh, no. You're gonna stay right here in this room. I'm going to go down and talk to Mr. Clatterbuck and see if I can get this mess straightened out. I came out here to buy horses, not to fight duels over some silly woman."

"Call me what you will. I still think that I should intervene."

"That sure would make me look good, wouldn't it? Like I couldn't handle my business. Like I had to run a skirt in front of me to intercede for me. I don't think Mr. Clatterbuck would take it that way. According to Cloyce, he's as much a bug on this southern chivalry shit as Royce is. I'm going to see what I can do. You just sit tight, lady."

She watched as I went out of the room. I didn't slam the door, but I didn't pull it to none too gently.

I found Mr. Clatterbuck in his office. The door was open as if he was expecting me. I paused inside the frame and inquired if he had a few moments to talk. He waved me forward. His face was grave. I was pretty certain that he knew what the situation was. I sat down.

He didn't offer me a cigar or a brandy as he usually did. I said, "Mr. Clatterbuck, I am sure that you are aware of the misunderstanding that exists between your son Royce and myself. I'd like to—"

He cut me off. "I'm not aware of any misunderstanding, sir. The facts that I have are that you have insulted my son and that he has appealed to your chivalrous nature for redress of that insult."

"I had no earthly idea how I insulted him. He was paying far more attention to Mrs. Pico than she cared for. I simply told him to stop it."

"My son got no such indication from Mrs. Pico. I challenge you, sir, in that you were jealous of the attention that my son was paying and took it upon yourself to interfere with a relationship that was none of your business."

"Mr. Clatterbuck, you and I are starting to get crosswise. That is the last thing that I want.

Now, I have no intention of fighting your son in a duel. We don't have duels in Texas. We have gunfights and we don't think they are funny and we don't think that honor or chivalry has anything to do with it. But that aside, I came here to buy a couple of stud horses from you and I would like this other nonsense to be swept out of the way so that we can get on with our business."

He sat there listening to me in his full black suit and his brocade vest and his four-in-hand tie. He said, "Sir, you have just referred to the gentlemen's code as nonsense. Perhaps you will not think it's so when you are facing either a blade or the barrel of a pistol."

I shook my head slowly. "Mr. Clatterbuck, would you get it straight once and for all? I am not going to fight your son. I am an experienced gunman. I don't want to kill your son and I certainly don't want him to kill me. Let us find a way to reconcile this matter."

He put up his hand. He said, "Sir, there are only two ways to reconcile this matter. Either you will withdraw your statement that you made to my son and apologize, or you will engage him on the field of honor. That is the long and the short of it."

I was becoming heated. I said, "Mr. Clatterbuck, I can't withdraw my statement because it was made at the request of the lady. I made the statement with full intentions and I certainly am not going to apologize for something that I do not consider a wrong. And I certainly am not going to fight your son. Now, are you going to sell me those two horses?"

He leaned back in his chair and placed his hands across his ample belly. He said, "Mr. Grayson, I will not sell you so much as a bale of hay while you conduct yourself in such a manner. Thoroughbred horse racing is for gentlemen and you have not proven yourself a gentleman."

I looked at him for a moment. I said, "So the only way you are going to sell me those horses is if I fight your son, because I am not going to withdraw my statement?"

"I will make you a proposition. If you fight my son—we do not prefer to call it a fight, sir, it is a matter of honor, it is a duel—if you engage on the field of honor with my son, I will sell you, or your heirs, those two horses, that dun and that roan, for the original price that you have offered, eight thousand dollars."

I stood up slowly. I said, shaking my head, "This is the damnedest way that I have ever done business in my life. First the gunfight and then the horse trade. In Texas, it's usually the other way around."

Mr. Clatterbuck ignored my remark. He said, "My son Cloyce, who is acting as Royce's second, is awaiting your choice of grounds and the other particulars."

I said, "Mr. Clatterbuck, the circumstances being what they are, I think that Mrs. Pico and I should move into a hotel in town. I feel that it is going to be a little awkward around here with this business between me and your son."

Mr. Clatterbuck stood up. He said, "Sir, that would be an insult to my hospitality. We have a small cabin on the place. My son Royce has already taken up residence there awaiting your pleasure. I can assure you, sir, that neither you or Mrs. Pico should feel the least discomfort or be the least bit ill at ease staying on here until this affair is concluded."

I gave him a thin smile. I said, "Mr. Clatterbuck, your version of honor and chivalry certainly takes some funny turns. I'll be sleeping under your roof and eating your food with the full intention of shooting your son. Do you understand that?"

"Those are the terms of the contract that my son has engaged you in."

I said, "And you're still going to sell me those horses for eight thousand dollars, even when they bring the lifeless body of your son in here? Is that correct?"

He drew himself up. He said, "You have my word, sir."

I laughed slightly. I said, "Well, I've been in

some squirrelly deals before but this beats any of them."

As I turned to go, I said, "Now, I have to find me a second, if I understand the rules of that book correctly."

Mr. Clatterbuck said, "You would understand, sir, that I would be unavailable, and of course, your lady friend is disqualified. Perhaps you would like to ask around among some of the grooms. Most of them are southern by birth and are familiar with the code."

I looked at him for a long time, wondering if he knew how silly he sounded and looked. I said, "Oh, I'll figure out something. Maybe I'll send home for one."

He said, "Sir, even now my son Cloyce is awaiting your instructions. We expect this affair to take place in the morning at first light."

I almost let myself get angry. "What the hell's the big hurry?"

"It's better these matters get settled with dispatch."

I gave him a long look just before I turned to go out the door. I said, "Dispatch just might be the word that fits the situation."

Laura was gone when I got back to my room. Instead, the elderly Negro who saw to my wants was tidying up the room, making up the bed again. He had placed the book, the *Code Duello*, on the bedside table. I guessed he figured that it would make good bedtime reading. Jasper was his name. I got the bottle of whiskey and a glass and sat down in the chair. I poured myself out a pretty good slug and then drank most of it down.

I said, "Jasper, have you ever heard of this dueling business?"

He was a very soft-spoken old man. He said, "Yass sir. I've heard of it. But I don't be studying on it none. I don't have no truck with that kind of white-folk's stuff. Folks shooting each other and stabbing each other with them big long old knives. No, sir. I heard of it, but I don't want no truck with it."

I said, "Does everybody down here in this part of Louisiana go for that kind of stuff?"

He kind of ducked his head and smiled a little bit. He said, "Well, I reckons that just thems as reckons themselves to be gentlemens. Sometimes I'm glad I ain't no gentleman. Terrible burden on the soul and the body."

I asked, "Are the Clatterbucks gentlemen, Jasper?"

He straightened up from his work at the bed and gave me a look. He said, "Why, yass sir. They's the finest gentlemen in the world. Yass sir, ain't no question about that."

"How do you know that, Jasper?"

" 'Cuz they tolds me so."

A thought came to my mind that made me

167

smile. I said, "Jasper, do you know what a second is?"

He thought about it for a moment and then scratched his head. "The next best horse?"

"No, I'm not talking about the runner-up in a horse race. I'm talking about in a duel."

He said, "Well, no sir. I don' knows that I knows all about that."

I said, "Well, how would you like to be my second, Jasper?"

He said, "I don' knows that I's understands all abouts that, sir."

I said, "All you've got to do is to deliver a slip of paper down to Mr. Cloyce Clatterbuck's room. You can do that, can't you?"

He said, "Well, yass sir. I reckon I can. I's just a messenger then, just a carrying boy. Is that right?"

I said, "Well, yes. But officially you are my second."

"Well, yass sir, I can handle that. Yass sir."

I got out a roll of money and peeled off a ten-dollar bill and said, "Well, Jasper, let's seal the bargain. You take this ten spot."

His eyes got big in his head. He said, "Aw, no sir. I can't take that. We ain't supposed to take tips from the guests of Mr. Clatterbuck."

I said, "This is not a tip, Jasper. This is payment for being my second."

He said, "Well, yass sir." He tentatively reached

out his hand and took the ten-dollar bill and looked at it.

I said, "Now you go along, Jasper, and come back here in about an hour. No, make it an hour and a half or maybe two. Then I will have a piece of paper written up for you."

He said, "Yass sir. Yass sir, all right. Yass sir."

I smiled to myself as I watched him go out the door. I was thinking about what Mr. Clatterbuck's reaction would be when he found out that my second was one of his house servants. I was certain that he regarded the Negroes as a step below the horses.

After Jasper was gone, I sat there, sipping whiskey slowly, thinking. I could not figure a way out of this mess. I could not see me putting my back to Royce's and then stepping off ten paces, turning around and firing one of those flintlock pistols that I imagined he had a brace of. And I certainly couldn't see myself crossing swords with him. But the choice of weapons and the choice of grounds were mine. I sat there trying to think. Bullwhips? I figured that I could flay him alive with one of those. But it had to be a deadly weapon. Bullwhips were not deadly weapons. I mean you could kill a man with one of them, but it would take a while.

A fistfight? Well, fists aren't deadly weapons either. Besides that, a gentleman wouldn't go for that. As I thought, I got up, glass in hand, and slowly walked across to the window and looked out. My view was of the back part of the ranch, overlooking the stables and the corrals and the back pastures. Off in the distance, I could see a little copse of woods about four or five acres big. I had ridden around it on the ride that I had taken the afternoon before. It was obviously left standing as a weather break for the cattle. It was a good, dense thicket, longer than it was wide. I stood there looking at it and a thought suddenly popped into my mind. At first, I didn't pay much attention to it, but the more I thought about it, the more I liked it. It seemed far-fetched but I could pick the weapons and I could pick the grounds.

Now as far as the weapons went, I could pick six-shooters, but that went against my code, because I didn't think that Mr. Royce Clatterbuck would have much of a chance against me out in the open with a six-shooter, especially if I used my nine-inch Colt, which was accurate at about fifty or sixty yards. I could say pistols at sixty yards and he wouldn't have a hell of a lot of choice.

But as I looked at that grove of woods and thought about six-shooters, the thought kept coming back into my mind and coming back and coming back. It might be a way out. There might be a way for us to have a duel to satisfy his honor without him being killed and without me being killed. It was as good a plan as I could come up with, especially with the limited amount of time that I had.

I stood there studying it for about five more minutes and then I drank the rest of my whiskey. I twirled around and went out of my room and down to see Laura. She was dressing. I don't know whether it was for lunch or not, as she always seemed to be dressing or undressing.

I had her stop what she was doing and sit down. I explained my plan to her. At first she didn't get it, but as the realization came to her, she said, "Oh, my. Oh, my. Warner, I don't like the sound of that at all."

"Like it or not, Laura, it seems the best way out of this. It seems the best way for me to use the skills I have to keep from killing the son of a bitch and not get hurt myself."

She suddenly stood up. She said, "No, there is a much better way to settle this whole matter." Then, before I could say another word, she crossed the room, grabbed up one of her many valises, and then went to the chiffonnier and began to take out numerous articles of clothing.

I said, "What the hell do you think that you're doing?"

She didn't bother looking around. She said, "We're leaving. I'm packing."

I said, "No we're not, Laura. I can't run out on this."

"Warner, I will not have any of this manly heroic bullshit, as you call it. We're in the horse business. We're not in the southern dueling business."

"I want those two horses, Laura, and this is the only way that the old man will sell them to me."

She whirled on me. "Warner, these aren't the only two horses in the world. Get packed while I finish, and then I will see to having a coach arranged for us and we shall go back into town. We can take the first train to Tennessee that leaves. You have six farms that you are going to look at horses at. This is only one."

"Laura, the man will sell me those two studs for eight thousand dollars if I fight his son in this duel. I can never get that close to quality stock for eight thousand dollars. That would leave me twelve thousand dollars to buy one or two more studs. This is too good a chance to pass up."

"Too good a chance to get yourself killed?" Her eyes blazed. "Listen Warner, I've got too much time invested in you, not to mention what little feelings I have. I have no intentions of you risking your life."

I laughed with no humor. I said, "Laura, where have you been living the past four or five years? You've lived in Texas. Every day in Texas you risk your life if you're a man and you carry a gun."

She threw one of her dresses savagely at her valises. She said, "Oh, you and your damn guns. I'm sick of your guns. I'm sick of all guns."

"You didn't use to feel that way, Laura. You feel that way now because of that shot Jack Fisher put into your side when he was trying to scare the horse I was racing against him. You'd never been shot before and so you were upset. But I'm not going to pass up this chance."

"The hell you're not. We are getting the hell out of here and that's final."

I went over to her and, as gently as I could, I took her dresses out of the valise and closed it, putting it back under the bed where it had been. I said, "Laura, honey, this is none of your business. This is man's business. You let me tend to it my way."

She stood there facing me, her fists clenched, her mouth contorted. I could almost swear there were tears in her eyes. She said, "Damn you, Warner Grayson. Damn you all to hell. You can tear me to pieces easier than any man that has ever lived. Why do you do it? Do you take pleasure in it?"

"I'm not doing this for pleasure, Laura. Do I seem happy? Do you hear me laughing?"

"You could end up dead, you damn fool," she said.

"That's what you think? You think that he is a better man than I am? Do you think that that dandy in his coat and his silk shirt is a better man than I am? That he is going to be a better man in those woods? Come on, Laura. Give me a little credit."

I was right, her eyes were full of tears. One ran down her cheek. She said, "Please, Warner. Please. Let's leave."

"I can't leave, Laura. Get that straight. Leaving is out. I just want your support in this."

"I thought you thought more of me than that. I thought you thought more of my happiness than this."

"I do, Laura. I think that everything I do is for your happiness. I think that is what I do. I hate to say it under these conditions. I've never said it before, but I am always thinking of your happiness."

"Not like this, you're not."

I sighed. "We've said everything there is to say on the subject. Now I have to go and write up my terms and get them down to Cloyce so that he can deliver them to his brother so that they can understand them."

"Is there nothing else I can say?"

"Laura, I've thought of every way out of this I could. There is no way out of this. This is the safest plan."

"This is the safest way out that includes those horses. Damn those horses. Damn your guns. Damn this whole business. I wish you weren't

174

even in the horse-breeding business. Why can't you be a dentist or a storekeeper or something else?"

I laughed slightly. I said, "Laura, don't forget that you're drawn to horse breeders. You love horses. I think half the reason that you care about me is because I'm in the horse business."

She abruptly sat down on the bed and put her hands to her face. She said, "Oh, go away. Just go away."

I backed slowly toward the door. I said, "I hope that you come down to lunch. It's going to be a little rocky without you."

"Go away."

I closed the door softly behind me and went down the hall to my room. I found a pen and some paper and began to write up my terms, the conditions for this duel that Mr. Royce Clatterbuck's honor demanded. I hated to make Laura feel bad, I really did, but I didn't see that I had any selection.

7

At about two in the afternoon, I sent for Jasper and dispatched him with a note that I had written proposing the conditions and terms that it was my right as the challenged to claim. Lunch had been a strained affair. Royce had not been there, but Laura had shown up, as had Mr. Clatterbuck and Cloyce. We had tried to make casual conversation but it was hard going with this axe hanging over all our heads, or at least it appeared to be hanging over my head and over Laura's head and even in some way, over Cloyce's head. Mr. Clatterbuck seemed jovial about the whole thing. I thought that he was viewing me as another notch in Royce's dueling pistol handle. Of course, he hadn't gotten my conditions by then, else he might not have been so jovial.

After the note was gone by the hands of Jasper, I went down the hall and visited with Laura for a few minutes and then came back to my room to await the results of my second's efforts. At about four that afternoon, there came a light tap at my door. It was Cloyce again. I invited him in and offered him a drink. There was a bottle of brandy on the bureau and he helped himself to a hefty tumblerfull. Off to one side of the room there were two overstuffed chairs with a small table between them. We retired to these, sitting opposite each other. To my eye, Cloyce had an amused look on his face. We gave each other a toast. He said health and I said luck and then we both had a pretty good pull at our glasses. I lit a cigarette after offering him one, which he declined.

I asked, "You are in receipt of my terms from my second?"

He suddenly laughed. It was a nice sounding laugh. "My God, sir. You do have a way about you. I cannot tell you the expression on my daddy's face when he realized who your second was. I tell you sir, it was worth the price of admission just to have been there, even if the ticket had cost a hundred dollars. I have never seen the old man as irritated and out of sorts. Never mind the contents of your conditions, but to have them delivered by one of the house servants acting as your second. A Negro, sir. A Negro!"

"But your father was a Yankee. Wasn't that what he fought the Civil War about?"

"To begin with, my father never fought in any part of the Civil War. And secondly, he treats all of his hired hands, no matter what color they are, as slaves."

He continued saying, "Do not confuse my father with an emancipator, Mr. Grayson. My father is interested in only one thing: building an image of himself as a southern plantation gentleman."

I said, "Cloyce, several times you have made slighting remarks both about your brother and your father. You don't seem to think much of them."

"On the contrary, sir. I think a great deal of them. However, I deplore their actions and the thinking that results in those actions."

"Well, we are not here to discuss your family. We are here to discuss the duel that must be fought. As I understand that book you gave me, you are acting for your principal, who is Mr. Royce Clatterbuck. I assume that Mr. Clatterbuck has been advised of my conditions and terms."

Cloyce laughed again. "Oh, yes, he has been apprised."

"And what was his reaction?"

Cloyce thought for a minute. "I would say shock, Mr. Grayson. He is stunned. My father is flabbergasted. I would say that they are in disarray."

"Do they accept my conditions?"

Cloyce said, "Well, there it is, Mr. Grayson. They have no alternative but to accept your conditions. You are the challenged party. You have the right to a weapon of your choice and you have the right to the grounds. You have chosen both. You have fulfilled the condition that the weapons be of a deadly force; certainly revolvers are. And you have chosen the grounds. He can't argue with grounds that are his own. That patch of woods is part of his plantation."

"So the terms are acceptable?"

Cloyce took a sip of his brandy. He said, "Mr. Grayson, they have to be acceptable."

I nodded. "I'm glad to hear that. So you are officially telling me as his second that we are to fight this duel in that patch of woods with six-shooters? Is that correct?"

He nodded. "As my brother's second, I am so advising you. The hour that we choose is seven A.M. It will be good and light by then. Is that acceptable to you?"

I said, "I would rather have breakfast first. It's a little early."

He said gently, "It's generally not considered a good idea to eat before a duel in case you suffer a belly wound."

"I have no intentions of receiving a belly wound or inflicting one. Would you agree to eight A.M.? It seems a more civilized time."

He thought for a moment and then said, "Eight is as good a time as any other time." He smiled. "In fact, it might even give Royce a little more time to stew, which these conditions have him doing."

"Then let it be eight o'clock."

He nodded, "Eight o'clock in the copse of woods with revolvers, six shots each is agreed." He paused. "Now, may I ask you something, unofficially, not speaking as my brother's second?"

"Of course."

"Why have you chosen these particular conditions?"

"Just between you and me?"

"Yes. I could say on my honor as a southern gentleman, but I am not sure that there is really any such thing. However, I will give you my word that I have no interest in repeating your reasons."

I said, "It is the only way that I could figure not to kill your damn fool brother or run the risk of getting myself killed and still make the deal with your father at a very favorable price."

He laughed out loud. He said, "How very becoming of you, Mr. Grayson. I can understand you not wanting to be killed. I can even almost understand you not wanting to kill my brother. What I cannot understand is that you are willing to make a deal with my father."

"What is so hard to understand about that?"

"I would have assumed that you would have shrugged the entire matter off and left. That is what I expected you to do. Now I understand that you are going through with it so that you can buy some breeding horses from my father. Is that correct?"

"Yes."

He shook his head. "I guess I will never understand horse people."

"Are you not one yourself?"

He reflected for a moment. "I suppose that I am, in that I have grown up around them and have been exposed to them all my life, but I have no intentions of making horses my life. I am interested in law and medicine and I'm not sure that I understand what prompts someone to be such a devoted horseman. Can you tell me, Mr. Grayson? Why are you yourself a horseman and why are you willing to go to such lengths to be a horseman?"

This question had never been put to me so directly before or else I had never really given it any thought. I had become a horseman at a very early age and had never seen any reason not to go on being one. But his question deserved an answer so I said, "Well, I guess that it's because it keeps you out of the weather and there is no heavy lifting involved."

He said, "Believe it or not, that is the most sensible answer that I have ever heard."

I could not recall why I had thought of the young man as having a dour look. Sitting across from me, his features were gentle and refined. He laughed easily and he was very pleasant company. He was from a different cut than his brother and his father. I suppose that Laura would have found him a sensitive young man.

He said, "Mr. Grayson. I am going to tell you something that I ask that you hold in confidence."

"Of course."

His brow furrowed. He said, "You should understand that my brother is not really an honorable man. He will try to figure out how to cheat you in this duel. He has before and he will do it again. I don't know exactly how he will do it in this case, but he will find a way. I urge you to be on your guard."

I looked at him strangely. I was surprised but I still said, "Cloyce, I can assure you that any time guns are involved, I am always on my guard, but I appreciate you telling me. How has he managed to cheat in the past?"

Cloyce shrugged, "I can't give you exact details, except in one instance he forced the man he engaged to take a gun with only half a charge. Of course, the man was killed."

I said, "But what if the man had chosen the other pistol, the one with the full charge that your brother had?"

Cloyce said, "I don't know. I think something would have been arranged."

I said, "Any other advice?"

He said, "No, but I still think that it would be very wise for you to leave here and buy your horses somewhere else."

"Someone very near and dear to me has given me the same advice and I didn't take it."

He said, very thoughtfully, "Mrs. Pico is a charming and sophisticated lady. I can see why Royce's attention would have been extremely unwelcome. But I think that you would have been better served if you had made your feelings toward one another clear from the beginning."

I said, "You are wise for your age, Cloyce."

He took a step toward the door, setting his brandy glass down as he did. He said, "There is only one final piece of business to be decided. The woods run east to west. Which side do you prefer to enter from? My brother has expressed a preference for the east side, that is the side nearest to the house."

I shrugged. "I don't much care. I guess someone will get me over to the west end, either loan me a horse or take me over in a buckboard."

Cloyce said, "That will be seen to." He paused a moment more, looking at me. "Mr. Grayson, do you really intend not to kill my brother if you can possibly manage it?"

I nodded and said, "If I can manage it."

"It may be harder than you think."

I asked, "Do you think that your father will

sell me those horses at our agreed prices if I am forced to kill your brother?"

Cloyce nodded. "Oh, yes, of course. In fact, he is much more likely to sell you those horses if you kill Royce than if you humiliate him."

"What makes you so sure that I plan to humiliate him?"

He smiled. "I think I understand you better with each passing moment, Mr. Grayson. You are an unusual man. I don't get the opportunity to meet such men very often. It is definitely a pleasure. I think my father and Royce may very well learn a lesson from this."

I stood up. "You think I'm running a risk, don't you?"

"I think you would be running a greater risk if you went out to meet Royce on this so-called field of honor with a pair of dueling pistols. You might find your sights bent."

"Has that happened?"

"Let me say that it's been my observation that strange things have been known to surround Royce's duels."

"One last question. Does he like to fight?"

"Oh, indeed no. In fact, he is frightened to death. But it is all part of the mystique that he and my father have invented for themselves. My father was a small-time government official from New Jersey. He came here to a land of wealth aplenty. He came here with a license to steal. Believe me, he used that license to its full advantage. Most of what you see here has been stolen, Mr. Grayson."

"You seem a pretty decent fellow, Cloyce. Why do you stay here?"

"Because they are my family, Mr. Grayson. Be they whatever they are, they are still my family. I do not intend to end up here, nor do I intend to wind up like them, but they are still my family. Now I wish you good day until dinner this evening. That should be a hilarious affair, considering the temper that my father is in over your conditions and about your second. I will leave you with this final warning: if there is some way for Royce to cheat tomorrow, he will."

"Thank you for that final warning, Cloyce."

He left and I picked up my whiskey and sat down in my chair. I was thoughtful, to say the least.

Contrary to Cloyce's prediction, supper that evening did not turn out to be the hilarious affair he had forecast, primarily because Laura and I were the only ones at the dinner table. With only the two of us, the dining room seemed even bigger and longer than before. I sat at the head of the polished table with Laura to my right. I assumed that the elder Mr. Clatterbuck and Cloyce were with Royce, trying to figure out what sort of chicanery I was up to. Jasper waited table on us looking about as worried and uneasy as a man fighting off a sneeze while handling nitroglycerin. I tried a few good-humored sallies on him but he didn't respond.

Matters were still a little strained between Laura and me, so it was not the most pleasant dinner I had passed. She didn't again broach the subject of our leaving, but it was in her eyes. We were served roast pork and gravy, yams, and butter beans with fresh tomatoes and green onions. Under other circumstances, it would have been a delightful meal. Laura ate very little. For dessert, Jasper brought in angel food cake smothered in peach marmalade. He informed me that Mr. Clatterbuck would like to see me in his office as soon as were through eating.

The dessert was so larruping that I figured that I had to have a second piece, which also gave me a chance, since Laura didn't seem to be all that interested in hers, to direct her to go upstairs, get out her checkbook, and write out a check for eight thousand dollars to the Gables Thoroughbred Breeding Farm and bring it to me to sign. I figured to close the deal this very night. I was going to give Mr. Clatterbuck a check and get a bill of sale for those two horses. I wasn't going to give him a chance to renege pending on whether I did or did not kill his son.

Laura looked at me a little longer than I wanted her to. I said, "Laura, this is business and I'm the senior partner. So go write that check." She got up slowly.

"All right," she said.

I watched her leave the room. She had changed into the same severe gown that she had worn the night before. That was a measure of how down she was—the idea of wearing the same gown to the same dinner table was beyond her comprehension. I guess her mind was somewhere else.

She stopped just before she passed out of the dining room and said gently, "Warner, it's still not too late. We can still leave tonight. We can go into Lafayette, get a hotel room and take the train in the morning."

I said, "Laura, I appreciate your concern, honey, however, I have already explained my reasons. Now go fetch me that check. I didn't change my mind before and I'm not going to change it now."

She nodded her head slowly. "All right. I dread this, though, Warner. I dread this. I cannot tell you with what sorrow I dread this."

"How about you not burying me just yet?"

She turned away and I heard her evening slippers clicking down the polished wood of the hall toward the upstairs bedroom.

● ● ●

As soon as I had entered the office, the old man was up and waving a piece of paper at me. I recognized it as the conditions of engagement that I had written out and had sent by my second, Jasper. I had stolen the phrase from the book that Cloyce had given me. I thought it a rather strange term to apply to two men approaching each other with the intent of mayhem. Sounded more to me like something that you would write up before marriage.

Mr. Clatterbuck said, "Sir, what is the meaning of this tomfoolery? What do you mean by these conditions? I have never before in my life heard of such a manner of settling a gentlemen's dispute."

"You won't let me get sat down before you start in?"

That stopped him for a second. He waved me toward the big armchair. "By all means, have a seat and help yourself to some brandy and some cigars."

I poured myself a drink and sat down and, as always, I passed on the cigars. I asked, "Why do you call it tomfoolery, Mr. Clatterbuck? Is it any more tomfoolery than two men having at each other with swords? Is it any more tom-foolery than two men stepping off ten paces then turning and firing at each other with weapons out of another time and place? What do you find that's such tomfoolery about it?"

His face was flushed not with alcohol but with exasperation or anger. He said, "As I understand it, your conditions are that you enter one side of that small patch of woods in the near pasture and that my son enter it from the other end, both of you bearing six-shot revolvers and that you seek each other out."

"That's about the size of it," I said. "The one that comes out is the winner."

He blustered for a moment, searching for words. Finally he said, "Why sir, that is barbaric. Barbarous. Where are the niceties of the affair? Where is the conduct? Where is the honor? Where is the ceremony?"

"Where I come from, Mr. Clatterbuck, there is no ceremony, no niceties, and no honor attached to the reckless killing of a man. A killing of a man over nothing but some imagined slight. So if you want to be foolish about this matter, then I suppose that I can be equally foolish."

He said, "This goes against all that I have ever heard of the gentleman's code of dueling. Where will the witnesses be? Where will the judge be? How will we know if fair play exists? We won't be able to even see you. You will be hidden by the thickness of the trees and the brush of the forest."

I said, "It's pretty simple, Mr. Clatterbuck."

He said, "These conditions leave a great deal

of room for skullduggery, Mr. Grayson. What is to prevent you from hiding behind a tree and ambushing my son?"

"What is to prevent your son from hiding behind a tree and ambushing me? Or for that matter, what is to prevent both of us from hiding behind a tree? Might make for a long day for those of you waiting outside to see which one of us comes out the victor. This may not hold with your code, but it holds with my code. We don't take the killing of another human being very lightly, Mr. Clatterbuck. As far as I'm concerned, there are only two reasons to kill another human being. That is to save your own life or the life of another person. You don't kill a man over money and you don't kill a man over some imagined insult. You don't kill him over honor. I've never actually seen honor. Is that something that you can pour in a bowl, or put in a bucket, or in a box?"

His eyes gleamed with hostility. "I am not at all sure that you are a gentleman, Mr. Grayson."

I shrugged. "Let me set your mind at ease, Mr. Clatterbuck. I make no pretense of being a gentleman. I came here to buy horses, no other reason, and whether I am or am not a gentleman has nothing to do with our business."

While he was sitting there fuming and foaming, trying to digest that bit of information, I got the check out and laid it on the desk.

I said, "Here is a check for eight thousand dollars. That is the agreed upon price."

He barely glanced down at it. "Aren't you rushing things a little?"

"You agreed to sell me those two horses for eight thousand dollars, no matter what the results, if I fought your son a duel. So I thought we'd finish our business tonight as I'm liable to be a little rushed in the morning. If you will make me out a bill of sale for that dun and that roan, I'd be much obliged."

His eyes got mean and small. He said, "What makes you think that you will still be in the horse business later in the day tomorrow?"

"I may well not be in the horse business tomorrow, Mr. Clatterbuck. I may well be dead at the hands of your son. But my business partner will still be in the horse business and I will expect you to honor your commitment to me through her."

He made a motion at my check with the back of his hand and said, "Then there is enough time for that tomorrow."

"There is time enough for it right now. Why shouldn't we get this business concluded? Do you have any reason not to? We have agreed to it verbally, why shouldn't we continue with the conclusion of this business?"

His face pinked up a little more. He said, "Are you doubting me keeping my word, sir?"

"No, I'm not doubting you keeping your word. Are you about to get offended with me, Mr. Clatterbuck, and take as an insult what was only meant as business talk? Are you about to challenge me also? If you are sir, you are wasting your time. My quota is only one duel a day. You'll have to get in line behind your son."

"I have said that I would sell you those horses for eight thousand dollars if you fought my son. I did not, however, count on these barbaric conditions you have imposed."

I gave him a glance. "You wouldn't be trying to get out of our deal because you don't like my terms, now would you, Mr. Clatterbuck? One has nothing to do with the other. When you stuck this deal about me going ahead with this tomfoolery, you didn't say anything about the methods. As far as that is concerned, I could have said that we both hold hands and jump off a cliff and the one that survived was the winner. Now that would have been in the book. What do you say we do this business in a businesslike fashion. If you intend to keep your word, then now is as good a time as any."

He didn't like it one damn bit. I really had him hemmed up. He had no good reason not to go ahead and take my check and give me the bill of sale to complete the deal. Certainly I had, except for the actual doing of it, completed his requirements.

I asked, "Are you expecting me to back out in the morning, Mr. Clatterbuck?"

With a stiff jerk of his head he said, "You have described yourself as not being a gentleman."

"I said I wasn't a gentleman in your sense of the word, Mr. Clatterbuck. I didn't say I didn't keep my word. I have kept my word for thirty-two years and I intend to go on keeping my word. This time is no exception."

"Then are you implying that I won't keep mine?"

"Let's say that ain't either one of us is implying anything. Let's say that we are just trading horses. Let's say that I am giving you the price that you asked for and you're giving me the horses that I want."

He half rose from his chair. He said, "Yes, but there is this damn fool method that you have concocted. This damn fool answer to my son's challenge. I tell you, sir, this is not the gentleman's code."

I said, "The hell with your gentleman's code, Mr. Clatterbuck. Your son is going to kill me or I'm going to kill him. There is nothing gentlemanly about that. Here is your money. Give me a bill of sale. Or would you prefer that we withdraw from your house tonight and go into Lafayette and put it out that your son challenged me and then refused to meet my conditions? Conditions that I, as the challenged party, had the right to make?"

That nearly lit his fuse. Even his balding head got red. He finally sputtered, "Indeed, you are no gentleman, sir, and I will be well rid of you. One way or another."

I said, "I reckon that you have a choice as to which one or the other that it will be. You can rest assured of that, sir. My bill of sale?"

Cursing and swearing, he began jerking open drawers until he found a suitable form. He slammed it on his desk, opened up his registry book, found the pen and ink, and began filling in the necessary papers. It was a work of some minutes, but I was in no hurry. I sat idly by, smoking my cigarette and sipping brandy. I was content that I was making a good horse trade. I was hopeful that I wouldn't have to kill anybody in order to do it. But I did have in the back of my mind that perhaps a lesson would be learned from this. Of course, the words that Cloyce had spoke echoed in my ear, that Royce would find some way to cheat. That would bear some thinking.

Mr. Clatterbuck was finally through with his work. He thrust two bills of sale at me. He said, "There, and be damned to you, sir."

I took the papers, looked over them quickly, put them in my pocket, and stood up. I finished my glass of brandy. I said, "There's your check,

Mr. Clatterbuck. I hope that you sleep well tonight."

He said, "Oh, I think that I shall sleep very well tonight, sir, although I doubt that you will sleep at all."

"You may be surprised at how well I sleep tonight. I bid you good night."

I set my glass down and went out of the room. Behind me, I could hear him fuming and sputtering. I didn't give a damn. I had gotten what I came here for and I was very pleased about it. As I got to the door, I stopped and turned around.

I said, "One more thing, Mr. Clatterbuck. Those horses now belong to the partnership that I am a member of. We would like to leave the horses here and then pick them up on the way back. Would that be satisfactory? We would be delighted to pay the necessary room and board."

He said, "Are you attempting to teach me manners, young man?"

"My heavens, Mr. Clatterbuck. What a thought. But may I leave the horses here?"

He said with vicious glee, "You may well leave yourself here, sir."

I smiled at him, turned on my heel, and left. By the time I had gotten upstairs I stopped in my room long enough to collect my saddlebags. There wasn't anything in them but my revolvers and some ammunition and an extra bottle of whiskey, along with some extra tobacco. I had a valise against the wall, but I didn't bother with that. I closed the door behind me and went on down to Laura's room. I opened it without knocking. She was sitting up in bed with the lamp on, smoking a cigarette. She had a bottle of wine and a glass on the table beside her. She looked up as I came in.

She said, "What are you doing? Come to tell me some more about the manly pursuit of dueling or to blame me for it?"

I came in and went to the other side of the bed and sat down, dropping my saddlebags to the floor. Before I spoke, I took off my boots. I said, "No, believe it or not, I came for some peace."

"What are you doing?"

I said, "I plan on sleeping with you tonight."

"My, my. What will the gentry think?"

"Right now, I don't guess that I give a shit what the gentry thinks." I reached into my pocket and got out the bills of sale and gave them to her. I said, "Put those away with the checkbook and the other important papers. We now own two horses."

She didn't take them for a few moments. She said, "But at what price?"

"Don't be so morbid right now, Laura. Just take the damned papers and put them in the right place. Those are the bills of sale to two damned good stud horses that we stole."

"You call it stealing when you have to put your life on the line?"

"One has nothing to do with the other, Laura. I came in here for some peace. Will you please let me have it?"

She turned her head on the pillow and looked at me. Her features softened. She said, "Of course, Warner. Sometimes I can be such a bitch."

"I thought you called that taking a position." I laughed slightly.

She said, "Yeah, but it's the same thing. Women just tell men that it's different. Men will believe anything." She smiled thinly.

I yawned and then looked at my watch. It was a little after ten although it felt later than that. It had been quite a busy day. I stood up, took off my shirt and shucked off my jeans. All I was wearing was a pair of socks. I took them off and then lay down on the bed beside Laura. She leaned over enough to pour herself a glass of wine and then sat up, sipping at the wine, and lit a cigarette. She said, "What do you want to talk about?"

I said, "I really don't want to talk at all."

She leaned over and kissed me lightly on the lips. She said, "Just what is it that you want?"

I said, "I don't really want what you're thinking, I'm not in that kind of a mood. I'm in

197

more of a calculating mood. With that business tomorrow over my head I don't think I could give it my best effort."

She said, "Well, why don't we sit here quietly and talk for a while. Do you want some of this wine?"

I got up and reached down for my saddlebags. I said, "Like I want some swampwater." I got the bottle of whiskey out of my saddlebags and then let them drop back to the floor. I pulled the cork and had a shot of the good corn whiskey and then said, "Mr. Clatterbuck has informed me that I am no gentleman."

"Hah! I could have told him that."

"What is a gentleman, Laura?"

She said, "One thing that a gentleman is not and that's a man who claims to be one. Mr. Clatterbuck claims to be one, so therefore, he is not. So does his son, Royce."

"What if you don't claim to be a gentleman. Does that make you a gentleman?"

She said, "Not in your case."

I laughed. "I don't think I can take much more of this loving comfort. You're overwhelming me with all this sweetness and light."

"We could have left."

I sighed. "Don't start that again, please, Laura. Please don't start that again. I think that I can handle this matter. I think that I am handling this in the best way that there is to handle it. If

I didn't think that, then I would have handled it some other way."

"Are you sure that there's not some manly pride involved? You sure you're not jealous of Royce Clatterbuck's attention to me? Are you sure that it is just business?"

I said, "If I've got to be jealous of somebody like Royce Clatterbuck, then you're not the woman that I think that you are. I'm not saying that there is not a man out there somewhere that couldn't make me jealous, but it damn sure ain't Royce Clatterbuck."

She laughed and took my hand and held it. The movement made the cover slip down so that her breasts were revealed. I wasn't so sure anymore that I only wanted to talk for a while and then get a good night's sleep. Not with that enticement in front of me.

Laura asked softly, "Are you worried about tomorrow?"

I said, "No, not really. The only thing that bothers me is that Royce is an unknown quantity. I don't know how he will fight. I've never fought a man who duels. I've fought gunfighters but never a man who duels, so I can't be sure exactly what he will do."

"What are you going to do?"

"Well, I'm going to hope that I am better in the woods than he is."

"But they are his woods."

"Yeah, but . . . he's used to this thing out on the field of honor with the surgeons there and the seconds there and his daddy standing by watching, sort of bolstering him up, giving him confidence. This way, it's just going to be me and him. I'm calculating and counting on the fact that he is going to get a little lonely roaming around in those dark woods, never knowing when or if I am going to drop him with a shot."

She got an urgent tone in her voice. She said, "Warner, I don't want you to get silly tomorrow. You have the bill of sale for those horses, and I don't want to take any chances with that man. I know that you don't want to kill him, but just don't take any chances."

"Are you asking me to actually shoot him if I get the chance?"

"You're damn right. He'll shoot you if he gets the chance. You promise me that you won't take any chances. I know how good you are, Warner, how damn good you are. Wilson Young has even said that next to him, you're the best. So don't take any chances if you don't have to. Promise me that you won't. Don't get to feeling all silly and chivalrous because you are not chivalrous. You're a good man. Forget all this other nonsense."

I smiled, amused by her excitement. I said, "My, my, my. And you call yourself a Virginia girl? Tush, tush, tush. What would the members of your family say if they could hear you now?"

She said, "Warner, I'm serious."

I took another drink of whiskey and then leaned down and put the bottle on the floor. I slid down in the bed beside her, putting my arm under the cover and around her waist to draw her to me.

"So am I," I said.

I was full awake by six the next morning. Laura and I had slept very close together through the night. After we made love, I'd gone immediately to sleep, but I had been aware that she had sat up for some time smoking and drinking wine. Now she lay on her side, her hair ruffled, her face composed in sleep. I eased out of bed as gently as I could and proceeded to put on the same clothes that I had worn the night before. Hell, I was fixing to go for a walk in the woods. There wasn't any need to get all dressed up.

As quietly as I could, I slipped out of the room and went downstairs into the breakfast room. I had expected to find myself alone, but to my surprise, Cloyce was sitting there over a cup of coffee. We gave each other a good morning and I sat down. Jasper brought me a cup of coffee and asked what I would like for breakfast. I told him eggs, ham, and grits.

Cloyce raised his eyes. He said, "Still not worried about a belly wound, huh?"

I said, "No. If I'm going to get shot, I'd like to have my strength up. My mamma always used to tell me, 'Son, if you're gonna fight a duel, be sure to eat a good breakfast first.' "

Cloyce laughed. "Your mother must not have known too much about duels."

I didn't bother to tell him that I'd never known my mother. I said instead, "How is the other party? Is he not going to eat breakfast?"

Cloyce shrugged. "I haven't seen him."

"But you're his second."

"My duties only start when we begin the ceremony."

"There's a ceremony?"

"Oh, yes. Didn't you read it in the *Code Duello*?"

"Oh, you mean the part about where both seconds ask the two principals if the matter can't be resolved without bloodshed?" I laughed. "I can tell you my answer to that right now."

Cloyce looked amused. He said, "Unfortunately, Royce's answer would not be the same."

I asked, "Is your daddy going to be there?"

"Oh yes. He wouldn't miss this for the world. He will be in his element."

Jasper came with my breakfast and I asked him for a bottle of brandy.

Cloyce asked, "A little Dutch courage?"

I said, "No, actually, it's my habit to start the day with a morning whiskey. Nothing unusual about it, whether I'm going to shoot somebody or not."

"You seem mighty at ease, Mr. Grayson, for a man going into armed combat."

I said, "It's not the first time, Cloyce, and getting nervous about it ain't gonna help matters much. I've got a friend, Wilson Young. You might have heard of him. He was a pretty famous bank robber about five or six years ago until the governor of Texas pardoned him on account of the law got tired of trying to catch him."

Cloyce furrowed his brow. He said, "The name does ring a bell. Supposed to be quite a hand with a pistol."

"That's the one. Very few men in the world care to go up against Wilson Young."

"Was he your teacher?"

I shook my head. I said, "No one ever taught me a thing about guns. I think using a gun is a lot like making love—it either comes natural to you or you better take up another hobby."

Cloyce gave me a long look. He said, "I think my brother might be in a lot more trouble than he realizes."

I shook my head. "I'm going to try and not kill your brother."

Just then, Jasper returned with a bottle of

brandy and held it poised over my coffee cup. I nodded. He poured until I nodded again and then set the bottle down on the table.

I said, "Don't forget, Jasper, you've also got to act as my second. In addition to your duties as a waiter, you're gonna have to come out and act as a gentleman's gentleman."

He rolled his eyes and walked out of the room, shaking his head.

Cloyce said, "I'm afraid that you're going to have to second yourself. I don't think that my daddy is going to allow one of the house servants out on the field of honor."

He said it with such élan that I was forced to laugh. I said, "For some reason, I didn't think that Jasper would be coming along. Getting back to Wilson Young. Wilson was—still is—the most determined man to avoid a fight that I've ever seen. As he says, when there is no other alternative but to fight, make certain that the other fellow ends up being damn sorry that he came up with the idea in the first place. I've always taken that idea to heart."

Cloyce took a sip of coffee, put his cup down and then looked away. He said, "Perhaps for the first time in my life, I am fearful for my brother and if you knew how I felt about my brother, you would be surprised that I would care."

I said, "I have no interest in knowing the

inner workings of your family. Like I have been saying from the very first, I came here to do some business, some horse business. And what we are doing now is beyond my knowledge. Or how it came about or why it has to continue, but apparently that is the case, so I am going to play the cards that I've been dealt."

Cloyce looked at his watch. He said, "We should leave the house at seven-thirty. Horses have been brought. My brother will come from the other direction, from the cabin. Observers and witnesses will be coming from some of the nearby plantations. They are friends of my brother and of this plantation, but you can rest assured that they will be scrupulously honest."

I laughed. "They going into the woods with us?"

It was Cloyce's turn to laugh. He said, "I know I'm not." Then he thought. He said, "Tell me, in your conditions, you didn't limit the ammunition."

"In a situation like this, if you don't get your man with the first shot, or maybe the second, you're not going to need any more ammunition. The one thing that I would like to know, though, do you have any idea what time the next train headed for Tennessee leaves here in the morning?"

Cloyce smiled slightly. "I must say, Mr. Grayson, I admire your confidence. Yes, I happen to know that there is a train with a direct route

205

to Nashville, Tennessee. Leaves Lafayette at one o'clock. I would say that you would need to leave here no later than noon."

"Either way?"

"Either way."

I made quick work of my breakfast and then got up. It was a few minutes after seven—I didn't want to be late. I said, "You seem dressed rather casually for the occasion, Mr. Clatterbuck." He wasn't wearing a coat or a tie, just a white linen shirt with black trousers.

"Oh, I'll be properly attired when the time comes. How about yourself, sir?"

I said, "Not being a gentleman, I assume that I'm allowed to dress as I am."

"You are a most interesting man, Mr. Grayson. A most interesting man, indeed. I would say that Mrs. Laura Pico is fortunate to have you as her champion."

I gave him a look and said grimly, "If I was you, I wouldn't tell her that. She has taken a mighty dim view of these proceedings."

"As well she should, sir. As well she should."

I opened the door to Laura's bedroom to find her sitting at her dressing table looking at some papers. I recognized them as the bills of sale for the two stud horses. The minute she saw me, she quickly put the papers down and made a clumsy attempt to conceal them.

I said, "What are you doing, Laura?"

"Nothing. Nothing."

"Then why were you looking at those bills of sale?"

"No reason."

She was still in her nightgown. She looked as desirable as I had ever seen her. I walked over and stood behind her. I said, "Let me see those."

"You know what they look like. Why do you want to see them?"

"Let me see them. I didn't look at them carefully last night."

She sighed. "He didn't sign them."

"He didn't what?"

"He didn't sign them."

I looked over her shoulder as she produced the papers. Sure enough, where his signature should have been affixed, there was nothing. I swore softly for a few moments. I said, "Now I know what a southern gentleman is—a damn liar, a cheat, and a thief. Well, we'll see about this."

I stuffed the papers in my shirt.

Laura turned in her chair. She said, "Warner, there is trouble enough. Please, let's just go. Please."

"No, I'm going to see that the man keeps his word. He may not know it right now, but he's going to keep his word. It may cost him a son, but he will keep his word."

"Warner, don't be a damn fool. That old man is not going to let you kill his son. He's not crazy."

"Listen." I stuck my finger out at her. "He thinks I'm some hick, some rawhide saddle tramp from Texas that he can treat any way that he wants to. Well, he's got some news coming to him. They may know about chivalry and honor and all those other doodads, but I'm fixing to find out what all they know about fighting. I mean real, sure enough, down and dirty fighting."

Laura dropped her head and looked down at her hands. "It would come to this. Yes, I guess it would. Oh, Warner. Why did this have to happen?"

"It was none of our doing, Laura." I moved close to her, kissed her cheek, then her neck, and then her bare shoulder. I said, "This is not your fault. I spoke some hurtful words earlier, making it sound as if you had a hand in this. You didn't. It's the temperament of these people. They don't have the class of a pig with a curl in it's tail. There ain't a one of them, except Cloyce, worth wiping your feet on. I'll tend to them. I don't want you to worry."

I gave her another gentle kiss and then walked around the bed to where my saddlebags were. I picked them up, took out my gunbelt and strapped it on. For a moment, I debated between revolvers. In the end, I decided that it would be close, quick work and I chose the six-inch Colt. I checked the cylinder to make sure that it was fully loaded. It was. I shoved it in the holster. As an afterthought, I took a half dozen more cartridges, put them in my shirt pocket and buttoned it. Then I put on my hat. I was ready. I came back around and knelt down in front of Laura. Our heads were just about on the same plane.

I said, "You go ahead and get packed. There is a train that leaves Lafayette for Nashville at one o'clock. As soon as I get back, we'll have a light lunch or maybe not, I don't know. They may not want to feed us after what happens." I tried to make a joke out of it, but she wouldn't smile. "But anyway, you be ready to go and we'll be clattering down the tracks on our way to Tennessee."

She looked sadder than I had ever seen her. I thought she was going to cry. She said, barely audible, "I hope so. God, I hope so."

Before she could say anything else, I gave her a quick kiss and said, "I'll be back before you can even miss me." Then I got up, turned and went out the door.

8

It was about a three-mile ride to the patch of woods. Cloyce had two horses tied outside the back door of the house. We mounted together and he led the way. He had put on a black frock coat and a tie. I joked with him about how official he looked. He said, "Man has to take these duties seriously, sir. You must understand that."

I'd asked him what was going to happen and he said there would be quite a lot of rigmarole, most of which would make me impatient, but that it was all part of the ceremony that had to be gotten through before the real fun could start.

I swear, I thought that sometimes he was older than he looked—a great deal older. He sure as hell seemed older than Royce, who acted like he was about fifteen. We stopped at a rise in the grounds and saw the group waiting for us about a hundred yards back from the copse. They had dismounted and were standing in a bunch. I saw Royce and his daddy. There were three other men there. Except for Royce, who was simply wearing a white shirt and black pants, they were all dressed alike in black frock coats and white shirts, and damned if one of them didn't have on a stovepipe lid. Last time I had seen a hat like that it had been on a snake-oil salesman turned preacher—or was it the other way around?

We skidded our horses up and I dismounted and walked forward. Royce saw me but gave no sign. I made a beeline straight for Mr. Clatterbuck, pulling out the bills of sale as I did. He reached to greet me and I slapped the two papers in his outstretched hands. I said, "You forgot something, Mr. Clatterbuck."

He gave me a cool look. "This is not the time to discuss business, sir."

I said, "We ain't talking about business, sir. We're talking about lying and maybe not living up to our word, sir. You may get the chance to be the third man into those woods, if you're not careful, sir."

"Whatever do you mean, sir?"

"I mean, whenever I come out of those woods, you better have those papers signed, do you understand me?"

"I live up to my word, sir."

"And I'm here to see that you do."

I was aware of the other members of the party staring at us, but Cloyce took my arm and nudged me forward. The man in the stovepipe hat stepped forward. He didn't look to be much

211

older than Cloyce. He tipped his hat and said, "You would be Mr. Grayson, sir?"

"I would be."

"My name is Hawkins, sir. I am the judge. I am here to see that the rules of conduct are observed and that fair play is extended to both principals."

I said, "Good luck."

He said, "It now becomes my duty to ask each of the principals involved if this matter can't be settled without the spilling of blood."

I said, "Hell, yes it can. I don't see no point in spilling any blood."

Royce obviously took my answer for weakness, for he stepped boldly forward and said, "No, I demand satisfaction from this gentleman here and blood is the only answer to it."

Mr. Hawkins looked to me. He said, "Mr. Grayson, what is your answer?"

I said, "If the silly son of a bitch wants to get himself killed, then let's have at it. Cut out all of this foolishness and save the theatrics for the stage."

Mr. Hawkins looked somewhat taken aback by my direct manner of speaking. He said, "The conditions are a bit unusual. But as I understand it, Mr. Grayson, you will enter the woods from that end there, carrying a loaded six-shot revolver. Is that correct?"

"That's right."

"And you, Mr. Clatterbuck, will enter the

woods from the other end, carrying a six-shot revolver. Is that also correct?"

Royce nodded, curtly.

Mr. Hawkins said, "Do either of you care to examine the other's weapon?"

I said, "I don't care if he's got a Gatling gun, let's get after it."

Mr. Hawkins said, "Since it is some distance to each end of the grove, will you gentlemen ride or walk?"

I said, "I'm not much of a hand at walking. I'll ride."

"Then you will be accompanied by your . . . no you do not have a second. Therefore, Mr. Gilroy here," he indicated a young man dressed the same as himself except for his silly looking hat, "will accompany you and bring your horse back."

I said, "Oh, I don't need anybody to accompany me. I'll ride the horse back when I'm through." I glanced over at Royce as I said it and saw him grit his teeth. From somewhere, he had found a revolver. I noticed that it had ivory grips, but it only had a four-and-a-half-inch barrel. I wondered if he knew what he was doing.

I said, "I'm ready. Let's get on with this."

Mr. Hawkins turned to Royce and said, "Are you ready, sir?"

Royce nodded again curtly.

Mr. Hawkins said, "Then, let these proceedings

begin. Gentlemen, you may mount your horses."

I didn't plan to be the last one into the trees. I was on top of the horse they had loaned me and lit out to my end before Royce could get himself turned around. The words that Cloyce had used to warn me about his brother kept echoing over and over in my mind, though I could not for the life of me figure out how Royce could cheat. We would be two hunters in the same patch of woods, each hunting the other. He couldn't get behind me unless he did so fairly and squarely. He could not outflank me unless he did so fairly and squarely. I didn't see anything that he could do. However, I did have a plan that I thought might make certain that there were no shenanigans. I rode to the end of the copse and turned just enough so I was in sight of the group. I dismounted and tied the Thoroughbred that apparently hadn't made it as a racehorse to a small shrub and then started along the southern edge of the woods.

The copse backed up to a field of green wheat that was about four feet tall. I skulked my way through, low enough so that I couldn't be seen, until I had gone about a hundred or hundred and fifty yards. It was only then that I crept forward and entered through the low shrubs and brush that were the beginning of the tract of trees. As soon as I could, I got to a fair-size tree and knelt down behind it, taking time to get my breathing adjusted to where I wasn't making any noise. Then I squatted down and looked and listened. There was no sound except the twittering of the birds, and here and there, the rustle of some small animal.

I decided to work my way along the southern edge before penetrating much farther into the grove. To do so, I more or less scuttled quickly from one big pine tree to another. The grove was primarily pine, with some oak and some sycamore and an occasional willow, which seemed native to Louisiana. And, of course, there was a good deal of underbrush and a good many fallen logs, some of them rotten, having lain there for a hundred years.

I worked not quite a third of the way down and then ventured a hundred yards deeper toward the middle of the grove. I found a good place between two pine trees with a log lying in front of me. I crawled up to it and was about to peek over when it occurred to me that I still had on my hat. I quickly took it off and laid it on the ground.

As I was about to rise up, I would have almost sworn that I could hear the sound of voices— it sounded like men's voices. They seemed to be behind me and somewhat to my right, but I knew that couldn't be so. I assumed that Royce might have the unfortunate habit of talking to himself, but I doubted that he would do it at such a critical time. For a second, I was inclined to believe that I had misheard, then I heard a distinct metallic clink. It didn't sound like a spur or a horse's hoof. It sounded more like two pieces of metal. I raised up cautiously and peered around to my right. For a long time in the dim coolness of the grove I couldn't make out any sign of anything that could have been talking or making a metallic sound. Then, as I was about to shift back to my original position, I saw through the leaves of a small bush what had to be a man's boot heel. Listening intently, I heard a man's whisper. And in reply, another faint whisper. It very quickly became obvious to me that this was what Cloyce had meant about Royce's cheating. He had seeded the field with a couple of wild cards—two jokers that weren't supposed to be in the deck.

It did not make me angry, but it did make me very determined. I studied the situation for a moment. Royce would be coming from my left and he could be moving in my direction at any time. I rather thought, however, he was lying well back, waiting to see what came of me walking into his ambush. But I had thwarted the ambush by circling the grove and coming in closer to its middle. Now I was the one behind the back shooters.

I needed to move to my left about twenty yards, but there was a clearing in front of me, so I had to backtrack carefully until I could get in amongst some brush and trees and then move forward. By then the two voices were to my right and slightly ahead.

I moved forward until I reckoned I was about ten yards from where I had seen the boot heel. There was a fallen log lying across the fork of a tree. It was about four feet off the ground and I eased up behind it, my revolver in my hand. As I stood up, two men came clearly into view. They were squatting behind some brush and one had a rifle and one a pistol. Both had their hats off. I let them hear the *clitch-clatch* sound as I cocked my revolver. The sound startled them. They rose, whirling, bringing their guns up. I shot the man with the pistol, hitting him dead in the chest. He went over backwards.

The man with the rifle fired wildly, the shot whipping through the leaves, tearing up a lot of sky. By the time he had fired, I had already thumbed another round into the chamber and pulled the trigger. The slug took him below the neck and knocked him flat. Before he had hit the ground, I was down and moving toward Royce's end of the grove. He would be very curious as to what had come of his ambush. I wanted to be there to tell him about it. So much for gentlemanly combat.

As quickly and as quietly as I could, I edged away from the center line of the grove. After I had moved about fifty yards in the brush, I settled down in good cover to wait. I didn't expect to have to wait long.

He made no pretense at stealth, he just came hurrying and crashing his way through the brush. As he came near, he called out, "Bowie? Bowie? You and Josh get him? Josh?"

He had the revolver in his hand but he did not have it up. It was hanging by his side. I moved very carefully along a line angling to intersect his. As he got to within ten yards of the bodies, I suddenly stepped out behind him and stuck the revolver to his head.

I said, "Hello, Royce." He froze.

"In case you are wondering, this is a .42/.40 caliber revolver barrel right here at the base of your neck. It fires a .40 caliber soft-nosed bullet that makes a little hole going in and a hole the size of a washtub coming out. It's cocked. Now why don't you just flinch, you bushwhacking, no-good son of a bitch. You want to be insulted, Royce? I'll be glad to insult the hell out of you. Drop that gun."

He was frozen stiff. I didn't think that his fingers would move enough to let go of the revolver. I reached around with my free hand and plucked it out of his lifeless fingers.

I said, "Now, go up and look at your two friends. Names are Bowie and Josh, did you say? You had a mighty warm reception all set up for me, ain't that right, Royce?" I shoved him again. "I said get on up there and take a look at what dead men look like, boy."

He moved, but he didn't want to. He still hadn't turned around to face me. I kept shoving him along until he got up to the two men who were lying on their backs.

I said, "That's what you are fixing to look like, my boy. Do you understand?" He started to tremble. I could see his shoulders shake.

I took him by the shoulder and whirled him around so he could face me. His eyes were wide and frightened, staring. I said, "You are really something, boy. You are a piece of work, boy. You are a piece of shit, is what you are, boy. Well, ain't you got nothing to say, boy?"

He just looked at me and gulped. I said, "Get down on your knees, Royce." He didn't move.

I said it again.

He still didn't move.

I put the revolver between his eyes, the hammer still cocked. I put my finger inside the trigger guard. I said, "Get down on your knees, Royce." Slowly, trembling, he fell to his knees.

Then he spoke the first words. "Oh God, please don't kill me. Please, please, don't kill me."

I said, "Royce, lean forward and lick dirt."

His face looked puzzled. He said, "What?"

"You heard me. Lick dirt."

"Lick the dirt on the ground?"

"That's the only other dirt I see around here. You're shit—that's dirt. Don't you know the difference? Now lick it."

He didn't want to, but he finally bent over and made a motion. I pressed the Colt against the back of his head and forced his head down. I said, "Lick the damn dirt, Royce."

He raised up spitting and wiping at his mouth.

I said, "Now tell me what you are, Royce."

He said, his voice trembling, "Are you going to kill me?"

I said, "Tell me what you are, Royce."

"Are you going to kill me?"

"Not if you tell me what you are, Royce."

He said, "What . . . what do you want me to say I am?"

"What you are. You are a coward, Royce. Say you are a coward."

He swallowed. It was extremely hard for him. He said, "I'm . . . I'm . . . I'm . . ."

I prompted him. I said, "Coward is the word, Royce. Coward."

"I'm a coward." All of a sudden he started crying. Tears began to roll down his cheeks. His chest heaved. In a blubbering voice, he said, "Oh my God! What will my daddy and my friends think of me? Now I'm ruined forever. My God, now I almost wish you would kill me. I'm dishonored is what I am. Dishonored."

I said, "No, you're not dishonored, Royce,

because you never had any honor to begin with. I knew that you were going to cheat."

I jerked my head toward where the two bodies lay and said, "You got two men killed. That enough for you?" Without waiting for an answer, I suddenly slung his ivory-handled revolver off into the brush. I said, "You've got two good men killed. Must have been good men. You wouldn't have sent *bad* men, would you, Royce? Or did you think so little of me that you sent a couple of bums out here to bushwhack me?"

He didn't answer. I backhanded him across the face. A little blood ran out of the corner of his mouth. He knelt there, trembling and white-faced.

I said, "You would send good men after me, wouldn't you, Royce? You do think enough of me to send competent bushwhackers, don't you?"

His mouth opened, but he knew that there wasn't anything he could say that would answer my question because it wasn't a question, it was another insult. To help him along, I backhanded him again. His head jerked sideways. I said, "Royce, you may be the sorriest son of a bitch I have ever met in my life, and I have met some low-down scum, but you do take the cake. Lie down on your belly. Like a snake."

His voice trembled. He said, "What?"

I said, "God damn it, Royce. I am getting tired of telling you things two or three times. I am going to tell you once more and then I am going to knock you down. Lie down with your face on the ground."

He reluctantly got down on all fours, but before he lay all the way down, he looked up at me and said, "What are you going to do?"

"What the hell do you care?" I said. "Just lie down, shut your eyes, and press your face in the dirt. If you make a move, I'll gut-shoot you."

He was whimpering and then it seemed like he got an idea. He said, "Mr. Grayson, sir. I swear I didn't know anything about those two men. I swear I didn't. I did not put them there."

I sighed. "Royce, I'm ashamed of you, for God's sake. You're a low-down son of a bitch, you're a chicken-shit, no-good louse. Don't add lying to your list of poor qualities. I now know what a gentleman is. I'm looking at one. I'm ashamed of the sight."

He said, "But what is going to become of me?"

I said, "I will tell you this. If you get up, I'm gonna shoot your ears off. Now, I'm going to leave, and if I was you, I'd lie real still for about half an hour."

He raised his head so abruptly that I almost shot him. I said, "Hold on there, boy."

He said, "For God's sake, you can't do this. You can't leave me. My honor is at stake here."

I said, "You hide and watch me, boy. I'm gonna walk on out of here and I'm not gonna touch those guns that are over there by those two men. If I was you, I'd hide them in the bushes. I'd hide their bodies too, except I think that somebody will find them sooner or later."

His voice trembled. "What are you going to tell my daddy?"

"I'm not gonna tell him a damn thing. I think that the facts will speak for themselves."

"What if . . . what if . . . what if I tell him that those men were yours and that you got me trapped this way?"

I shrugged. I said, "That doesn't even make sense to you, does it?"

He said almost in a wail, "But I can't bear this dishonor! For God's sake, do me that boon and just wound me!"

I was already starting away from him. I said, "No, Royce. You'll have to talk yourself out of this one. I wish you luck, and all of it bad."

I left him yelling for me to wound him, do something to him. I called back to him. "Hell, Royce. You've got a cut lip, won't that do? How much blood has to be spilt?" I laughed.

Once I was free of the grove of trees, I walked swiftly to where I had left the horse, untied him, and then mounted. I had him in a run within two jumps, racing around the corner of the woods and heading straight toward where the party was waiting.

As I rode toward them, I saw Mr. Clatterbuck recognize me. I saw him raise his hands into the air, his fists clenched, either in despair or rage. I chuckled to myself. I rode the horse straight into their midst, then pulled him to a shuddering stop and stepped down.

The first words out of Mr. Clatterbuck's mouth were, "Where is my son? Where is Royce? Is he killed? Have you killed him, sir?"

I said, "Have you signed my bills of sale, Mr. Clatterbuck? In front of witnesses, you said you would."

He said, "What about my son? What about Royce? Where is my son?"

I said, "Sign those damn bills of sale, Mr. Clatterbuck, or I'll take you in there to find your son and you may not come back."

I turned to the others. I said, "Gentlemen, I call upon you to witness the fact that Mr. Clatterbuck is going back on his word."

He suddenly swore a mighty oath and jerked the two pieces of paper from his vest pocket. He hunted through his clothing until he found a stub of a pencil. Then, bending over to use his thigh as a writing surface, he scribbled his name to the bottom of each bill of sale. With an angry gesture, he handed them to me and said, "Now what about my son, sir?"

I could see the anxious looks on the faces of the others. I casually mounted the horse that I had been loaned and said, "There are two dead men in that grove of woods. Why don't you go in there and see if he is one of them." Then I turned the horse and started loping toward the house. Mr. Clatterbuck's cries echoed after me, but I never looked back.

Halfway to the house, I heard a horse coming up fast behind me. I looked back. It was Cloyce. I slowed to let him catch up. When he was alongside of me, I dropped my horse into a walk, as he did his.

Cloyce said, "What happened?"

I said, "He sent two bushwhackers in after me at my end, except I didn't come in my end, I came in behind them. I took your words to heart."

"What about Royce?"

"I'd say that he is suffering a little right now. The only mark he has on him is from where I slapped him across the face."

Cloyce laughed. "You mean, you didn't even wound him? You did nothing but slap him?"

"That's correct."

"What about the two men?"

"They're dead. They pointed guns at me. They were planning on shooting me."

"We heard three shots."

"One of them came from one of the men. The other two were mine."

Cloyce gave me a long slow look. He said, "Just that? Just one shot apiece?"

"I tried to tell you that this wasn't my first county fair."

Cloyce nodded. "Well, I guess Royce right now is wishing you had killed him. I don't know how he's going to handle this. I suppose that he will have to go away. That's funny as hell." He laughed and then asked, "Did he beg?"

I nodded. "First he begged for his life and then, when he figured out what had happened and what was going to happen, he began begging me to wound him."

Cloyce laughed again. He said, "That poor son of a bitch. He never did have a lick of sense."

I asked, "How come you're not like him and not like your daddy? As young as you are, how did you keep from being formed that way?"

He shrugged. "I don't know. I guess that I never cared for the same things that they cared for. My mother was a good influence on me. She made a reader out of me—I like books. I found that it was better than traveling. I learned a great deal more. I'm not even sure that Royce can read."

"I had a grandfather like that. I guess that was one of the biggest helps in my life. What do you think will become of Royce?"

Cloyce shook his head. "I really don't know, but if ever the word disgrace fit a situation, it's gonna fit this one. I'm not sure that they are even going to be able to get him out of that patch of woods. No sir. You rubbed his nose in it."

I grinned. "If you ever really want to get at him, ask him what it tastes like to lick dirt."

Cloyce jerked his head around and looked at me, his mouth open. He said, "You didn't make him lick dirt?"

"The hell I didn't."

Cloyce laughed in delight. "Oh, yes sir! Yes sir! I shall bring that one up on the appropriate occasion. Yes sir, you may depend upon it."

I said, "One thing, Cloyce, that I want to make certain of. We're going to be leaving on the next train. Your father has agreed to keep the dun and the roan out of that string of horses he showed me. I have bought them. We'll be back in about two weeks and I'd appreciate it if you would separate them from the rest of the stock and see to their care. Your father may not be feeling quite so charitable toward me now."

Cloyce nodded and said, "You need have no worries about that, Mr. Grayson. I'll take care of your horses." He stopped and smiled. "On top of everything else, you rooked the old man too? What did you pay for those two studs? Twelve? Fourteen thousand?"

I soundlessly formed the word eight with my mouth. He said, "Get out of here. You didn't buy those two horses for any eight thousand dollars."

I handed him the two bills of sale. He said, "Well, Mrs. Pico whipped us at poker, you disgraced my brother for life and beat the old man at horse trading. Mr. Grayson, I'm not sure that I want any further business with you."

I reached over and patted him on the shoulder. I said, "Cloyce, I think you and I are going to be getting along all right. I think you and I are a couple of the same kind of southern gentlemen."

He said, "I damn sure hope so, because I sure can't stand to be one of them other kind."

Laura was standing in the middle of her room when I came walking through the door. For a second she just stood there as if she didn't know what to do or say. Then she suddenly rushed at me full tilt. I caught her in my arms and kissed her. For almost a full minute, we clung together. Then she stepped back and looked at me. She said, "Are you all right? Have you got all your parts?"

I said, "All of the ones that you care about."

"You're not hurt?"

"No."

She put her hands on her hips. "You don't care at all how you worry me. What a damn fool thing to go and do."

"I'm back, Laura. I'm all right."

"Yes, but there was no guarantee. You're not bulletproof, you know. I swear, Warner Grayson, sometimes you exasperate me more than any man I've ever known. I don't know why you get yourself into the messes you get yourself into, but I can tell you this, I am getting damned tired of it. I have been up here fretting for two damn hours and it has not been pleasant."

I said as I sat on the side of the bed and reached down for the bottle of whiskey, "Well, I feel mighty guilty about that, Widow Pico. The truth is, I've been out having the time of my life."

She sat down on the bed beside me, put one of her hands on my thigh and her head on my shoulder. She said, "Warner, you scare me to death sometimes. How did it go? Did you kill the bastard?"

Between drinks and cigarettes, I told her the whole story. When I was finished, she was in a smoldering rage. She said, "That low-life, scheming son of a bitch and his daddy, too. My God, have these people no idea of honor? No idea of justice? No idea of fair play?"

I said, "I ain't worried about all that. All I'm glad of is that they didn't have no idea about how to fight."

She laughed at that and then she said, "Do you have any idea who the two men you killed are? Could there be any trouble about that?"

"Cloyce told me that they were a couple of ruffians from town that Royce used from time to time in some of his dirty work. Big brother wasn't quite as clean as his clothes would indicate. He got up to female trouble every once in a while. Sometimes he had to have a husband beat up and such as that. I would reckon that the Clatterbucks are going to do their dead-

229

level best to make believe that this day never happened."

She said, "God, I'll be glad to get out of here."

I said, "Let's get loaded up and leave. I'll go downstairs and see to transportation into town. Are you all packed?"

She said, "Oh yes. I am ready to leave this damn place."

9

By one o'clock, as I had promised Laura that morning, we were on a train, chugging our way out of Lafayette, Louisiana. There weren't too many people on board. We had passed up lunch at The Gables plantation. Neither one of us had felt like staying any longer than we had to. None of the dueling party had returned to the house. I didn't know where they'd gone and didn't much care. Only Cloyce and, of course, Jasper had been there to see us off. One of the grooms had driven us to the station. Cloyce had reiterated that he would take care of the horses until our return. He stood in the circular driveway waving as we left in the carriage.

Laura said, "That Cloyce seems like such a nice young man."

I said, "If it hadn't been for him, I might well have walked into that ambush blind. I might have believed that bullshit about honor and chivalry and the code duello. If I had, I'd have been cold meat by now."

She shook her head. "Somehow I don't believe that. I don't believe that you would not have availed yourself of every opportunity to have

231

the odds on your side, the way you do everything else."

I said, "Still, it was handy having some fore-knowledge. Funny thing, though. I completely misread Cloyce. He first struck me as a sulky, sour-faced kid. And he turned out to be the most grownup one of the bunch."

"That's funny. That is exactly what I thought of him at first. When I was playing poker with them, he seemed to hate to lose, even though we were playing for very small stakes."

I said, "People will fool you, won't they?"

"Not you."

"By not doing exactly what you say, Widow Pico?"

She gave me one of her looks. She said, "You're gonna keep on with that Pico business, aren't you? You're gonna keep rubbing salt into that wound, aren't you?"

"I swear, right now, a mighty oath that I will never mention it again the rest of this trip."

"That's what you say."

"That's what I'm gonna do."

We rode in silence for a while, both of us thinking about the last few days. It had certainly been an interesting start to the trip. I had never expected that my first horse purchase would involve a gunfight. I hoped that matters would improve as we moved north.

Laura said, "Warner, do you think that it was

all right leaving those horses there? I mean, you have paid the man for them. Might he do something to them? Lose them or hurt them in some way?"

I shook my head. "No. He wouldn't do that. In the first place, it would be illegal and I would have the law on him and take him to court. Secondly, Cloyce is going to look after the horses, and thirdly, that old man is so embarrassed right now, he doesn't know what to do. Those horses are going to be the last thing on his mind. Besides, we don't want to cart the horses all the way up to Virginia and then back."

"Well, if you think they will be all right." There was an uncertainty in her voice that I didn't much like.

I said, "Laura, how many times do we have to agree that I tend to the horse end of this business and you tend to the female end of it. You do the female end real good. You don't do the horse end worth a damn."

She slapped me on the thigh with a stinging smack. "Oh you."

I said, "Woman, one of these days, you're gonna hit me once too often."

"I've heard that before."

We enjoyed being away from The Gables plantation and the various members of the Clatterbuck family. It had been an unpleasant and dangerous, though profitable, expedition. It gave me a good feeling to know that I still had twelve thousand dollars left in the kitty for the balance of my horse buying trip. Chances were that I might still be able to get a couple of pretty good studs for that money. Or I might blow the wad on one really outstanding animal. The point was that I knew for certain that I had a basis for a good bloodline with the two stallions out of Cajun Rose. Well, really out of Slewfoot Bob via Cajun Rose.

The train rolled and swayed, clicking along. Outside, the country was rolling green. We were headed northeast, traveling at a pretty good clip. We weren't due in Nashville until late that night. I hadn't yet told Laura that we had a connecting train we had to take to head north some sixty miles outside of Nashville to the small town of Dixon, outside of which the breeding plantation owned by a man named Sutherland was located. That meant one more transfer of all her gear— valises, trunks, hat boxes, and God only knew what all. Overhead, my saddlebags were rattling along in the rack. Laura hadn't mentioned anything about the guns going off. I had a bottle of whiskey in one side and a bottle of Mr. Clatterbuck's brandy in the other. His brandy was about the only thing that I liked about the old man, that is besides the two horses. Well, and his son, Cloyce. For a moment, I wondered what Royce was doing and how fast his mouth was working as he tried to talk himself out of the mess he was in, but then, I didn't really care.

Laura turned to me after a time. She took one of my hands in hers. She said, "Did you really mean what you said?"

I tried to think what I might have said that I might not have wanted to mean. Finally, I was forced to say, "What? What do you have in mind?"

"You very gently told me, when it was obvious that you were going to have to fight the duel, that I was not to blame myself. That I had not caused it. You were very tender about it. You said that you had spoken in heat and anger when you accused me of flaunting myself. Did you really mean that?"

"Oh, hell. Laura, often times a man will say foolish things. Of course it was your fault that I got in the damn duel. You know that and I know that. I was only trying to make you feel a little bit better in case I got killed."

Her face flushed and her eyes widened. For a minute I thought she was going to bite me. Instead, she said, "Warner Grayson, someday justice will be visited upon you, and I certainly hope that I'm there to see it."

"As near as I could figure out, justice got visited upon me for all my sins, all my wrongs, and all of my evil deeds the day that I met you, and I have been suffering on the rack ever since. If ever a man was given his comeuppance on this earth, it has been me in the person of you."

She tried to look grim but she couldn't keep a smile from twinkling at the corners of her mouth. She said, "Oh, you talk so tough. You would really like everybody to believe that you are such a very mean, tough brute, wouldn't you?"

"I am a mean, tough brute. Where did you ever get an idea to the contrary? If you don't think so, I'll show you." For emphasis, I bent down, put my head in her bosom and ran my right hand up under her arm and started tickling her. It was the most sensitive place on her. She was fighting, wiggling, and suppressing squeals and screams. Laura was surprisingly strong, and it was all I could do to hold her down. She finally got me by the hair and got my head back up, jerking my hand loose from under her arm.

She was panting when she said, "Oh, you are mean! You are a devil, Warner Grayson, and I am going to pay you back for this."

I said, "Not before I do it again. That's just half the payment for the old knee trick you played on me. In fact, one of these days I think that I'm going to tickle you to death, and I think that it can be done. You can't breathe when you're being tickled."

She said, "Don't you ever do that again."

Of course, I very promptly did it again at the very instant that she said it.

• • •

We got into Nashville about ten o'clock that night. Fortunately, they had one of the new dining cars on the train and we had a good meal. By the time we got to Nashville, we were both plenty tired of rocking back and forth on the train. All either one of us wanted to do was to get in a bed and get some sleep. Laura insisted that she had to take a bath, but I didn't much care.

With some difficulty, I found a big buggy for hire that would carry us to the best hotel in Nashville. We got there about ten-thirty, and, after getting us a room, got Laura's gear unloaded. She went up to take a bath while I went into the bar of the hotel for a few drinks. Our train the next morning, the Kentucky and North, left at ten A.M. Mr. Sutherland would either meet us or have someone to meet us at the depot in Dixon as the Clatterbucks had. I hoped that the results would not be the same.

It was a big, fine, handsome, old hotel with a lobby full of sturdy quality furniture. They even had Negro men in uniforms to carry your bags, fetch things for you, and to run errands. They called them bellhops. That's because when the clerk at the desk rang a bell, one of them would jump right up and come forward. I had seen the same thing in big hotels in Houston and Dallas, but they didn't seem to have the hang of this bell-hopping business like these southern hotels did.

I walked on into the bar. It was well lighted with lamps and moderately crowded for that time of night. I felt considerably out of place— not that I hadn't been in my fair share of bars, but this was the first one that I had been in where everybody but me was dressed in a white linen suit or a black broadcloth suit. And everyone had on white shirts and ties and those damn plantation hats. I couldn't see the point of the hats. They didn't have the flare like a Western hat, where the brim curves, and they were made out of Panama straw. I'd found out, while we were at the Clatterbucks, that they wouldn't hold water, which meant you couldn't give your horse a drink out of the crown, and they were too stiff to use to take hold of the handle of a coffee pot on a bed of coals. I didn't see the point to them other than to keep the sun off the back of your neck. They didn't look comfortable to me. A hat sometimes got to be an old friend. The one that I was wearing was a Ten-X Beaver, light tan, that I had paid $29.95 for from the M. L. Leddy Company of San Angelo some three or four years back. It was just now getting broken in real good and I considered it as fine a hat as a man could buy. But in that place, I was the only man wearing one like it.

I stepped up to the bar and ordered corn whiskey and settled down to look the place over. To tell you the truth, I was still feeling a little off balance. It was hard to believe that barely more than twelve hours previously, I had been engaged in mortal combat with three men. I didn't feel bad about shooting the two, because they had obviously been intent on shooting me. But I did feel that I had been forced to shoot them. Cloyce had assured me that the kind that they were would have come to a bad end anyway.

We hadn't been out but a few days and already I was anxious to get the trip over with and get back home. I knew that the best part for Laura was coming up, when we finally got to Virginia. Just thinking about her in her home setting made me smile. Sometimes all that toughness and all that hardheadedness melted away and she could be such a little girl. She had been that way for a few minutes when I first talked about this trip and mentioned Virginia. Her parents were dead but she still had kinfolk there. We were to stay with her Aunt Euless. I had never heard of anybody named Euless before and I had joshed her about it, which she took in good humor. She also had an Aunt Rowena and Uncle James that lived nearby. I wasn't exactly sure without consulting a map where all these places were, but the town that we were headed for that was near the horse breeding operation was called Shelbyville. I remembered it as being some eighty or a hundred miles from Richmond. Her kinfolk lived in and around that area, so we were going to be able to kill two birds with one stone.

I wasn't as optimistic about the Virginia stock as Laura was. I think her memory of the horses that she had seen when she was a little girl had gotten better and better down through the years. What I had read in the various breeders' magazines I subscribed to was that the Virginia Thoroughbreds were not among the top in the big racing meets that they had throughout the bluegrass country. I was hopeful, for her sake, that I would be able to buy a stud from Virginia. I don't think anything that I had done or could do would please her more.

I finished my drink and then had another, turning to watch the plantation owners as they drank and played cards. They were a prosperous looking bunch. They, whoever "they" were, said that cotton was king. I guessed that it was. At least, everybody had to wear clothes. Of course, these gentlemen also raised sugarcane and beef stock. I kind of got the impression that the business of horse racing was more a hobby for them than a business. I hoped that was the case and would continue to be the case. I knew that Clatterbuck had not been all that hard to deal with—I didn't think that he knew much about his horses. I hoped that I would continue to run into rich amateurs the rest of the trip.

There was a four-handed poker game going

on near where I was standing. I had noticed the players eyeing me from time to time. When I was finished with my second drink, one of them got up and approached me.

He was a man in his middle age dressed in a white linen suit. He said, "Sir, we are playing a four-handed poker game, which, if you are a poker player, you understand is not the ideal game. We wonder if you would care to sit in for a few hands."

It is damn seldom that I would turn down a chance to play poker, especially against some gentlemen who appeared to have enough money on the table to pay for our trip. But I was tired and the only thing that I wanted to do that night was to lie in bed and hold Laura close, think peaceful thoughts, and know that there was no trouble on the horizon for the morrow. So I thanked the gentleman politely and explained that I was just passing through and that I would be having one more drink and be on my way to bed.

But he didn't want no for an answer. He asked me if I would play just a few hands and by then perhaps someone else would come in. I grudgingly agreed. I sat down. We didn't bother with introductions—you didn't do that in saloon poker. We were playing stud poker—one card down and four up. On the first hand, I caught a pair of kings. That's a pretty good hand going in in stud poker. Before the hand was over, I was beat by a pair of aces after I had built a pretty good pot. That hand cost me about sixty-five dollars.

Because of Laura's wishes, I had taken my gunbelt off after the business with Royce. It was now up in our room. I thought that it was mere coincidence that I should start off with a pair of kings back to back and then get beat at the very end. The next hand I caught an eight in the hole and an eight showing and then, on the fourth card, I caught the third eight. The only hand that I could see that could beat me was a pair of jacks. Nevertheless, I was wary of these strangers. None of them appeared to be wearing a gun, but there are all kinds of places in those suits for a man to hide a derringer. And a derringer at close range would do just as much damage as is necessary. I bet the three eights on the last card, betting fifty dollars. The man had three jacks. I had lost a hundred and eighty dollars in a very short time.

Now there is something that I can do that I am not particularly proud of. It was taught to me by Wilson Young and it was taught to me with the full understanding that I would use it in just such circumstances.

I felt like the circumstances now deserved it. What I had here was some more of these southern gentlemen who seemed to think that cheating was part of chivalry and honor. Well, I thought that maybe tit for tat was a part of it also. On the third hand, I kind of laid low. On the fourth hand, it came my turn to deal. Now, I don't tell people how I do it and I don't talk about it, but through some long practice, I can make those cards walk and talk—some of them even sing. You may think that you have cut the deck so that it can't be stacked, but unfortunately, you will only find out later that you made a false cut.

On this hand, I gave one of the gentlemen three eights just for meanness and the other one three jacks just for meanness and arranged to give myself a spade flush. The whole proposition was based on the fact that I would drive out the other two that I didn't give anything so that the cards would fall right for me to catch that fifth spade.

The betting got pretty hot and heavy when the third eight hit and even more so when the third jack hit. What surprised me was that only one of the other four had dropped out. The way that I had the cards stacked, the other one needed to drop out also. He didn't have a damn thing as far as I could tell, and yet he was calling twenty-dollar bets. It was now time to deal the fifth card and I was depending on luck. I didn't much care for that and I didn't know what the damned fool had stayed for anyway. Then of course, I realized that he had stayed just in case I had scalded the deck to mess me up. What he didn't know was that there was a spade that I could deal seconds on. In other words, I could slip the top card back with my thumb and deal the card below it and you could never tell which card I was dealing. The only way that you could catch it was as the card underneath the top card came off, it made a little snicking sound. But I was pretty slick with it.

Sure enough, I dealt the next round and gave myself that fifth spade that I would have ordinarily gotten if the man had dropped. The table consisted of a hand with three eights, a hand with three jacks, and I had a spade flush. Of course, the man with three jacks had only two of them up and the man with three eights only had two of them up. The jacks bet first and he bet twenty dollars. It was my bet and I raised that fifty. The man holding the pair of eights showing looked at me and grinned.

He said, "All black, huh? Ya sure that one in the hole ain't a club though?"

I said, "There's only one good way to find out."

He slowly folded his hand. He said, "I don't think I need to know that bad."

The man with three jacks was watching me closely. In my mind, I thought that he was trying to decide if I was a sharper, but one cardsharp could seldom recognize another. I, however, didn't look the part. I looked like some dumb old cowboy who came in and donated the game almost two hundred dollars. He didn't think that I had the spade flush. He figured that what I had was a skin full of whiskey and a lot of money. He called my fifty and raised me a hundred back. I called his hundred and raised him two hundred dollars.

That gave him reason for pause. For a long time, he looked at his cards and then looked over at mine. He had nearly three hundred dollars in the pot already. Did he want to send another two hundred dollars after it or not? He couldn't make up his mind. I was gonna win the hand, but I wouldn't mind taking him for two hundred dollars more.

Now you might say that I only had the moral right to cheat to get even, but I defend that I had the moral right to teach them a lesson in cheating.

Just to help his decision along, I made as if to take a tiny peek at my hole card. Then I pulled it up a little farther as if I had to see all of it, then blinked. That was all I did, I just blinked. The card fell back face down.

It was all the man needed. He called my two hundred dollars and raised me two hundred more. I just called him.

They were a mighty sad, sick looking lot when I showed that fifth spade.

The man with the three jacks said, "My God, sir. You were looking down my throat. You knew that the best I could have was a pair of jacks. Why did you keep raising me?"

I said pleasantly, as I drew the money in, "Well, I guess I was under the impression that the idea in poker was to win as much as you could."

They protested loudly when I got up taking all the money with me. I bid them good evening and gave the bartender a twenty-dollar bill and told him to keep them satisfied with drinks. I then went upstairs.

Laura was just finished with her bath. She was wearing a robe and had a towel around her head—she had washed her hair. She said, "Where in the world have you been?"

I had a hand full of money, about six hundred dollars. I dropped it on the bed and said, "Oh, just learning some of your famous southern customs."

She said, "Have you been playing poker?"

I smiled at her. I said, "No, I wasn't playing. I was cheating."

"You cheat at poker? That's . . . dishonorable."

"Not when you get cheated first." I went up to her and put my arms around her. She was kind of damp. I said, "Ma'am, you smell mighty good. That's about six or seven hundred dollars lying there on the bed. What will that buy me?"

She bit me lightly on the neck. "That might buy you a kind word, but nothing more than that."

I said, "You're pretty expensive. What would it cost to get into your britches?"

She laughed and slapped me on the shoulder. She said, "Warner, don't be crude."

I felt under her robe. I said, "You're not wearing any britches so I can't get into them."

"You certainly are presumptuous, sir. Do you always walk into a lady's bedroom and begin fondling her?"

"Only when I have the money to tempt her. I know the way to your heart, you little vixen."

She tilted her head up to be kissed and I obliged her. At that second, there came a loud knock on the door and we pulled apart. I turned to stare and the knock came again. I didn't know anybody in Nashville and I certainly didn't have any friends there. I looked at Laura and she shrugged.

She said, "Might be the room clerk."

"I doubt it."

With a few quick strides, I reached my saddlebags, opened one of the flaps, and took out the six-inch-barrel Colt and stuck it in the waistband of my pants. Then I motioned her to get back out of the way. The knock came again, just as I reached the door.

Two of the gentlemen that I had been playing poker with were standing there in their white linen suits and silly panama hats. This time I noticed that the one that had held the three jacks had one of those little mustaches like Royce had. It was curious that I hadn't noticed that before. This time, I also noticed that in his white linen vest, he was carrying a derringer in the pocket usually reserved for a watch. I could barely see the handle protruding.

I said, "It's a little late to be calling, isn't it, gentlemen?"

They couldn't see Laura the way that I was holding the door.

The one with the mustache said, "Well, sir. We think that you deserted the game at an inopportune time."

I said, "Oh, I found it to be a very opportune time for me. I was ahead."

"Well, that's the concept of the matter right there, sir. You see, we think that it would be only fair that we get a chance to get our money back."

"Well, we seem to have a difference of opinion about that."

The man with the mustache let his hand wander up toward his waistband. He was getting dangerously close to the butt of his derringer.

I said, "Well, gentlemen. I certainly don't want no trouble. But the fact is, my wife won't let me play any more poker."

They looked incredulous. The man standing behind the one with the mustache, he was a little heavier and a little younger, I would have put him in his mid-twenties, said, "Am I to understand, sir, that you don't do your own deciding as to when to play at games?" He had a sneer in his voice.

I said, "I'll tell you what." I suddenly swung the door open so that Laura was exposed standing at the side of the room. I waved with my hand. I said, "The money is over there on the bed. Now, you have just challenged my ability to handle the little woman. Well, I am going to give you a chance to try your hand, sir. That money is right there on the bed. If you can get by her, you just go right ahead and take it."

They didn't know whether to take me seriously or not. For a minute, they looked at me and then at Laura and then at each other. Laura was trying to keep from smiling. She was trying for a stern expression.

I said, "Gentlemen, go ahead. Help yourself. She is not armed. I note that you have a derringer there, sir."

The one with the mustache said, "Are you saying that we are to enter this room and take this money off that bed if we can get by your wife, sir?"

I stepped back, clearing the way for them, and said, "Yeah, if you can get by my wife."

They hesitantly entered the room, both making sort of a halfhearted attempt to tip their hats to Laura. They moved kind of crab-like, facing her more than me. As they got near the bed I pulled the revolver out from behind my back and the next sound that they heard was the *clitch-clatch* as I pulled the hammer back.

They stopped. They froze. They very slowly turned.

I said, "Gentlemen . . . meet my wife."

The one with the mustache said, "What . . . what are you talking about? You are holding a gun on us."

"That's who I'm married to—this here revolver. Reckon you can get by her? That one over there, the one standing by the wall? That's someone I picked up off the street, but this one here in my hand, this is Mary Lou. She is my true love. Ya'll still want the money?"

They began ever so carefully walking sideways toward the door, this time facing me with their backs to Laura. I let them get out of the room and listened to them hurry down the hall. I slammed the door shut and turned the key. I said, "Laura, I sure hope these southern gentlemen that you have been telling me about pick up in caliber the farther north we go. So far, they ain't showed me much."

She was staring blankly at me. She said, "Who the hell were they?"

"Couple of cardsharpers that ran into a better cardsharper."

She asked, "Where the hell did you learn to cheat at cards?"

I said, "You always thought Wilson taught me how to shoot a gun. He didn't. He taught me how to cheat at cards."

For an answer, she went to the bed and scooped up the money and put it in the pocket of her robe.

I said, "You're stealing my money? What are you going to give me for that?"

She gestured at the revolver in my hand. She said, "There's your true love. See what Mary Lou will give you."

I went over and grabbed her in my arms. I said, "Well, if anything, she's a damn sight warmer than you, but then, what wouldn't be?"

The trip to the Sutherland Breeding Farm outside of Dixon turned out to be a bust. Mr. Sutherland and his wife were nice folks but he didn't have the kind of horses that I was looking for. Apparently he had fallen on hard times in the last year or two and had sold off most of his top quality breeding studs and mares. The journals and magazines that I subscribed to from the racing fraternity had indicated at one time he had a bloodline that anyone would have been proud of. Now he was down to fringe horses. He offered me several for anywhere from two thousand to three thousand dollars. They were good horses, but they were not the kind of horses I needed to form a solid basis for my breeding line. They would have been fine for a man who was looking to expand his operation in quantity, not quality. It was with regret that I had to decline Mr. Sutherland's business.

We spent a hospitable two nights with them and then they took us to the train depot in Dixon, where we embarked on the balance of our journey.

Ahead lay Kentucky, specifically Louisville and two breeding farms with its environs. That was the real home of the bluegrass Thoroughbred horse. It was the home of the most famous race track in America, Churchill Downs. I was excited. Laura was excited too, but I think that she was more excited that we were one step closer to Virginia.

I think that was the real purpose of her making this trip. I hoped that her going home again after all these years wouldn't prove to be a disappointment to her.

As we rattled along on the train, watching the lush Tennessee countryside turn into the equally lush Kentucky country, I kidded her a little more about the southern gentlemen. I said, "Thus far, one has tried to kill me and one has tried to cheat me at cards. Are you sure you didn't just make up all this southern bullshit?"

She said, "I sometimes think, Warner, that you bring out the worst in people."

That certainly made me laugh. "Well, if you're an example, then I guess that I will have to agree with that."

She gave me a dirty look. She knew that she was on unsound ground.

We got into Louisville, Kentucky, at about eight in the evening and put ourselves up at a fine hotel called the Southern Select. We took a suite of rooms with plans to visit the first of the breeding farms the next day. I had made no arrangements with the owner of the breeding farm, a man named Tom Claibourne, as to exactly when we would arrive. I had written him that we would get word to him as best we could and that we would hire a carriage and drive ourselves. I understood it was about a twenty-mile trip. He had written back and offered us accommodations for as long as we cared to stay while looking at his stock.

That night, Laura was all in a tizzy about what clothes to take, asking me how long did I expect that we would be there. She advised me that we had not seen the true southerners, outside Virginia, naturally, until we had enjoyed the hospitality of a Kentucky plantation.

My doubts were of such magnitude on that subject that I did not even bother to reply.

She had insisted that I take the white linen suit that she forced me to buy, and wear it at dinner. I was agreeable to that only because I was thankful that the damn woman hadn't forced me to buy one of those damn plantation hats.

Mr. Claibourne's farm was duly famous. He had produced one Kentucky Derby winner in 1880. That was no small accomplishment. Men would gladly spend several lifetimes, theirs, their sons', and their grandsons', trying to produce one Kentucky Derby winner. He had not only won it, but he had horses that were runners-up on several occasions. In addition, many of his horses had won derbies in other states. I feared mightily that I was going to be seeing bloodstock that was well out of the range of my pocketbook.

True to form, Laura was fearful that I would spend all the money allotted for the studs and not have enough left to buy a Virginia horse.

She said, "Now Warner, I want you to promise me that you will not commit all of our funds until you have at least looked at the horses in Virginia."

It was no good, me trying to argue with her on the subject. No good trying to explain to her that if I could strike a bargain on the right kind of horse, I had to make the deal while I could. It was damned hard trying to buy this kind of breeding stock, because it was just now coming into full fashion in states like Oklahoma and Texas as well as states that were as far away as Indiana and Kansas. Even up into Ohio, New York, and all of those northern states, Maryland especially, they were finding the Thoroughbred horse a fine vehicle to breed, to race, and to bet on.

I felt like one of those California forty-niners who had gotten there first. I knew that I was ahead of the pack—I wanted to stay that way, so I could not promise her that I would pass up any good horse just so that I could buy one in Virginia.

I knew that she wanted to show off for her kin-folks, and I didn't blame her, but not at the expense of the horse ranch that we were trying to establish.

Occasionally, my mind went back to the ranch in Tyler. I was homesick for Texas, there was no question about it, but I knew that matters were in good hands with Charlie and Les and my two vaqueros. What was important now was to get this business done, get back home, and then get some stallions and some mares together. They needed to start throwing some colts and even some fillies that we could be proud of in the days to come. I hoped to see Churchill Downs before we left, but for the moment, as I told Laura that night before we prepared for bed, my mind was on business.

She said that she could understand that but she hoped that I would take the opportunity to enjoy the southern culture while I had the chance. She agreed that so far my experiences had not been the best, but she assured me that they would improve.

I said, "Does that mean that we will run into a breed of folks whose eyes are a little farther apart? Most people that I've seen so far look like they take the expression kissing cousins a step or two closer."

She said, "I'm a southerner."

I got into bed. "I rest my case, but not your body. Come here."

The next morning, we set out right after breakfast for the drive out to Tom Claibourne's horse breeding operation. I had rented a smart little buggy and we had a stylish trotter pulling us at a good clip. I figured that we would make the short journey either by lunch or shortly thereafter. As we went through the town, I noted that Louisville was a very pleasant looking city of some twenty-five or thirty thousand inhabitants. It was sparkling clean. They even had folks out cleaning up the garbage and trash along the side of the street. You seldom saw that in most places I'd been.

Within three hours, we were sweeping up the lane leading to Claibourne's house, running between white painted fences. The whole place was neat and ordered and clean. We pulled up into the circular drive and a servant came running out to take the head of our horse. The Claibournes had a fine looking house but it was nothing like that of the Clatterbucks, which reminded you more of a hotel than a house.

We had barely descended from the buggy before Tom Claibourne himself was coming out the front door to greet us. He was a tall, spare man who appeared to be in his fifties, wearing whipcord riding britches and a blue work shirt. As near as I could tell, he was the first southerner that I had seen who wasn't in white linen or black broadcloth. He wasn't even wearing a plantation hat.

We had arrived in time for lunch and we made a good meal out of steaks, vegetables, and some fruit salad. Mrs. Claibourne was a friendly, plumpish woman in her early forties and she and Laura had a good time giggling and laughing. After lunch, Mr. Claibourne and I went out to the stables.

Tom Claibourne was a friendly enough man and a good host, but he was a no-nonsense man when it came to trading horses. We were there two and a half days and two nights. Most of that time I spent trying to haggle him down from his price of ten thousand five hundred dollars for a bay stud that I badly wanted. The stud was twelve years old and was a direct male descendent from his Kentucky Derby champion, Shamrock Dilly. The bay had retired early from racing because he had two white hooves. White hooves, as any horseman knows, splinter and crack easily, and this had cost the horse his racing career.

I tried every trick I knew but Tom Claibourne would not come off his price. If I paid it, it would only leave me fifteen hundred dollars to buy a horse in Virginia, and all I would be able to buy for that would be a Shetland pony.

He understood my predicament and tried to show me another bay who had come down from his champion on the distaff side through the mare, but in my opinion the horse was too small, standing only sixteen hands tall. Claibourne was willing to sell me the horse for only sixty-five hundred dollars but I was still reluctant because of his size. The horse himself had not had a very distinguished racing career because of that very fact.

If the horse had been a hand higher, I'd have bought him like a shot, but that extra hand meant a lot of distance in the stride of the horse, and a Thoroughbred has got to have a stride. I was able to buy only horses that had not themselves had distinguished racing careers. If they had, I'd not be able to touch any of them for my twenty thousand dollars. Horses who were descended from champions and were themselves champions were much too valuable to sell. They were kept on and used as breeding studs to perpetuate the line. I was starting at the bottom and I was having to gather up the leftovers, trusting my knowledge and skill and insight to make buys that other folks had overlooked.

Claibourne's argument about the small bay was that if I mated him with some big mares, in a couple of generations I would wind up with some fine racing stock. He said the horse had all of Dilly's blood, that he was a solid little horse, only short.

In the end, I had declined, even though at his age I could expect to breed the horse for ten more years. A couple of generations was only about three years, but we had Virginia and I hoped to find what I was looking for there.

It was with regret that we said goodbye to the Claibournes and went back into Louisville to try our luck at the other breeding farm that I had received an answer from.

As we drove into Louisville, I told Laura about the little bay and why I had turned him down even though Tom Claibourne had dropped the price down to six thousand dollars. Laura had thought I was wrong. She said that he was such a pretty horse.

I said, "Laura, pretty ain't got anything to do with it in race horses. Pretty works in girls, but pretty won't get a Thoroughbred to the line first."

She said, "He doesn't seem short to me."

"He's not too small for a saddle horse, Laura, but Thoroughbreds are big horses. They've got to be. They are big and they're long. They've got to be big enough and long enough to be able to run. Too big and they can't run, too little and they're at a disadvantage. This horse was a shade too small."

"But you've got plenty of money left for Virginia?"

I said somewhat sadly, "I've got too much money, unfortunately, left for Virginia. I'm not very hopeful about this new breeding farm we are headed for tomorrow."

I had been completely correct in my assessment of the second breeding farm, a place called Garden Hills. The bill of particulars they had sent me concerning their available stock had interested me only as something to make a comparison against. The cheapest horse they had was only fifteen thousand dollars, so they advertised, and by the time we got out to pay them a call, that horse was gone. The cheapest thing that they had left was twenty thousand dollars. We had lunch and supper with them and then drove back into Louisville the next morning, having only wasted one day and a little embarrassment to find out that, yes indeed, we were paupers when it came to being in the Thoroughbred racing game. I was more than a little discouraged. I had seen some magnificent animals, animals that I could never hope to afford in the near future, and yet I was going to try to produce a line of stock to run against them. I was doing some real tall hoping, as near as I could figure.

Laura, bless her, tried to bolster my spirit by talking about what I could do if given the chance and that I would have the chance. She knew that they were empty words, just as I did. You didn't win horse races on talk. You won horse races by putting a horse on the track, and we were a long way from putting a horse on the track. I did appreciate her trying to lift my spirits and keep my hope up, but the fact was, we were shopping with a short pocketbook.

The next morning we would take the train to Virginia and Laura could hardly hide her excitement about her first visit home in something like ten or fifteen years. Seeing her excited and happy like that did lift my spirits. There wasn't any point in us both being down and I was glad it was her that was happy. I hoped that she still had as much confidence in me a year or two hence when our first colts started dropping out of our mares. There were two ways to go broke, I had been told, in the Thoroughbred business—when you got in it and when you got out of it. I could understand that. I had also been told that one of two causes could ruin you—bad judgment or bad horses. Seemed to me that they went hand in hand.

At that high-priced farm outside of Louisville, in talking with the owner, John Bowers, I had complained about my lack of capital. He'd said, "You ought to feel lucky. All that means is you'll lose less money."

10

The train for Richmond left at eight o'clock the next morning and we damn near didn't make it, what with all of Laura's paraphernalia and the fact that she insisted on sending her aunt one more telegram just about the time the train was pulling out of the station. We weren't really going into Richmond. We would detour there to go to Shelbyville. It was fortunate that the two horse farms I was to visit were located there and that her Aunt Euless, who she was so fond of, lived only some fifteen miles distant. Her Aunt Rowena and her Uncle James lived not far from her Aunt Euless.

I had hoped, and told Laura so, that we would stay in a hotel and not with her relatives. For some reason, she would not comment on the subject, even though I had pressed her several times for her thoughts on the matter.

But then, as we were well settled on the train and about an hour out of Louisville, she said something that almost knocked me down. She said, and she put her hand on my thigh first, "Now Warner, I hope that you won't be too severe with me on this, but I have written my aunts and they are under the impression that we are married."

Well, you could have knocked me over with a feather, especially in view of the fights that we'd had over her going by the name of Pico. The only thing that I could think to ask her was when had she written her aunts to that effect.

"When I knew we were going, about a month ago."

"And you have been going around calling yourself Mrs. Pico? Arguing with me about it, having a fight to the death over the name, and meanwhile you had already written to your aunts to advise them that your name was Grayson?"

She had the good grace to blush and look down. She said in a timid voice, "Well, yes."

I looked at her and shook my head. I said, "Laura, you are the damnedest piece of work I've ever seen. I can't even call you a piece of work because I don't think you're finished yet. I don't know what you are finally gonna turn out to be when they get done making you. I do know one thing. You are the hardheadedest, stubbornest, most contrary liar that I have ever met."

She said, flouncing her head a little bit so that her hair shimmered, "You don't have to take it like that, Warner. I thought that you would be pleased that I would be going by the name Grayson."

I said, with as cold a tone as I could manage, "I would like you to go by the name Grayson lawfully, as a married woman, as my wife."

She turned her head and gave me a timid smile. She said, "But you will pretend with me—just for this little while, won't you?"

"No."

She looked startled. "What?"

"You heard me."

"Oh now, Warner, please don't say that. You would embarrass me to death."

"Doesn't make any difference, missy. You've made your bed, now lie in it."

She fluttered her eyelashes at me. "Warner, please honey. My aunts are old, genteel ladies. They wouldn't understand. You'll do this for me, won't you?"

"Laura, if you had told me this a month ago, I'd have been more than happy, but you gave me pure hell, including a knee in the nuts, over this very thing. And now you want me to go along with what you will probably call a little white lie. I'll be damned if I'll let you be called Mrs. Grayson. I'll call you the widow Pico at every opportunity. I'll even ask you about John in front of them."

Her face flamed. She suddenly dug her elbow in my side. She said, "Oh, no you won't. You damned well better not. Listen, Warner Grayson, I'll do what Royce Clatterbuck couldn't do. *I'll* shoot you."

I rubbed my sore ribs. I said, "You're afraid of guns, remember?"

"I'll make an exception in your case. Now are you going to do this for me or not?"

"Give me one good reason why I should."

She looked at me for a long moment and then she slipped her hand up behind my neck and pulled my head down and kissed me on the lips. A long, searching kiss. A long, searching, probing kiss. When she let me go, she said, "Is that a good enough reason?"

I sighed. "Don't you ever get tired of getting around me that way? Don't you ever get tired of being a woman one minute and a bully the next? I mean, you can't claim to be the weaker sex if you're going to use that weakness on me."

"Warner, a woman's got to do what a woman's got to do."

"Yeah, but you're always doing that to me."

"That's because you're the one that I love."

I gave her a grimace. I said, "Yes, Mrs. Grayson."

She smiled. "Why thank you, Mr. Grayson."

"Oh, go to hell, Widow Pico." She dug her elbow in my ribs again. I said, "All right, all right. Mrs. Grayson. Mrs. Laura Grayson. The wonderful wife of poor, downtrodden Warner Grayson."

She said, "You're going to love my kinfolk."

I was still rubbing my ribs. I said, "Not if they are anything like you."

She said, "Oh, they are not anything like me. They are very genteel and nice."

"I'll believe it when I see it."

It became clear to me that that was why Laura had been noncommittal about whether we were going to stay in a hotel or stay with one of her relatives. She first had to find out if I would allow her to represent herself as my wife. Now that she had gotten permission, I assumed we would be covered up with relatives and kinfolk. She said that she had about a dozen cousins in the area. Well, things could have been worse. Virginia wasn't very big, but her kinfolk could have been on one side of the state and the horse farms on the other. Of course, if that had been the case, I would have sent her to visit her kinfolk while I went to see the horses.

I made it clear to her that while I did want her to enjoy seeing her kinfolk my main interest had to lie in looking at livestock. She said that she understood. Of course, Laura had the habit of saying that she understood something and then later denying she had ever even heard the matter mentioned. But I pressed this point home to her. I said, "Laura, it could be that I will have to stay in Shelbyville at a hotel and inspect what these horse farms have to offer while you get your visiting done. We've been away from home for a good long while now and I am starting to get an itch to get back."

She said that she understood and I hoped that she did. She said, "Honey, I am bringing home a tall, handsome Texan. At least give me the chance to show you off just a little bit."

I said, "What are you setting me up for, Laura?"

"Why, whatever do you mean?"

"That's not the way you talk."

She hugged my arm as the train rattled along. "That's the way I feel. I don't always tell you everything about the way I feel."

I said, "Ha!"

I was content, though, that she said the horse business had to come first.

We got into Richmond at about eight that night, too late to catch a train for Shelbyville, which was just as well. I did manage to prevail upon Laura to leave most of her paraphernalia in the baggage room of the depot so that we wouldn't have to fool with it going to the hotel and back the next day.

We spent the night at a nearby hotel, both of us feeling the need for a bath. Richmond was an up and coming city. We got a suite with a bathroom that went with the room. It had a big bathtub and Laura suggested that we take a bath together, but I was damned if I was going to do any such a thing. There are some things that a man likes to do by himself and taking a bath was one of them.

I said that I didn't mind playing afterwards, but I wasn't about to get in there with a hot, soapy woman and find that exciting.

By nine the next morning, we were rattling along on the relatively short journey into Shelbyville.

Now it was my turn to be excited. It was the end of the trail, though I was still one or two horses short. I kept thinking about that little bay that Tom Claibourne had. The more I thought about it, the more I thought that some use could be made of him, but for the life of me, I couldn't think what. He was too small and his get would be too small.

When we finally pulled into the station at Shelbyville, Laura was all aglow. I've never seen a woman that excited in all my life. She went rushing down the steps of the train and into the arms of one of those elderly, motherly looking ladies that you automatically associate with apple pies and starched aprons and doilies on the parlor chairs. It was Aunt Euless.

Well, naturally, it was a mixed up, scrambled affair with a bunch of excited talk. Then her Aunt Rowena and Uncle James came up and it got worse. First we were going to do this and then we were going to do that, with me all the while trying to explain my purpose for the trip. It seemed like I got lost in all that kinfolk business. There seemed to be about a dozen cousins there, most of them female and most of them bearing an amazing resemblance to Laura, and I came in for my fair share of neck-hugging and kissing. I must say that I was not averse to the better part of it.

Her Aunt Euless was as sweet as Laura had described her. Her Aunt Rowena was very much the same, though she was thin and hard boned and hard featured like Laura. Her Uncle James was a tall, spare man going bald—which was revealed when he took off his hat. He seemed like a nice enough fellow and looked almost as bewildered as I felt.

Finally it was decided that Laura would load up with her Aunt Euless and go the ten miles to her farm and such cousins and other relatives would meet there for supper that evening.

I was going to rent a horse and get a hotel room and visit the nearest of the two breeding ranches. After that, I would ride out and try to make it in time for supper. The last I saw of them was Laura and her Aunt Euless in one surrey with one of her aunt's hired hands driving. Another buggy held Uncle James and Aunt Rowena contending with Laura's luggage.

She had left half of it behind for me to lug to the hotel. There were two more buggies filled with more cousins. I sure hoped that Aunt Euless had a big enough dining table, though I reckoned that the young folks would eat second table. I know I wouldn't have wanted to make a habit out of feeding that bunch.

When they were gone, I gave a boy a quarter to take Laura's gear over to the hotel. I went over myself to get the best room I could, though it wasn't much. Shelbyville wasn't much larger than Tyler, although it did have an entirely different look. I was pleased that I didn't see so many of those damned plantation hats. The men seemed to favor a kind of a bowler, which I guess they thought seemed a little more citified. Virginia was pretty far north when you stopped and thought about it. Damned near the nation's capital, Washington, D.C.

All I knew was that I still had horses to buy.

When the boy finally managed to get all of Laura's gear piled up in the room, I gave him an extra half dollar in sympathy for his efforts and then took myself to the livery stable and rented myself a traveling horse—something that I had heard called a Tennessee Walking Horse. They said such an animal had a good gait and would get you there and back in good comfort. I was headed for the Shiroh Breeding Farm owned by a Mr. Matthew Shiroh and his wife. The stable hand said it was a mighty big place and grand, too. They didn't seem to have such a southern accent in Virginia, more the way Laura talked, with a kind of force behind every word. Very precise spoken they were. They seemed to have trouble with my Texas twang, something else that made me realize how far from home I was.

They put me on the road to the Shiroh farm and I was content to set out and keep my hopes and my pocketbook where they both belonged until such time that I would have reason to get them up.

It was only about a seven-mile trip and they were correct about the Tennessee Walking Horse. He had a gait called a running walk that was about as fast as most horses could gallop. The flat walk was a stylish gait that moved you along at a clip about like a quarter horse trotting, but much smoother. I swear, you could have sat on his back and drank a cup of tea.

It was in some comfort that I arrived at the lane that turned off to the Shiroh farm, which was nestled back in the soft Virginia hills. Of course, it was spring and all the flowers and the trees were in bloom and blossom. A gentle breeze was blowing and I could tell why Laura was so partial to her home country and why she had such fond memories of it as a child. I went up the lane in good style, noticing to my left and right the sleek-looking Thoroughbreds grazing, and here and there a yearling colt frolicking and gamboling and generally feeling his oats.

The Shiroh home place was a big, white, rambling frame structure. It looked like it had been there for a number of years, though it was still in excellent repair. Out beyond, I could see lines of stables with corrals and small catch pens where animals were trained and worked.

I dismounted in front of the house and waited for a moment. No one came to meet me so I tied the Tennessee Walker to a concrete post with a ring in it and went up the big wide steps onto the veranda of the house. As I was about to knock, the door opened and a gentleman pushed open the screen door and stepped out.

"Would you be the gentleman I am expecting from Texas?"

I put out my hand and introduced myself.

He said, "I'm Matthew Shiroh. I was watching for you, but you slipped up on me. Mighty sorry that I wasn't out to greet you."

He was an elderly gentleman that I put in his mid to late sixties. He was wearing a white linen suit, all right, but his shirt was open at the collar and he wasn't wearing a hat. His gray hair was thinning a little on the top and he was stooped and thin, but there was a vitality about him that told me he was still very much in the game.

Mr. Matthew Shiroh was one of the most respected names in the Thoroughbred breeding business. He had founded many a line of famous horses. In other parts of the country, his two sons were equally well known for their breeding stock. I had chosen to come to the source.

We went into the house and into a well worn parlor that looked like it had gotten good using by people that could appreciate it. Mr. Shiroh won my heart immediately by bringing out a bottle of what he called sipping whiskey and two glasses. We sat down in a couple of easy chairs with a small table between us. He put the bottle and the glasses on the table and said, "Help yourself, Mr. Grayson. There is a saw-bones in town that says that I am supposed to go light on that stuff, so I'll let you do the pouring. May the guilt for my intemperance be on your head, sir."

I had to laugh at that. I started to pour him a very light one but then I glanced up at his face, which was looking stern, so I poured a little more and the face mellowed a little. I poured a little more and it mellowed even more. I poured him a half a tumbler to match mine.

We lifted glasses and damned if he didn't make the toast to luck as I did. I knocked mine all the way back as befits the toast while he took a good swallow. I reckon in earlier days, he would have done as I had.

I had warmed to the man immediately, which had absolutely nothing to do with his horses or my chance of buying any of his horses. Nevertheless, if I wasn't going to do any business, I figured that I would just as soon not do any business with comfortable company like Mr. Matthew Shiroh.

He said, "I understand from your letter—well, two letters wasn't it, and a telegram—that you have come all the way from Texas traveling through several states with the express purpose of getting into the Thoroughbred horse racing business. I have just one question to ask you, sir."

I said, "What would that be, sir?"

"What kind of damn fool are you?"

I laughed. I said, "Would it be fair to ask you the same question, considering that you are in the horse racing business?"

He said, "Well, I was dropped on my noggin as a baby. What's your excuse?"

"I was kicked in the head early on."

"Sounds like solid enough reason to me." He raised his glass.

We drank and then I settled back and said, "Mr. Shiroh, I'm kind of on a tight schedule. My par—" I stopped. I didn't know when the opportunity might come up that Laura would have occasion to meet Mr. Shiroh or he might know her kinfolks, so I said, "My wife is visiting

274

kinfolk near Shelbyville." I went on to explain who they were, and as it turned out, it was wise that I had played it safe, because he knew nearly all the family.

He said, "You must remember, young man, that I have been right here for pretty close to sixty-seven years so there ain't a baby gets born or an old man like me that goes on over across the river that I don't know about."

"And I reckon you know where all the good horses are, also?"

"Truth be known, I've got most of them right here." He gave me a wink.

His next question was, "How big of a bank-roll you got?"

I didn't figure there was going to be much profit in lying to him about the question I most feared, so I told him the truth from the beginning to the present, leaving out, of course, the business about the Clatterbucks. When I was through, he just nodded.

"So, what you are is a man that is doing a lot of wishing."

"Yes sir. That would be pretty close to the truth, but it don't cost nothing."

"Well, young man. I'm fearful that I have to tell you that what you have will let you buy half a stallion on this farm. And that is the fact of the matter, sir."

"Well, I am much obliged to you for the drink,

Mr. Shiroh, and for the information." I went ahead and asked him about the other breeding farm I was going to visit that was run by a fellow named Wentworth.

When I was through, he said, "He'll sell you a horse, maybe even two, for the amount that you have left, but you don't want them. Not to my way of thinking, that is."

"Tell me something, Mr. Shiroh. Did you make your money in horses or did you have money and then get into the horse business?"

It made him smile slightly. He said, "Sir, I believe you are asking me if I am a dilettante. You are asking me if I dabble in horses as a hobby. The answer is no. I made my money in horses. They are valuable to me. They have been my life's work."

"I am glad to hear that, sir. I have run into quite a few dabblers, as you call them, and it's a pleasure to talk to another horseman."

"Young man, I recognized you as a horseman the second I saw you get off that Tennessee Walker."

"I know that I can't afford any of your horses, but could I look at them?"

"Well, of course you can look at them, sir, but also stay for supper, with welcome, and stay the night."

"Oh, I wouldn't want to impose on you, sir. Not after it is clear that we can't do business."

He said, "Oh no, no, no. I'm an old man. My dear wife has departed me and these nights are lonely. I'm not much of a solitary drinker and it would be a pleasure to defy that old sawbones's advice. Stay and we'll have a good supper and enjoy good conversation. I love talking horses with a man who knows horses and I know that you know horses."

We went out to his stables and I swear that he had thirty of the best looking studs I had ever seen. I could see why his stable had such a reputation. He had some horses that were ten years old that looked like they could go to the track the next day. He had some three year-olds that he was readying for the track that would be working early the next morning. He had an oval race track, a mile training race track, right there on his property. This man was in the horse racing business. He had grooms that very obviously knew what they were doing. He had his own farrier shop. He had developed a special horseshoe for his own race horses that he could change depending on the conditions of the track, depending on whether it was sloppy or muddy or firm or what. It was very easy to be impressed.

On top of that, I enjoyed the old man and it appeared that he enjoyed me, too.

Toward the end of the day, he took me into the broodmares' barn and walked me over into a corner to a box stall. He said, "I want to introduce you to an old lady." Inside the stall was a big, black, aging mare who was as elegant as anything that I had ever seen. He had one of the boys lead her out. She had perfect lines and perfect conformation, and Lord, was she tall. She was seventeen and a half hands tall if she wasn't eighteen.

He said, "Let me introduce you to Lou Ann's Lady. Lou Ann was my wife's name. This mare has dropped more fast running horses than any mare you've ever seen. She's an honest twelve years old and I think with luck, we've got three or four more years to drop colts. I wouldn't sell this mare for fifteen thousand dollars. But young man, I'll sell her to you for six thousand. That's half of what you have left."

I said, "Mr. Shiroh, I appreciate your compliment, but I am looking to buy stud horses, sir. I have all the mares I need."

He said, "A lot of folks make the mistake of thinking that they have to start a line with studs. This lady will do you fine. I'm an old man and I don't want to breed her again. I am a horse trader so I'm not going to just give her to you, but I am going to make it possible for you to buy her. Now let's go back on in the house for supper. You be thinking about it."

I was already in trouble. I was supposed to have tried to get to Aunt Euless's that night, but

I knew that I wasn't going to make it, not with the opportunity to visit with Mr. Shiroh and learn from him and drink his fine sipping whiskey.

We ate in the kitchen, served by a big, fat Negro lady who laughed at everything that Mr. Shiroh said. She served us as fine a smoked, honey-cured ham as I had ever eaten, along with hominy grits, yams, and fresh sliced tomatoes. I tell you, when I walked away from that table, I was nearly going sideways. That woman plum stuffed us full.

As we went back into the study, I asked Mr. Shiroh how he managed to stay that thin eating like that.

He got kind of a sad look on his face. "I don't eat that way very often, young man. Kinda lonesome eating by yourself."

"Well, it's coming onto dark so I guess I had better be heading on back into town."

But he wouldn't hear of it. He insisted that I stay the night. He said, "There are more bedrooms in this place than we know what to do with. I'll send Lulu, that's the fat lady that tried to get you as fat as she is, to turn down the covers on the bed. You spend the night here with me and think about that mare. I'll even ship her to Texas for you and send a groom along with her to make sure that she gets there safe. I'll even let him stay with you for a couple of weeks until she gets used to you. I'm kinda fond of that old lady. She has made me many a dollar. Maybe I'd like to see her make you many a dollar."

"Mr. Shiroh, you haven't known me but a few hours. I can understand that you are a kind man, but why are you bestowing so much kindness on me?"

We were sitting in the parlor sipping whiskey. He gave me a look and said, "Because I am so tired of the phonies and the dilettantes in this horse business. When I see one that is a real horseman, I want to give him a leg up. That's the only answer that you are going to get to that question. And I'm not going to give you that mare or anything else, because I am still a horse trader."

I didn't argue with that because I understood it. I'd done a few favors in my life as a horse trader too, but I had never given anything away.

I was up early the next morning and out at the stables as it was becoming dawn. Some of the grooms were taking horses out to work them around the track. Mr. Shiroh had told me the night before that he wouldn't be up that early, that he didn't get up and around much before eight o'clock.

He said, "My old bones won't stand the chill of the morning like they used to. I used to like nothing better than to watch a young colt with vapor coming out of his nostrils. But now it is more than I can stand. Damn, don't ever grow old, Mr. Grayson. You'll regret it."

For a little while I watched as some of the grooms galloped the colts around the track. Breezing they called it, letting a colt work easy and nice and smooth. They were marvelous looking animals. After that, I wandered into the barn and had another look at Lou Ann's Lady. As I looked at her, a thought nudged into the back of my mind. God knows this mare was perfect. She had conformation, she had a record, she had everything. Of course, she also had quite a bit of age. But this thought started plaguing me.

I suddenly turned and walked back into the house. Lulu was in the kitchen, making a pot of coffee. She said, "You sit yourself down, young sir, and I'll get you some coffee and make you some breakfast right away."

I said, "Lulu, I am in a terrible rush. I believe that I will just settle for that cup of coffee. If I'm gone before Mr. Shiroh gets up tell him that I'll be back."

I waited for the coffee and then didn't even finish the whole cup. Within fifteen minutes, I had saddled the Tennessee Walker and was on the road to Shelbyville. Me and that Tennessee Walker covered the road in miraculous time.

I went straight to the depot and got a telegram off to Tom Claibourne outside of Louisville. I had to pay an extra five dollars to have it delivered at such a distance.

My telegram inquired if the small bay was still for sale at six thousand dollars. If so, I wanted to buy the horse and please wire me back immediately because I would be waiting for an answer.

For the next two hours, I walked the streets of Shelbyville anxiously. I didn't know how I was going to get that little bay stud up on that big black mare, but I knew that if I did, that big mare would drop some mighty fine sized colts. And they were going to be plenty swift afoot. Why I hadn't thought of it before I didn't know. But I knew that the mare more than the stud dictated the size of the get, be it colt or filly. That bay stud and that wonderful old mare were a perfect match. They might not fall in love, but I didn't care. If they could mate and breed, that was all I cared about.

I thanked my lucky stars that providence had led me to such a man as Mr. Shiroh. As near as I could figure, he was the first honest man that I had met on this trip.

I made a stab at eating breakfast at the hotel, but didn't do a good job of it because I was so anxious. Instead, I ended up at the bar drinking beer instead of coffee and finally wound up with a couple shots of whiskey. I guess I had made four trips back to the telegraph office before the wire that I had been expecting arrived. It was going on to two o'clock in the afternoon by that time. The wire said that Mr. Claibourne was still willing to sell the horse and did I want to take delivery in Louisville or did I prefer to pay the shipping costs and have the horse delivered to me in Tyler, Texas. Mr. Claibourne assured me that he would send a groom with the horse and guarantee his safe delivery. He estimated the shipping costs at around three or four hundred dollars.

That wasn't much of a decision to make. There was the problem of collecting the two horses from the Clatterbucks and I didn't need another horse on my hands to complicate matters. Besides, I figured to allow the gamblers who had so graciously donated six hundred dollars to me to pay those costs. I immediately wired him back with the instructions to draft on my bank in Tyler for the six-thousand-dollar purchase price and the shipping costs. I asked that he send the horse on its way in about a week's time, as I figured that would give me a chance to get back to Tyler to receive him. I could not resist mentioning in the telegram that I had found the perfect mare to mate the stud to, just as he suggested. I closed by saying that I would stand by for his return telegram if all conditions were agreeable to him. Twenty minutes later his answer came back saying that he understood and all the terms were acceptable and that I had bought a stud horse. He wished me luck.

I went out of the telegraph office feeling pretty pleased with my day's work. Now all I had to do was go back and make sure that Mr. Shiroh hadn't changed his mind. But, as I mounted the Tennessee Walker, I was sure that he hadn't.

I had instructed Mr. Claibourne to draft on my bank in Tyler because of the difficulty involved in stopping in Louisville and getting a check to him twenty miles off into the country. If I could, I intended to give Mr. Shiroh a check and complete our business on the spot. I only hoped that mare hadn't died of old age before I got there.

I found Mr. Shiroh out by the track watching some of his horses work. He was leaning on the railing and I walked up and stood beside him.

He gave me kind of a sideways look and said, "Well, you're some hell of a house guest. Leave before breakfast and I bet you didn't even have a good lunch. What did you do, go into Shelbyville to find your wife? I bet you are in big trouble because you were expected for supper last night and you stayed here just to play on an old man's sympathy and get him to sell you a horse cheap. Now, ain't that about the size of it?"

I said, "Mr. Shiroh, it ain't no fun fooling somebody if they're on to you as fast as you got on to me."

"You catch a little hell from the missus?"

I said, "No sir, what I did was I went into town and got off a telegram and bought the smallest stud that I could conceive of buying. I figured that he would make a perfect mate for Lou Ann's Lady. And if we still got a deal, I've got a checkbook in my pocket."

He was smoking a cigar and he turned around to look at me and smile. His old, weathered cheeks creasing, he said, "Damn it, I made you that deal in a moment of softness. You ain't going to hold me to it, are you?"

I said, "Yes, sir, I am afraid that I am going to have to. But look at it this way—it will mean that your fame will spread to Texas."

He said, "I know that you are a Texan and I dread hurting your feelings but I don't think that there is such a thing as being famous in Texas."

I just laughed. "This money is burning a hole in my pocket, Mr. Shiroh, and I am anxious to give it to you and have a bill of sale for Lou Ann's Lady."

He said, "Did you have any lunch?"

I said, "No, sir. I have been so worried about

completing this transaction that all I have had today is a half of a cup of coffee from Lulu, and a good many beers and several whiskeys."

He said, "Well now, let's go into the house and tend to business so that maybe you will settle down and eat some lunch."

An hour later, I owned the biggest, most graceful, most beautiful broodmare that I had ever seen. True to his word, Mr. Shiroh threw in the shipping and the groom for nothing. He said, "As a matter of fact, I might come down there with that mare and look your operation over and set you straight in the Thoroughbred business." I made him promise and shake on it.

I said, "Mr. Shiroh, if you are not spending the night in my house in Tyler in two weeks, I'll never again believe the word of a southern gentleman."

He laughed and said, "They ain't sold you on that southern gentleman bullshit have they? Young man, that is a contradiction in terms. You can't be southern and a gentleman at the same time. That is a myth that a lot of folks invented as an excuse for their poor way of doing business and their generally poor way of doing anything. A southern gentleman is nothing but poor white trash in a white linen suit."

"Does that include you?"

He laughed. "I will leave that to your discretion,

sir. Now let's go in and eat a late lunch. I'm a little hungry myself."

I said, "You ought to be. It's nearly four o'clock in the afternoon."

Mr. Shiroh wanted me to stay the night, but I knew that I was probably already in trouble with a lady named either Laura Pico or Laura Grayson. I begged off and pointed out the difficulties that I was laying up for my future harmony if I was to stay and take advantage of his hospitality for another night. He was willing to let me go on the condition that when our visit was up with her relatives, we would come and stay a night with him. I assured him that we would.

It was late in the afternoon and I thought that I was facing a twenty-mile ride, but he knew where Laura's Aunt Euless's place was and drew me a map that made it come out closer to fifteen. He said that if I set that Tennessee Walking Horse to its pace, I could be there in two hours.

I bid the old gentleman a fond goodbye and then mounted up and took off. His directions were accurate and I would have arrived on time if I hadn't gotten lost by my own ignorance and wasted time asking directions at a farm house. As it was, it was only about half an hour after sundown when I arrived at Laura's Aunt Euless's place. It was a big, grand, two-story frame house, a fine country house. There was no problem telling how many rooms that the place contained because there was a light on in every room as near as I could figure. Aunt Euless seemed to be in a combination business as I saw beef cattle and dairy cattle and fields of garden truck and corn and such. It looked to me like she ran an integrated operation.

I rode slowly up the driveway toward the front porch. Judging from the number of buggies and horses tied out in the front, half the county was there. I am not by nature a bodacious man and I shrunk from entering that den of whirling kinfolk and relatives. Nevertheless, I dismounted my horse, tied him up, and loosened his girth. Then I started up the steps in as good a cheer as I could manage.

I was about to knock, when the door was suddenly flung open by Aunt Euless herself. She reached out and grabbed me by the arm and sucked me into the hullabaloo of the gathering like a stick being drawn into a whirlpool in the water.

She said, "Wherever in the world have you been? You're about to miss supper. Now, there are all kinds of folks in the world that you have got to meet. They are your kinfolk."

Fortunately, Laura saw me about that time and came forward. She was looking her best in a light pink frock, her hair done up in a way that

I hadn't seen before. She had a string of jewels around her neck. As a normal course, she wasn't given to wearing jewels and gewgaws, but she seemed to be outfitted for the occasion.

She took me in hand and we went on a whirlwind round of the room. To this good day, I could not repeat the names of half of the people that I met. But all of them were kin in one way or another.

Aunt Euless had a fine and comfortable home. I could see how Laura grew up accustomed to a certain amount of luxury. I could see now why she'd found my little four-room cabin down in south Texas so distasteful.

As it turned out, I was a little behind on the news. It seems as though we were on our honeymoon. We had only been married about a week before we left on this trip. I cut my eyes around to Laura when I was first informed of this news by one of her giggling cousins, but Laura maintained a modest gaze in the opposite direction.

Finally, all the toing and froing and all the meeting and greeting were over with and we sat down to dinner. Aunt Euless's dining table wasn't nearly as long as the Clatterbucks', but what it lacked in length, it more than made up for in the weight of the viands and the vittles that covered it.

Aunt Euless turned out to be one of those sweet

old ladies who would kill you if she got the chance. It was "just one more slice of turkey," or "one more slice of ham," or "one more helping of potatoes and gravy," or "one more piece of apple pie." I swear the woman was dangerous.

When I was finally able to stagger away from the table, I was not a well man. She meant for the best, but then I've been on horses that nearly killed me that meant what they were doing for the best.

With supper finally over, little by little the cousins and second cousins and nearby friends and neighbors who had come to see the long-lost waif return to the fold gradually began to drift away. The party settled down to me and Laura, Aunt Euless, Aunt Rowena, and Uncle James.

It had become pretty clear during the evening that not a whole lot of drinking went on in the house. I had a couple cups of the punch they served. Why they called it punch I'll never know—it sure in hell didn't pack any. My saddlebags were still on the Tennessee Walker out front and there was a jug of brandy and a jug of whiskey in them. Besides that, the horse had been standing too long out there without being fed and watered, so I made my apologies and went outside. I gathered him up and started toward the barn. It had taken all I could do to keep Aunt Euless from sending for a hired hand to take him to the barn for me.

She couldn't understand why such a gentleman like myself would want to tend to a horse, but then I don't reckon that Aunt Euless had ever wanted a drink as bad as I did.

As I walked toward the barn, I heard somebody coming behind me and turned to see Laura carrying a lamp.

She said, "Were you planning on blundering around in the dark? I know what you're doing. You're going for a drink, aren't you?"

"Yeah, want to join me?"

She giggled. "You know I don't drink."

"Not unless it's available. By the way, what day is it?"

She thought for a minute and said, "It's Wednesday, why?"

"I don't want to get too close to Sunday while we're here. I've an idea that we would spend all day Sunday at the church."

She came up and linked her arm in mine. She said, "Don't you just love my family?"

"Just to death," I said, "just to death." I said it with as phony a southern accent as I could manage. "Just love them plum to death."

Naturally, that called for a dig in the ribs with her elbow. I said, "One of these days, I'm gonna have those elbows of yours filed down. They're a little sharp for my taste."

She lit my way into the barn to help me find a stable for the Walking horse. I took off his saddle and bridle, poured him out some feed and turned him in to get some rest. He had done a couple of good days' work.

As we turned around to leave, Laura said, "By the way, where the hell have you been?"

"I've been doing what I said I was going to do—looking into the horse business here in Virginia."

"And?"

I knew how excited she was in the hope that I would buy a Virginia horse. I said, "Well, I can't say right now."

"Did you or did you not buy a horse?"

"You know I bought a horse. You saw me buy two horses in Louisiana."

She stopped and stamped her foot. "Damn it, Warner, answer my question."

I stamped my foot. "No damn it, I'm not gonna answer your question. I may show you, the day after tomorrow."

"What is that supposed to mean?"

"Exactly what I said."

"You're not going to tell me anything, are you?"

I said, "That depends on what you'll give me."

"Not in my Aunt Euless's house."

That made me want to laugh. "I bet it wouldn't be a first."

"Why, of all the nerve. How dare you suggest such a thing. I was a girl of sixteen when I was here."

"So?"

She jerked at my arm. "Oh, you."

I was carrying a bottle of whiskey in my hand. We had gotten outside the barn when I stopped and pulled the cork and had a long pull. It went down mighty smooth. I offered the bottle to Laura but she shook her head.

I said, "You scared that your Aunt Euless is going to smell it on your breath?"

She reached out and jerked the bottle out of my hand. She said, "Don't you dare me, Warner Grayson. Don't you ever dare me." With that she took a good healthy pull.

I took the bottle from her. "Wait just a minute. Don't be getting drunk on me or I'll be catching the blame for it."

I took another drink and then we walked on toward the house. She said, "Are you going to tell me about the horses or not?"

I said, "Let me hide this bottle right here next to the stoop. I might need to come out and get a breath of fresh air later."

"If you don't tell me about the horses, or horse, I'm gonna tell Aunt Euless where that bottle of whiskey is."

"Of all the things that you've done that I should have killed you for, this would be the very thing that I *would* kill you for. You better not do any such thing."

I took one more drink and then hid the bottle in the flowers that grew around the front part of the house. We mounted the steps and went back inside.

Uncle James was yawning widely, making it clear that he was about ready for bed. We sat and talked for a few more minutes until Aunt Rowena and Uncle James went upstairs. Finally, Aunt Euless wore down and she took herself off. She gave me a kiss on the cheek and said that she was going to regard me as her own son-in-law. I didn't know quite how to take that, but I guessed that it was all right. Then she gave Laura a hug and a kiss. Laura told her that she knew where everything was, nothing had been changed in all the years, and then Aunt Euless went on upstairs.

I was sitting on the divan and Laura came over and snuggled up next to me. She said, "It's been so wonderful to come back here. Haven't you enjoyed it?"

I had to admit that I had. Not wanting to appear too soft or let it get out of hand, I went ahead and told her how happy it made me to see her enjoying herself so much.

She pulled my head down and gave me a gentle kiss. She said, "You know, you're not such a bad son of a bitch after all."

"And you have such a lovely way of putting things."

We spent another night there and then came the morning, when Aunt Euless drove Laura and all of her luggage back to Shelbyville with me following behind on the Tennessee Walking Horse. I left them at the hotel to get their good-byes done with, while I took the rented horse back to the livery and paid for his use. I rented a smart-looking carriage for two passengers, with a lively stepping trotter to take us out to Mr. Shiroh's place. I arrived back just in time to get a slobbery kiss from Aunt Euless and then watched her leave, while Laura stood on the boardwalk with tears in her eyes. Beside her was the pile of luggage. I knew that there was a good bit stored in the room in the hotel, which we had rented for three nights and hadn't slept in for a minute. I was amazed to see how much she had managed to take to her Aunt Euless's place. I got one of the boys from the hotel to take her gear up to our room except for one valise that she would need for an overnight stay.

She looked at me. "Where are we going?"

I said, "Well, since you're supposed to be a partner, I thought it was about time that you went along with me on one of these horse-buying trips and honestly made yourself useful."

She said, "Oh, good heavens. I don't know if I can do with just this one bag."

"Oh yes you can. This is all you're taking. We'll be back tomorrow."

We set out on the drive to Mr. Shiroh's, getting away from Shelbyville at about ten in the morning. The countryside was lovely and the weather was perfect. Laura was full of questions, none of which I would answer.

Laura was as taken with Lou Ann's Lady as Mr. Shiroh was with Laura. I didn't, however, let Laura see the big mare until we'd had lunch with Mr. Shiroh and let her be exposed to his grand old courtly manners. Mr. Shiroh made Mr. Clatterbuck's imitation of a southern gentleman look like a jack-ass standing beside a Thoroughbred. I had met many a man in my day, but I didn't recollect that I had met many I would have liked to become. Mr. Shiroh and my grandfather were the only two that I could think of.

We went out into the barn and Lou Ann's Lady was led out. Laura could only say, "Oh my! Oh my. *Oh my.* Isn't she beautiful?"

Perhaps I had made a mistake. If I had brought Laura with me the first time, I swear that Mr. Shiroh would have given me the horse for free. He beamed like a kerosene lantern. You could see the delight in him and you could see the delight he took in being around a beautiful woman like Laura. I kind of got lost in the picture, but I didn't care. It was a great treat and a privilege to see them both having such a good time.

When she had looked Lou Ann's Lady over from one end to the other and had patted her and smoothed her and the mare had nibbled at her neck, she came over and put her arms around me and hugged me hard. She said, "Thank you. Thank you. We're taking home a real Virginia lady."

I glanced over my shoulder at Mr. Shiroh. He had overheard her remark. He was smiling like he couldn't stop. I said, "I kinda thought I was taking home two."

"Well said, sir. Well said," Mr. Shiroh whispered.

That evening while Laura was resting before supper, Mr. Shiroh and I took a stroll out to the stables at his suggestion. As we walked, he told me something that surprised me. He said, "Young man, I never expected to sell that mare. Have you figured out why she is called Lou Ann's Lady?"

It didn't take me much time. I said, "I reckon that must have been your wife's horse."

"You are correct, sir. And she would have wanted you and that fine young lady to have her. I am delighted where she is going and who she is going with. But I have something else that I want to show you. Something else that I want to talk about."

I was glad that we didn't speak for a moment or two when we walked into the stables. I was touched by the fact that he would have let me have his wife's horse. Mr. Shiroh gave me an odd feeling. After all, I was virtually a stranger to the man, yet he trusted me this way. I doubted, though, that that'd been the only horse his wife had. I was sure she had had many.

We walked into one of the stables that we hadn't been in before. It was obviously reserved for stallions. The stallion barn has a different odor to it and a different feeling. There is a kind of tension and excitement and a power that you don't get in a barn full of broodmares. This one was electric with those ten or twelve stalls full of heads looking out at us curiously. Stallions aren't timid. They will thrust their heads through the top half of the door and look at you with big deep eyes questioningly, wondering what the hell it is that you are doing in there. They don't mind challenging you with their eyes. That is the nice thing about a stallion.

A groom appeared out of nowhere, quietly inquiring of Mr. Shiroh if he could be of any help. Mr. Shiroh said, "Lead number four out."

We stood there in the middle of the stables

while the groom went to the number four box stall with a halter and led out a chestnut so deeply brown-red and shiny that you could almost see your reflection in his coat. He carried his head high, his ears were alert, his neck was long and full. He had beautiful hind-quarters. His legs were in perfect symmetry. My God, he was beautiful.

I couldn't help myself. I whistled under my breath and said, "Lord love us."

Mr. Shiroh smiled and said, "That's something, ain't it? That's So Long Sam."

"So Long Sam?"

"That's what a lot of horses got to say as he left them, 'So long, Sam.' He just left them until the finish line. I could show you his record, but I'm not gonna take the trouble. I think that you have eye enough to see what kind of horse that is."

"Well, yes sir. I believe I do. My God, what a stud horse. What would he be? About ten?"

"He's a-coming eleven."

"Then his racing days haven't been over too long."

"I raced him until two years ago. I raced him because he didn't want to quit. I have never had a horse that hated to lose as bad as Sam. He never could stand for another to get his nose in front of his. He'd jerk the reins out of a jockey's hands and ride his own race. He's the most natural winner that I have ever owned. If the greatest horse in the history of the world was decided on by heart, it would be Sam. Not that he hasn't got the speed and the lungs and the endurance to go with it. He never won a big race but he won a lot of others and he gave a lot of much higher-bred horses a run for their money."

I stood there shaking my head in envy. I said, "My goodness, what an animal. What an animal. How I would love to own an animal like that."

Mr. Shiroh said abruptly, "Well you can't. Not now you can't. You're too young to afford a horse like this. A horse like this costs twenty-five thousand dollars."

"What's his lineage?"

He said, "His lineage goes back to the winners of so many derbies that you couldn't count them. He is as pureblood as a pure-blood can be—he's blue blood."

I said, "I would imagine that he fetches a pretty good stud fee."

Mr. Shiroh said, "Well, that was one of the problems. Sam wasn't ready to quit racing. Occasionally he'll get his mind on a mare but for the time being he is still chomping at the bit, hoping to get back out on that track. That is where his heart is. I think Sam needs a vacation. I think Sam needs to see some of the country before he settles down. What do you think?"

I was bewildered about what he was talking about. I said, "Are you talking about taking him on tour to some of the tracks around the country?"

He said, "No. I know this old boy from Texas—a young horse breeder. I'm thinking about sending him along with that Texas boy. What would you think about that?"

I was befuddled. I said, "I don't know what you're talking about, Mr. Shiroh."

"Well, you don't look dumb but you certainly are acting like you are. I plan to send this horse to Texas with you. I plan to let you use him as a stud horse."

I stood there dumbfounded. "Mr. Shiroh, I can't afford this horse. At best, if I sold everything that I have, I'd be hard pressed and still short of buying this horse."

"Ain't selling you this horse, boy. I'm going to send him down with you to Texas and I want you to breed him. You can't breed him to Lou Ann's Lady because she is his half-sister. But I'm impressed with you enough to believe that you have some good broodmares down there. You've talked about them and I think that you have some quality broodmares that would throw a colt from Sam that would turn out to be a pretty fair running horse. Mind you, there is a condition. I want the pick of the litter."

I said slowly, "Mr. Shiroh, at the risk of insulting you sir, a horse ain't like a dog where you get the pick of the litter, where you get a choice of six or seven pups. There ain't gonna be but that one colt as a general rule."

"Don't you reckon that I know that? What I am saying is that I get the first one that gets dropped. You get the second, I get the third, you get the fourth. Get my drift?"

I was overcome. I didn't know what to say. I said, "Mr. Shiroh, you haven't known me a complete twenty-four hours yet. Why on earth would you be willing to trust me with a horse of this value? Sir, you don't know that much about me."

He said, "I'm reminded of a story about General Robert E. Lee, a Virginia man, you will recall. General Lee was at a church supper and somebody handed him a freshly baked potato, which he promptly dropped. The man said, 'Hot, huh?' and General Lee said, 'No, it just don't take me that long to examine a potato.' Do you take my point, Mr. Grayson?"

I looked down at the stable floor. I said, "Mr. Shiroh, you have paid me a great honor, sir. I will not let you down."

"Besides, you told me that your grandfather was a Bible-reading man."

"Yes sir."

"A God-fearing man."

"Yes sir."

"And you are married to a fine Virginia woman."

The lie almost stuck in my throat, but with that horse at stake, I forced it out. I said, "Yes sir."

He said, "Of course, I am not going to give you a bill of sale. The matter is settled. The horse will continue to belong to me. If I die, I will have made provisions for the bill of sale to be sent to you. But for the time being, you give old Sam a change of scenery and he will take to those Texas mares like he hasn't been doing here. Now, why don't we go on in to supper?"

What he had said was nothing new to me. Very often, a racing stallion had trouble adjusting to becoming a stud. The fire was still up in his blood, the desire to run still in him, the competitive spirit still raged. He was not ready to settle down to making little race horses. And Mr. Shiroh was quite right. Very often a change of mares or a change of country could turn the trick. I had no doubt that I was going to give it a chance.

I tell you, as we walked back to the house, I was floating about a foot off the ground. Before we went in, Mr. Shiroh said, "I'll be shipping him with Lou Ann's Lady. Might be that I'll be taking a trip to Texas sometime to see how things are getting along down there."

There was no way I could convey the earnestness that I put into my invitation that he do just such a thing. I had come to admire and respect and care for that old man in as short a time as I'd ever come to think that highly of anyone, except Laura.

I did not mention So Long Sam during dinner—neither did Mr. Shiroh. We had a wonderful meal of fried chicken and potatoes, green beans, and salad, which Lulu served us with a giggle. I asked Mr. Shiroh if she giggled all of the time and he said, "For twenty years, my wife and I both tried to break that woman of giggling. There's no chance. She once told us, 'Lawds, Lawds, when ya this fats, ya naturally get de giggles.' Must be some truth in it."

That evening, I took Laura out and showed her So Long Sam. For once in her life, she was speechless. She could not believe that the horse was being, in effect, leased to us in return for half the get. Neither could I, as far as that went. To her credit, she realized just how lucky we were.

We stood there in the stable, hugging each other and looking at that beautiful animal. He didn't much care to be stared at, and every once in a while he would snort and fling his head around and stamp his foot as if to say,

"What the hell are you looking at? Ain't you ever seen a race horse before?" Well, I had seen race horses before, but never one quite so perfect.

We slept that night on a beautiful down tick and lay close to each other, feeling as peaceful as, I think, we had in many a day. Laura had not had a good visit since she was sixteen. Now she could go back to Texas knowing that her kinfolk were all right and proud of her.

I said just before we started to go to sleep, "I bet that they were surprised that you could catch such a man as me, weren't they?"

"I told them to never mind your looks, that you were enormously wealthy."

We had to take an early-morning goodbye from Mr. Shiroh. It was a sad parting, but we had a train to catch. We both beseeched him to come to Texas, that nothing could possibly please us more. He assured us that he would.

We drove away in the buggy, waving back to him. He had my check for six thousand dollars for Lou Ann's Lady. I wondered if he would ever cash it.

11

It was a tight fit, but we did manage to get aboard the ten o'clock southbound train. We would not be retracing our steps on the route home, as our journey north had taken us along a zig-zag path through the different horse farms. Now our route would be as direct a one as could be had to Lafayette, Louisiana.

Laura was just plain tired. If anybody could have been said to have worn themselves out having a good time, it would have been her. She was asleep almost as soon as the train left Shelbyville. I contented myself with a morning drink and a smoke and watched the town fall behind us as we headed south and east toward Richmond.

We arrived in Richmond about two o'clock that afternoon and I saw immediately to the business of sending a telegram to Mr. Clatterbuck advising him when we would be arriving in Lafayette. I said there was no need for them to trouble themselves to meet our train as we would put up at a hotel and I would either rent a horse or a buggy to come out and fetch the dun and the roan.

I was not uneasy in my mind about returning to the Clatterbucks'—I had a bill of sale and Mr. Clatterbuck had my signed check and I didn't think there was a man on the place that could give me any more trouble than I could handle. Still, there had been some unpleasantness and God knows I had shamed his son—but that had been a matter of Royce's choosing, not mine.

We rolled along through the dark night, lying fully clothed in what they called Pullman berths. Mine felt like a rehearsal for being in my own coffin. In fact, I did not find the ride enjoyable and spent a good part of the evening in the smoking car where they kept the bar open late.

The next morning, as we were rolling out of Memphis, Laura began to get a little excited. She was ecstatic about the stallion and the mare from Mr. Shiroh's farm. I assured her that she would be just as excited about the little bay once we got to Tyler. She didn't come right out and say it, but she had apparently given her kinfolk the idea that we had quite a spread in Texas. Naturally, you want to believe about half of what anybody from Texas told you, and that included transplanted Texans like Laura even more so than the real thing. But she gave it out, the way she told it to me, that it wouldn't be long before our colors and the name of our stables would be as well known across the south as any now running.

In view of the fact that our stable didn't even have a name, I wondered how she had gotten by that.

She said, "Well, I named it."

I found that fairly interesting and inquired as to what our stable's name was.

She said, "Why, Grayson Farms, what else?"

I looked around at her. I said, "Where does your name come into that?"

She said, "I feel fairly certain that it will be my name."

"By the way, the next time you decide that we are having a honeymoon, I wish to hell you would let me know. I nearly got caught short at that family reunion of yours when folks kept coming up and congratulating me on our marriage and asking me how the honeymoon was going. I'm not so sure, Laura, that there is such a thing as a honeymoon with you."

Giving my hand a squeeze, she said, "Just wait and see."

By the time we had finished lunch, got back to our seats and had a drink, I could tell the train was starting to slow. Then before I knew it, the conductor was coming through saying "Lafayette. Lafayette, Louisiana. Next stop. Fifteen minutes. All off for Lafayette."

I stood up and rummaged through my saddlebags and pulled out my gunbelt and began strapping it on standing there in the aisle.

Laura looked up at me, startled. She said, "What are you going to wear that for?"

"You never know, Laura. You never know."

She said, "I really wish you wouldn't. It makes me nervous."

"It makes me a helluva lot more nervous not to wear it." I got it settled on my hips and then sat down.

She said, her voice trembling a little, "Do you really think that you're going to need it?"

"No, but if I'm going to need it, I'll need it mighty bad and I would rather have it on me than someplace else."

The train came shuttering and squealing and clanging and puffing and smoking and steaming into the depot at Lafayette. We waited till the couplings had quit taking up and all the rattling and banging was over before we got to our feet. I took down my saddlebags and Laura's valise and then led her off the train. Her other luggage would be stored in the depot baggage room awaiting our departure westward to Tyler.

I was looking around expecting to find some form of conveyance that would carry us into town to a hotel when I heard a loud hail.

"Warner!" The voice yelled. "Warner! Mr. Grayson, over here."

309

I looked. It was Cloyce. He was driving a surrey. He was standing up in the seat waving.

I looked around at Laura and said, "Looks like we got met after all."

We went bowling along the road to the Clatterbuck plantation. I sat up on the seat with Cloyce and left Laura to the solitary splendor of the elegant coach. I could not say that I was happy about us both going out to the Clatterbucks, but Cloyce had insisted that the next train wasn't until the morning and we might as well enjoy their hospitality for the night. He promised to see us to the train in plenty of time and provide help for me to get the dun and the roan to the depot. Before we left, I had arranged with the freight master to rent half a stock car to accommodate the two horses on their trip to Tyler.

Nevertheless, I felt uneasy and had suggested that Laura stay at the hotel in town and that I would accompany Cloyce out to The Gables plantation. He wouldn't hear of it. He said the whole family would be disappointed if a bright light such as the lovely lady were denied them in their drab existence. Yes, he actually said that.

I got the feeling from him that there was a degree of shame felt by all for the treatment afforded me on my last visit and that they were eager to have this opportunity to make it up to me. On those terms, I could hardly say no. Still some instinct left me uneasy. I finally put that down to my naturally suspicious nature. You trade horses long enough, especially when you start out as a kid, and suspicion and uncertainty and wariness become your middle name.

We rolled up to the house and the same black servant, not Jasper, came out to take the head of the horse while we dismounted. We went up the stairs of the porch—me with my saddlebags slung over my shoulder and carrying Laura's valise. Cloyce opened the big door into that barn of a parlor and we went in. It was no less big, the furniture no less massive, and the echo was no less loud. We passed to the back of the house toward the stairs that would lead up to the bedrooms.

As we passed the door to the dining room, Cloyce said, "Oh, Warner, just a moment. Dad's in the dining room and has some business he would like to discuss with you. Could you spare a moment or two?"

I said, "Well, let me see to getting Miz Laura settled and then I'll be right on down."

He said, "Couldn't you come now?"

"Cloyce, I can't exactly let Laura carry her bag up herself."

I expected him to offer to do it, but instead he stood by the door to the dining room—that huge, long dining room with a table long enough that you could have damn near run a straight away quarter horse race on.

He said, "Oh, all right. I'm sure that Dad can wait. It will be the same bedrooms for both of ya'll."

I nodded thanks, still feeling funny. I took Laura upstairs, put her in her bedroom and dropped my saddlebags that still contained my nine-inch Colt revolver.

I said, "I don't know what's going on here, but let's don't make ourselves too comfortable too quick."

She had a concerned look on her face. She said, "Warner, be careful."

I said, "Laura, I'm always careful. I was born careful."

I gave her a light kiss and then turned, went out the door and down the stairs, and joined Cloyce at the dining room door.

He said, "All set?"

I nodded. "What does your Daddy want to see me about? I thought all of our business was done."

"Oh, I think he's just got something to show you." He reached out and pushed the big door open and motioned me through. I stepped in and then stopped. The door opened at about the middle of the long table. Up to my right was Mr. Clatterbuck and beside him was

Royce. Mr. Clatterbuck was dressed in a black broadcloth suit, black tie and a brocade vest. He had a double-barreled twelve-gauge shotgun pointed straight at me.

I froze.

Very slowly my hand started up toward the butt of my revolver, but almost at that instant, I felt Cloyce's hand close over mine. I glanced back at him. There was a kind of sheepish look on his face.

He said, "I'm sorry, Warner."

"What the hell is going on here?"

Mr. Clatterbuck said in a loud voice. "You'll damn well soon enough find out what's going on around here. Now put that repeating revolver of yours on the table and get yourself on down to the other end."

I glanced at Royce. The man had hate written all over his face.

"What are we fixing to have here, Royce? Another confrontation? Do you want your mouth slapped again? You didn't learn enough the last time around?"

Mr. Clatterbuck waved his shotgun around at me and shouted, "Goddamn you, sir! You will shut your mouth and march down to the end of that table after first depositing that revolver that you use so well on the table. Cloyce, take it out of his holster."

I looked at Cloyce—looked him clear in

the face as he slipped my revolver out and slid it on the highly polished surface of the table.

I said, "Well, Cloyce. What do you have to say for yourself?"

He shrugged. "I'm sorry, Warner, but after all, I am a Clatterbuck. When it comes to family, well . . ." He didn't finish, but I knew what he meant.

I said, "So this is what you people still continue to call honor? May I be told what is going to happen here?"

Mr. Clatterbuck said, "We're going to damn well fight that duel that should have taken place before. Only this time, Mr. Warner Grayson, we are going to fight it fair. You're not going to be able to hire two ruffians from town and hide them in that grove of woods of your choosing, I might add sir, so that they might waylay my son. I now know the truth of the matter and by God, this time, you will fight fair."

I almost staggered backwards at the man's words. I looked at Royce and he had an evil smile on his face. I looked at Cloyce. He wouldn't meet my eyes.

I said, "Am I to understand that I put those two men there and then killed them?"

Mr. Clatterbuck shook his shotgun at me. He said, "Enough of this kind of talk. At that end of the table, you will find a dueling pistol. It is the mate to the one in front of my son. This duel will be conducted with proper regard to the rules and with dignity and honor."

"Oh, yes. There is real dignity and honor attached to an engagement, as you people choose to call it, when one has a shotgun pointed at him."

Mr. Clatterbuck said, "Sir, this shotgun is to insure that you fight by the rules of conduct—that you fight by the code. Now, by God, get down to the other end, sir."

I looked at him for a long time. I didn't seem to have much choice. I walked the four or five paces to the end of the polished table.

Royce was at the other end, some twelve yards away. In front of both of us was a flint-locked dueling pistol. I looked at the pistol and the words came back to me about half loads and misfires always seeming to happen to Royce's opponent.

I glanced at Cloyce and caught his eyes and then looked back at the pistol and then back at him. He gave a barely perceptible shake of his head. It was answer enough.

Even if I got off a shot it was doubtful that the pistol was charged with enough powder for the ball to reach Royce, much less do him any harm. So what we had here was a shooting gallery.

Royce was a fat duck at the other end of the table. He could take his time, knowing that he

315

was in no danger, and put one right in the middle of my breastbone. This wasn't a duel. This was a slaughter.

I stood there, my brain going a mile a minute, trying to consider what options I had. My revolver was six yards away, lying on the table. I would never reach it in time before the old man blasted me with the shotgun, something that I felt like he was dying to do.

I said, "Mr. Clatterbuck, this is out and out murder and you know it. What are you going to tell Mrs. Pico? What are you going to tell the law when they come to inquire? How do you expect to get away with this?"

He smiled an evil smile. He said, "Mr. Grayson. The law in this town will side with me against the outsider. There is no way, of course, to know what has transpired in this room. Now you have as fair a chance as Royce does. He didn't have the fair chance last time."

I said, "Oh hell. Cut out the bullshit, Clatterbuck. You know damn well that your cowardly son stuck those two ruffians in those woods. Those were his bushwhackers. Their intent was to kill me so that he wouldn't have to face me. Are you so blind that you don't realize that your son is a coward and a bully?"

Mr. Clatterbuck went red in the face. He raised the shotgun. His voice was shaking.

He said, "By God, sir. I've half a mind to cut you in two with this weapon."

I said bitterly, "I'd just as soon you did. At least it would be quicker. I doubt that your son can shoot straight enough to kill me. Most likely he'll just give me a mortal wound and I'll last four or five days in pain and agony."

Mr. Clatterbuck said, "My son is in as much danger as you are."

I said, "Oh, yeah. I've got a feeling that if I shot this gun, the bullet would roll half way down the table."

Royce drew himself up and said, "That is a canard and that is a lie and you are a bounder and a cad, sir."

I said, "And you are a son of a bitch." I looked at Cloyce. I said, "I don't know what you are Cloyce. One thing I know, you're not a man of principle, not any more. I'm disappointed in you, Cloyce."

He looked down. He couldn't meet my eyes.

Mr. Clatterbuck said, "Enough of this prattle. Gentlemen, this is an affair of honor. Mr. Grayson, pick up your pistol, sir."

I looked down at it. I was damned if I would, but Royce was picking up his.

Mr. Clatterbuck said, "Gentlemen, cock your pistols."

Somewhat grudgingly, I picked up the heavy flintlock. Hell, for all I knew, it might be fully loaded. I half way debated about shooting Clatterbuck and then taking my chances with Royce. Clatterbuck had the shotgun—that was what I was the most afraid of. Besides that, I didn't think that Royce could hit me.

Clatterbuck said, "I told you, sir, to cock your weapon."

"What if I choose not to take part in this playacting?"

"Then I, sir, will march you into the pasture and blow your no-good head off."

I said, "Well, at least I won't have to listen to any more of this damned bullshit about manhood and chivalry and all that other southern nonsense that ya'll were so full of the last time. Now I see you for what you are. A couple of murderers. Royce, have you ever fought a fair fight in your life? You and I both know who hired those two bushwhackers and set them in that grove of woods, don't we?"

He was standing there with the dueling pistol in his hand, both hammers cocked back as it was a two-barrel pistol. However, he did not have his finger inside the trigger guard.

"Royce, come on. Why don't you tell your daddy the truth? Though I'm fairly certain that he already knows it."

Mr. Clatterbuck said, "This affair is going to proceed." He suddenly jerked out his watch. He said, "In one minute, I shall direct you to aim your weapons and then at the count of three, I will order you to fire. Mr. Grayson, you had better cock the hammers of your pistol. This is your last warning. I am starting the minute now."

With my mind racing, trying to think of every option that I could, I cocked the hammers, one after the other. I said, "Am I to understand that we have two shots each?"

Mr. Clatterbuck said, "If needed."

I smiled at Royce. I said, "I don't reckon that you will need more than one, will you, Royce? Unless you use the second one to finish me off."

Mr. Clatterbuck said in a loud voice, "Thirty seconds, gentlemen."

I said, "This is murder, Cloyce, and I call upon you to witness. You know that this weapon of mine is not loaded or not fully loaded."

Mr. Clatterbuck said, "Fifteen seconds."

Right at that instant, the door to the dining room suddenly burst open. All eyes went to it.

Laura stood there, holding—in both of her hands—my nine-inch-barreled Colt.

Without pause, she raised it.

12

It was as of we were frozen.

Mr. Clatterbuck stood where he was, shotgun half pointed toward me. Royce was at the end of the table, the dueling pistol at his side, Cloyce was a little way down the table from me. Laura's hands came up, the big nine-inch revolver gripped hard. I could see her face— it was dead calm. The hammer to the Colt was back.

There was no hesitation.

She fired. The shot boomed like a cannon in the cavernous room. A splotch of blood splattered Mr. Clatterbuck's brocade vest. A look of horror spread across his face, his jaw dropped. He tried to raise the shotgun. Laura fired again, this time pulling the trigger in double action. She hit him again. The heavy slug staggered him backwards to the wall. He hit against the curtains and slowly slid down to the floor.

By then, I could see Royce starting to react. I was two steps back from the end of the table with the useless gun in my hand. I launched myself across the varnished top, blessing the hands that had polished it so slick. I slid like a pig on ice and as I slid, I fired both barrels in Royce's general direction. As I expected, they made no more than a pop. But they were not using smokeless powder, and the eruption of noise and smoke served to obscure me as I slid along until my hands found my Colt revolver.

I never paused even as I heard Laura's gun fire again. I fired two quick shots directly into Royce as best as I could see him through the smoky haze.

He staggered backwards, hit the back of the room and fell, his dueling pistol falling helplessly at his side.

I swiveled after I had shot him and turned on Cloyce. He was backing rapidly toward the end of the table that I had just vacated.

I said, "Stop!"

He froze.

I carefully climbed down off the table and went up to Laura. I looked at her for a second. Her face was very white, but the hands that held the big revolver were steady as a rock. I took it carefully out of her hands. They dropped to her side.

I stuck the gun in my belt and put my arm around her. I said, "Honey, go out into the hall now. Let me clean this up. Go out and call for Jasper."

Dimly, as if she were in a trance, she went out the door. I watched her for a moment and then I came back in the room and I motioned for Cloyce.

I said, "Go see to your daddy and your brother, you son of a bitch."

Moving slowly and watching me warily, he walked the length of the table. He knelt first by his father who had been shot three times—twice in the chest and once in his ample belly. I could see that some of the old lessons that I had given Laura when I had been trying to teach her to shoot had stayed with her. She had aimed at the biggest part of the target. Old man Clatterbuck was quite dead.

Cloyce then went and knelt at the side of his brother.

He looked around at me and shook his head. He said, "I must admire you, Mr. Grayson. Even after the confusion and the awkward position you were in, it was one hell of a shot. Both holes are very near his heart. I doubt that he ever knew what hit him. You warned us. I will give you that, sir."

He stood up.

I still had my revolver in my hand. I said, "And now there is the matter of you, Cloyce. What am I going to do with you?"

He shrugged. "I know that you cannot condone my actions and I don't expect you to understand them. It came down to family, Mr. Grayson. They were wrong. They were terribly wrong, but they were still my family."

"There is going to have to be a sheriff come out here. The law is going to have to look into this. I want to know right now, are you going to tell the truth?"

He looked me steadily in the eye. "Yes."

"You know that the dueling pistol that I was given held only a partial load?"

He looked me steadily in the eye. "Yes."

"You know who placed those two men in the trees?"

"It was Royce. Yes, Mr. Grayson, I was here. I knew that they intended to kill you, to murder you. I plan to tell the sheriff exactly that. But neither my father nor my brother was a murderer. They couldn't bear the disgrace that you had brought them."

"I reckon that you have that a little backwards, Cloyce. Who brought what disgrace on who?"

"I stand corrected. They could not stand the disgrace that they brought upon themselves. In my father's defense, I will say that he chose to believe the lie Royce had told him, that the bushwhackers had been yours. Of course, I knew better, so did Royce, so did my father. He chose not to believe that, though. He could not let himself believe it. You may never understand this. In fact, I'd be surprised if you ever did."

I put my gun in its holster. I said, "In a strange way, Cloyce, I do understand. I also feel terribly sorry for your father and your brother, but even more so for you, for you know much better."

He looked down at the floor. "It goes without saying that my life will never be the same. In effect, I was an accessory to your attempted murder. I will tell the sheriff that."

"Then I suggest that you get someone started for town to get the law out here. I'd like to get this mess cleared up, take my horses, and get the hell out of Louisiana."

He half smiled. "I can't say that I blame you."

I went upstairs and found Laura sitting on the side of the bed, staring into space. I sat down beside her and put my arm around her. For a long moment, neither one of us said anything.

Then, in almost a whisper, she said, "I heard Mr. Clatterbuck's loud voice coming up from down below. At first, I didn't pay any attention to it. Then it kept on so I listened at the door and peeked through the crack, just enough to see what was going on . . ." Her voice trailed off.

My saddlebags were lying on the bed. I pulled out the bottle of whiskey and pulled the cork and then handed it to her. She downed a good strong pull. I took the bottle and had one myself.

In a little stronger voice, but still not looking at me, she said, "I realized what was happening. I knew that they were going to kill you. I knew that I could not allow them to kill you. I had to stop them. I came back here, upstairs. I knew that you had another gun in your saddlebags. I knew how to cock it, I knew how it worked. I took it and went downstairs. You always taught me to assess the situation and to judge where the greatest danger was. I thought that Mr. Clatterbuck with the shotgun was the greatest danger."

I patted her shoulder encouragingly and pulled her near me. She went on, "I knew that you had to cock the revolver. I saw the shotgun swing and I did what you always told me. I pointed my hands where I wanted the bullet to go. I pointed at his chest. I saw it go all red. Then I worked the trigger like you told me. It happened again and it happened the third time. Then I knew that you were in the fight and that I didn't have to worry anymore."

I handed her the bottle and urged another drink on her. Some of the color was starting to come back into her face. She turned back to look at me and said, "Warner, what am I supposed to feel right now?"

I put her head on my shoulder and said, "I don't know what you feel, but I feel so grateful for what you did. You saved my life, Laura, for

I was as dead as a doornail if you had not done what you did. You saved my life."

She turned her head and looked at me. "But you have saved mine so many times."

"Yes, but this is the real big one that counts."

"What am I supposed to feel right now? Right now, I don't feel anything at all."

I said, "You'll be numb for a while and then you'll be sorry, but in the end, Laura, you will know that you did the right thing. That man was going to kill me with that shotgun or his son was going to kill me with that dueling pistol. The one that they gave me was rigged up to not shoot. Had you not come here with me, had you not heard the loud noise, the loud talk, I would be dead now."

She pulled her head back and looked at me. She said, "You would have gotten out of it."

I said, "No, Laura. I had no way out of it. I had no gun. I had two guns against me. I don't know if Cloyce had a gun—that would have been three. I had a shotgun and a two-shot dueling pistol against me. My handgun was six or seven yards from me. The only thing that I had was that useless dueling pistol that they had given me. All I used it for was a smoke screen."

"Will I feel very bad about this?"

I suddenly laughed. I said, "Not unless you wanted me dead."

"Warner, I am being serious."

"So am I, baby, so am I, sweetheart. So am I, Mrs. Grayson."

She half smiled at that.

"What happens now?"

"The law will have to be involved. In the end, nothing will come of it."

All of a sudden, she collapsed in my arms and started crying. I had been expecting it. I held her in my arms and rocked her and kissed her wherever I could reach.

There was not very much trouble with the law. Mr. Clatterbuck had not carried as much weight as he had thought. To his credit, Cloyce explained to the sheriff the whole shabby setup, going back to the original duel and the placing of the two bushwhackers to try and ambush me. The sheriff himself was not of the Clatterbucks' southern gentlemen variety. He was more of a man given to reality and he did not believe that gunfights were suitable fodder for playacting, especially when you were using real bullets. He completely exonerated me and, of course, Laura. A hasty coroner's court found that the Clatterbucks had died by mischance in attempted murder of another person.

On the afternoon before we were to leave, the sheriff and I sat in his office. Cloyce had been taken into custody and even at that moment was in a jail cell. The sheriff asked me what I wanted done with him. I asked that Cloyce be brought into the office for my answer.

Once he was in the office, I told the sheriff that I did not hold Cloyce responsible. I said, "Sheriff, I am not much of one for allowing a man some complicated reason for not knowing the difference between right and wrong. But in Cloyce's case, I think that he was torn between family and what he knew to be right, that he really had very little decision. If you are willing to let him go, I am willing to let him go. I don't think the man will cause any further trouble. There is that plantation that has to be run. There are people with jobs at stake."

I turned to look at Cloyce. I said, "Cloyce, you ever reckon to get that confused again?"

He gave me a faint smile. "No, Mr. Grayson, I can't say that I anticipate myself ever doing that again. I knew it was wrong, yet I went ahead and did it. I cannot see myself not having learned from this. I've known for years that my father and my brother were crooks and thieves and murderers. I was afraid of what that would make me out to be. Now I accept what they were. I know that I am different."

I said, "You are different."

I stood up. I said to the sheriff, "I'm much obliged to you for your work, sir. Now I've got horse business to attend to, so if I'm free to go and Mrs. Pico is free to go, we'd like to get our stud horses into town and make arrangements to ship them and ourselves back to Texas."

He shook my hand and wished me well.

We left the next morning at ten o'clock for the seven-hour trip through Shreveport, through Longview, and then on to Tyler. The horses, the dun and the roan, were riding in comfort behind us. Laura and I were eagerly looking forward to getting back to our own bed, Rosa's cooking—God help us—and to our own life.

The day before, while grooms from the Clatterbuck place were bringing in the dun and the roan, I had busied myself sending a very important telegram to Charlie Stanton with some very detailed instructions that I was certain would bowl him over. I expected him to carry them out.

After that, I had gone shopping. That morning, before we left the hotel to catch our train, I had shaved and put on the new suit that Laura insisted I buy. I had it sponged and cleaned. She could not believe her eyes—that I was going to wear that suit on the train.

She could further not believe that I was insisting that she wear her smartest gown, especially the white one that I liked so well. It was not quite as daring as some of her off-the-shoulder ones, but neither was it demure.

Naturally, she was eaten alive with curiosity,

almost to the point of frustration, but I refused to say a word other than to explain, uncharacteristically, that I wanted to look good when we arrived back in Texas.

Justifiably, she found that hard to believe, given my normally sloppy dressing habits, but in the face of no new evidence, she was forced to believe it.

She was still wondering and still asking questions as we boarded the train for the last leg home. There would be a surprise waiting for her in Longview.

By the time she had shaken the dust of Lafayette off her feet, she was back to her gay, cheerful self, wondering how many of her bags and boxes had been lost by the railroad and threatening to sue everyone from the president of the line to the conductor and the baggage handlers.

She was also beginning to plan how she was going to run the Thoroughbred farm. After all, she had actually seen a Thoroughbred up close now. No, she had actually seen two, and that made her an expert. I didn't bother to point out that she might need a little more experience, such as getting a sixteen-hand stud to mount an almost eighteen-hand mare, or how to get a stud whose mind was still on racing to get his mind on the mares. I did say that I thought I would leave the actual physical part of the breeding to her, as I thought that she was actually more of an expert at that than I was.

That got me, naturally, an elbow in the ribs. I resolved again that I was going to file down those sharp instruments of the devil at the first opportunity.

As we rode, I looked around at Laura, admiring her, thinking fondly of what she had done, loving her. I asked her what she felt now about guns.

She took the question seriously, knitting her brows and studying for a few moments. Finally she said, "Warner, of all the things that I hate, to admit that you are right is the worst. But I have to admit that a gun is just what you said it is—a tool." She turned to face me. She put her hand up to touch my cheek. "I'm very glad that I used that tool. I'm very glad that you're here with me."

I said, "Sister, in a little while, you are going to be a lot gladder. By the way, what did you say your last name was?"

She gave me a sardonic look. "The honeymoon is over, sweetheart. We can go back to calling me Mrs. Pico now."

I said, "All right, Widow Pico, let's do that for the time being."

The train stopped in Longview for about fifteen minutes. We got there about two o'clock in the afternoon. Laura and I were sitting in the back of the car like we always did. Five or six minutes after we pulled in, there was a commotion and I saw a man in a black frock coat and a black city hat who appeared to be in something of a dither, being pushed onto the train. Behind him, I could see Charlie Stanton. They came down the aisle toward us. Charlie was grinning like he had just swallowed a possum. The man in black was clutching a Bible and looked bewildered.

I stood up. I said, "Laura, get up."

She looked up at me and she looked up at the man in black and she looked up at Charlie Stanton. She said, "What's going on?"

"I said stand up."

There were two ladies sitting in the seats in front of us. I said, "Ladies, would ya'll like to be witnesses to a wedding?"

Naturally, it set them to tittering and oohing and ahhing. I said, "If ya'll don't mind, stand up and face us, please."

I looked at Charlie. I said, "Charlie, work your ways up and get behind us, standing beside me. You're going to be my best man."

Laura was on her feet now. She was staring at me in amazement. She said, "What the hell is going on?"

I said, "Shh. That's no way to talk on your wedding day. Keep a civil tongue in your mouth, woman."

She said, "Are you completely crazy? I have no intention of getting married on a . . ."

She got no further for the train suddenly jolted as the engine surged and the slack was taken up on the couplings. She didn't know that the minister had been paid to marry us en route to Tyler and then take the train back.

But I did.

She grabbed at the seat in front of her. "Warner, have you gone crazy. We're on a train. We're moving."

I said, "I got a best man. I got a fiancée—that's you. I've got a minister here—what's his name, Charlie?"

Charlie said, "This is Mr. Howard."

I put out my hand and shook his. I said, "Reverend Howard, are you ready?"

He was a thin tremulous little man, maybe in his late forties. He looked about as bewildered as Laura. He said, "I suppose I am, though this is mighty irregular."

I said, "Does it matter in the sight of God if you get married in a moving vehicle or not?"

"I suppose not. I don't believe there's anything in the Bible against it."

I turned to the two women. "Are you ladies willing to be witnesses to a marriage on a train between Longview and Tyler at thirty miles per hour?" They started giggling again. One of them said that they didn't mind at all.

I turned to Charlie and said, "Charlie, are you willing to be a best man on a moving train heading to Tyler? I believe that we're up to about forty miles per hour about now."

Charlie said, "Well, you're the boss. Naturally I am willing."

"Well, I know I'm willing." I looked at Laura. I said, "You know, we've always done things kinda fast. I think it's kinda fitting that we should get married at forty miles per hour. What do you think?"

She said, "You are the craziest damn man I have ever met in my life."

"What's it to be? Pico or Grayson?"

A little smile played around her lips and she said, "At least that would make it one argument less."

"Pico or Grayson?"

She smiled. "Grayson."

I turned to the preacher, "Reverend Howard, do your stuff. Charlie, here's the ring. Hand it to me when you're supposed to."

Laura leaned over to look. She said, "Where did you get that ring?"

I said, "I bought that ring when you weren't looking."

"Why are we getting married on the train?"

"Because I wanted to marry you as soon as we got back in Texas—I didn't want to get married in Louisiana and this was the first stop in Texas where I could take on a preacher."

She looked at me. She said, "Why don't you tell Reverend Howard to hurry up."

I looked at Reverend Howard. "Reverend?"

Reverend Howard said, "Dearly beloved, we are gathered here today in the sight of God to join together this man and this woman in the holy bonds of wedlock."

His voice could just barely be heard above the clatter and rumble of the train. But we didn't need to hear the words. When he stopped speaking, we both said "I do." I put the ring on Laura's finger and I kissed her and said, "Let's go home, Mrs. Grayson."

Books are produced in the United States using U.S.-based materials

Books are printed using a revolutionary new process called THINKtech™ that lowers energy usage by 70% and increases overall quality

Books are durable and flexible because of Smyth-sewing

Paper is sourced using environmentally responsible foresting methods and the paper is acid-free

Center Point Large Print
600 Brooks Road / PO Box 1
Thorndike, ME 04986-0001 USA

(207) 568-3717

US & Canada:
1 800 929-9108
www.centerpointlargeprint.com